La Petite Mort Club

The Voyeur Series

Books 1-4

Ellis O. Day

I love to hear from readers so email me at
authorellisoday@gmail.com

http://www.EllisODay.com

Facebook
https://www.facebook.com/EllisODayRomanceAuthor/

Twitter
https://twitter.com/ellis_o_day

Pinterest
www.pinterest.com\AuthorEllisODay

Book 1

The Voyeur

CHAPTER 1: ANNIE

Annie finished making the bed and gathered the sheets from the floor, keeping them as far away from her body as possible. These sex rooms were disgusting and Ethan was a jerk making her work as a maid. She almost had her Bachelor's Degree in Culinary Arts, but he'd refused to hire her for the kitchen—too many men in the kitchen. The only job he'd give her at La Petite Mort Club was as a maid and unfortunately, she needed the money too badly to refuse.

She stuffed the dirty sheets into the cart and hurried out the door. She had almost thirty minutes before she had to clean the next "sex room." She hid the cart in a closet

and darted down a back hallway, staying clear of the
cameras. Julie, the woman who supervised the daytime
maids, was a real bitch. If she were caught sneaking away
from her duties, she'd be assigned to the orgy rooms every
day. Right now, they all took turns cleaning that nightmare.
She swore they should get hazard pay to even look in those
rooms.

She slipped through a doorway and hurried to the
one-way mirror. She stared at the couple in the next room.
From her first day here, she'd been curious about the
activities at the club. She was twenty-four and wasn't a
virgin but she'd never even imagined some of these things.

The woman in the other room was tied to a table,
legs spread and wearing some sort of leather outfit that left
her large breasts free and her crotch exposed. She'd shaved
her private parts and her pink lower lips were swollen and
glistening from her excitement. The man strolled around
the table as if he had all night. He still had his pants on but
had removed his shirt. His arms and chest were well
defined but he had a slight paunch. His erection tented his
pants and Annie felt wetness pool between her legs. She
had no idea why watching this turned her on but it did.
Ever since she'd accidentally barged in on a man and
woman in the Interview room, she couldn't stop watching.

The guy in the other room trailed his hand up the
woman's inner thigh, skimming over her pussy. The
woman thrust her hips upward and Annie ran her own hand
between her legs. The man's mouth moved but Annie
couldn't hear anything and then he slapped the woman

across the thigh hard enough to leave a red mark. Annie jumped. She wasn't into that, but she couldn't take her eyes off the woman's face. At first, it'd contorted in pain but then it'd morphed into pleasure. The man hit her again and then bent, kissing the red welts—running his tongue across them as his fingers squeezed her nipple.

Annie clutched her thighs together, searching for some relief. Her panties were soaked. It wouldn't take but a few strokes to make her come. She started to slide her hand into her pants.

"Having fun?" asked a deep voice from behind her.

She spun around, her heart dropping into her stomach. "Ah…I was just finishing cleaning in here." Damn, she should've closed the door but she hadn't expected anyone in this area. The rooms were off limits on this floor until tonight and she was the only one assigned to clean here.

He shut the door and locked it before strolling toward her. She'd seen him around the Club, but more than that she remembered him from the military photos her brother, Vic, had sent to her. She carried one of the three of them—Vic, Ethan and this guy, Patrick—in her purse. He'd been attractive in the picture, but now that he was older and in person he was gorgeous. He had dark green eyes, brown hair and a perfect body. He stopped so close to her his chest almost brushed against her breasts. She was pretty sure it would if she inhaled deeply. She bit her lip to keep from taking a deep breath and testing her theory.

"Don't let me stop you from enjoying the show."

"I…I wasn't. I should go." She started to walk past him but he grabbed her hand.

His grip was warm and strong but loose enough that she could pull free if she wanted. She didn't. Even though she only knew him from her brother's pictures and letters, she'd had many fantasies about him when she'd been in high school. Her gaze dropped to the front of his pants and her mouth almost watered. He was definitely interested. She dragged her eyes up his body, stopping on his face. He smiled at her.

"There's nothing to be embarrassed about. Watching turns us all on." He kissed the back of her hand and she jumped as his tongue darted out, tasting her skin.

"I…I should go." She didn't move.

"No, you should watch." He dropped her hand and grabbed her shoulders, gently turning her toward the mirror. He ran his hands up and down her arms. "Watch."

The man in the other room was now sucking on the woman's breast as his fingers caressed her pussy.

"Would you like to hear them? Or do you like it quiet?" His voice was a rough whisper against her ear.

"Sound, please." She wanted to hear their gasps and moans. She wanted to close her eyes and pretend it was her. She shifted, squeezing her thighs together.

He chuckled as he moved away. She felt his absence to her bones. He'd been strong and warm behind her and for a moment she'd felt safe, safer than she had since her brother had come back from the war, broken and sad, and her father had started drinking again.

The woman's moans filled the room and Patrick came back to stand behind her, this time placing his hands on her waist.

"I'm Patrick," he said against her ear.

She couldn't take her eyes from the scene in front of her. The woman was almost coming as the man thrust his fingers inside of her.

"What's your name?" He nipped her neck and she jumped.

"I...I..." If she told him her name, he might say something to Ethan. Ethan would kill her if he knew she was in here watching.

"Tell me your name." His lips trailed along her neck and she tipped her head giving him better access.

The guy was kissing his way down the woman's body. Annie wanted to touch herself, to make herself come but Patrick was here.

He nibbled her ear. "Why won't you tell me your name?"

"I...I'll get in trouble." She rubbed her ass against his erection, hopefully giving him a hint.

"Tease." His hand drifted down her stomach, stopping right above where she wanted him to touch. "Tell me your name or I'll make you suffer." He unbuttoned her pants and left his hand—warm, rough but immobile— resting on her abdomen.

"I can't." She stood on tip-toe, hoping his hand would lower a little but he was too tall or she was too short.

He had to be almost six foot and she was barely five-foot four. "I could get fired and I need this job."

"Darling, Ethan won't fire you for fucking a customer."

"We aren't. We can't." She spun around. She hadn't thought this through. He was her fantasy come to life and she wanted him even if it were only this one time, but Ethan would find out and then she'd be in deep shit.

"Don't worry. I'm a member and you work here, so we're both clean." He hesitated, his hands tightening on her hips. "Are you protected?"

"What?" She had no idea what he was talking about.

"Ethan makes sure everyone at the Club is clean but only the...some of his employees are required to be on birth control." He ran his hands up her sides, getting closer and closer to her breasts. "Are you on birth control?" His gaze dropped to her tits. "If not, it's okay. There are other things we can do."

Oh, she wanted to do everything his eyes promised, but she couldn't. "I'm on the pill but we can't. I need this job. I have to go." She tried to move but her feet refused to obey, so she just stared at his handsome face.

"Are you sure?" He bent so he was almost eye level with her. "I promise. Ethan won't care. A lot of maids become...change jobs. The pay's a lot better." His eyes roamed over her frame. "Especially, for someone as cute as you."

Ethan would kill her before letting her become one of his pleasure associates.

"I could talk to Ethan for you." His hands moved up her body, stopping right below her breasts.

Her nipples hardened and she forgot everything but what he was making her feel. He ran his thumb over one of them and she leaned closer, wanting him to do it again.

He did. He continued rubbing her nipple as he spoke. "I could persuade him to let me…handle your initiation into club life."

Her heart raced in her chest. It could be just her and him doing all these things she'd seen. Her pussy throbbed but she couldn't do it. She wouldn't do it. She couldn't have sex for money. Her parents were both dead but they'd never understand and she couldn't disappoint them. "No. I can't do that…not for money." Her eyes darted to the door. She needed to get out of there before she did something she'd regret.

"That's even better." He smiled as he stepped closer. "We can keep this between us. No money. Only a man and a woman." He leaned down and whispered in her ear, "Giving each other pleasure. A lot of pleasure. In ways you haven't even imagined."

There were moans from the other room and she glanced over her shoulder. The man's face was buried between the woman's thighs.

Patrick turned her around, pulling her against him and wrapping his arms around her waist. "Are you wet?"

"What? No." She struggled in his arms, her ass brushing against his erection again.

"Oh fuck. Do that again." He kissed her neck, open mouthed and hot.

She stopped trying to get away. She wanted this…this moment. She shouldn't but she did, so she wiggled her butt against him again. He was hard and long and her body ached for him. It'd been too long since she'd had sex. She needed this.

"Would you like me to touch you?" His hands drifted over her hips and down her thighs.

She'd like him to do all sorts of things to her. She nodded.

"Say it." His words were a command she couldn't disobey.

"Yes."

"Yes, what?" He untucked her shirt from her pants.

"Touch me. Please." She was already pushing her hips toward him. She wanted his hand on her, his fingers inside of her.

"Are you wet?" he asked again.

She inhaled sharply as he unzipped her pants.

"Don't lie to me. I'll find out in a minute."

She'd never talked dirty during sex and she wasn't sure she was ready to do that with a stranger. Her heart skipped a beat. Maybe, she shouldn't be doing any of this with a stranger. She grabbed his hand. "Maybe, we shouldn't."

The woman below cried out and the man straightened, wiping his face and unbuttoning his pants.

"Watch. The main event is about to happen." Patrick's hot breath tickled her neck.

Her gaze locked on the man's penis. It was large and demanding. He straddled the woman, grabbing his cock.

"Don't you want to feel some of what they feel?" He nibbled on her ear and then neck. "I can help you."

She may not know him, but she trusted him. He was a former marine. He'd been a good friend of Vic's. He wouldn't hurt her and she needed to come. She let go of his hand and he slipped inside her pants, caressing her pussy through her underwear. His fingers were long and strong. She closed her eyes, leaning against him as he stroked her.

"You're already so wet and hot." His breath was a warm caress on her ear. "But, I'm going to make you wetter and then, I'm going to make you come." His other hand shoved her pants down, giving him more room to work. "Open your eyes and watch the show."

She did as he said. The man was inside the woman, thrusting hard and fast. The woman was moaning and trying to move but the restraints kept her mostly helpless.

"Fuck, you're soaked." Patrick's hand cupped her and she arched into his touch, rubbing her ass against his erection. He shoved his hand inside her underwear, his fingers running along her folds until he slipped one inside.

"Oh." She grabbed his hand—not to push him away, but to make sure he didn't leave.

He smiled against her hair. "Don't worry, baby. I won't stop."

As he stroked his finger inside of her, his hand brushed against her clit, but she wanted more. She needed to touch him, feel him. She turned her head, wrapping her arms up and around his neck. He kissed her. It was desperate and wild, but he stopped too soon.

"They're almost done. You don't want to miss it."

She turned back to the mirror. The man below continued to fuck the woman as Patrick finger-fucked her. His other hand slipped under her shirt to her breast. His lips sucked her neck as he rocked his erection against her ass. He was everywhere, and she was so close. The muscles in her legs constricted. Her hips tipped upward.

"Wait, baby," he groaned in her ear, as he pushed a second finger inside of her. "Just a few more minutes."

His fingers were stretching her and it felt wonderful. She moaned, long and low as he thrust harder and faster, almost matching the pace of the man in the other room. She could almost imagine it was Patrick's cock and not his fingers inside of her.

"Oh…oh," she cried out. He was pushing her toward the edge. Her body was spiraling with each pump of his fingers. She was going to come—right here while watching that couple. It was so dirty and so wrong and it only made her hotter.

The woman below screamed and her body stiffened. The man thrust again and again and then grunted his release.

"Show's over." Patrick nipped her neck at the same time he pressed down on her clit with his thumb, sending her shooting into orgasm.

She trembled and he pulled her close, his hand still cupping her pussy and his fingers still inside of her. When her heartbeat had settled, he removed his hand and bent, pulling off her shoes and removing her pants before lifting her and carrying her to the wall.

"My turn." He wrapped her legs around his waist.

A phone rang.

"My work phone. I...I have to answer it."

"When we're done." He unzipped his pants.

"Annie, answer the phone. I know you're around here. I can hear it ringing you stupid bitch," yelled Julie.

"Oh, shit." She shoved Patrick away, and ran across the room, grabbing her clothes off the floor. "It's my boss. She'll kill me if she finds me like this."

"I'll take care of Julie." He headed for the door, zipping up his fly. "Don't move." He grinned over his shoulder at her. "You can take off your pants again, but other than that, don't move."

"No. Please." She raced over to him, grabbing his arm. "I need this job." And Ethan could not find out about this.

"She won't fire you. She can't. Only Ethan can fire you." He bent and kissed her.

His lips were gentle and coaxing this time and her body swayed into him. He pulled her even closer and she could feel his cock, thick and heavy, pushing against her. Her pussy tightened again in anticipation.

"Damn it, Annie. This is going to be so much worse if I have to call your stupid phone again. Get out here!" Julie was only a few doors down.

She tugged on Patrick's hand. "Please, hide." She glanced around, looking for somewhere that would conceal a six-foot, muscular man.

"I'm not going to hide from Julie."

"Shhh, lower your voice." She pulled him toward the wall by the mirror where the curtain hung.

He stopped moving, refusing to let her lead him, but he did lower his voice. "I told you, I'll take care of Julie." He caressed her cheek. "You don't have to be afraid. You won't lose your job."

"Damn it." She shoved him. "You don't understand." He didn't know who she was. He didn't know about her and Ethan's history. "I'm going to lose this job, my chance for a career and my home." Her voice cracked and tears welled in her eyes. Ethan would try and force her to take his money but she wouldn't. She wasn't her father. She would not accept his charity. "All because…because…" It was too humiliating to say out loud. She was horny and had wanted to watch two people get it on. She was such a freak.

"Hey, don't cry." He wiped a tear from her cheek. "I won't let any of that happen. I promise."

The doorknob turned. "Annie, I know you're in there. Open this door."

"Please, hide." She was begging and by the disgusted look he sent her it wasn't doing any good and then he sighed and moved past her.

"You owe me big time for this." He slipped into the bunched up curtains, that would cover the mirror when they were closed.

"Thank you, and be quiet." She pulled on her shoes, hurried to the door and opened it. "Julie, were you looking for me?" She tried to look innocent or perhaps stupid, but Julie's hard, blue eyes skimmed over her.

"Who's in here with you? If you're fucking one of the kitchen or maintenance staff you're both fired." Julie pushed past her and strode into the room.

The woman was as wide as she was tall and Annie hated her—not because of her looks but because she was a tyrant.

"There's no one here but me." She glanced at where Patrick hid, praying he'd stay put and that Julie wouldn't somehow sniff him out. She swore Julie could scent out men a mile away.

Julie stopped near the mirror. She was only a few feet away from Patrick. Annie's heart tried to escape from her throat.

"So, you're a voyeur." Julie spun around. "I should've guessed. Curious but afraid, just like a little mouse." She walked toward Annie, her ample hips swaying as her eyes roamed over Annie's form. "You're a bit rumpled. Rubbed one out, did you?"

Annie's face heated. *Not exactly.*

"Come with me. We're going to tell Ethan all about this."

"No. Please don't. I'll clean the orgy room for a month, two months." She followed Julie out of the room and down the hallway. Ethan couldn't find out about this. It'd be too embarrassing. He was like a brother to her.

CHAPTER 2: PATRICK

Patrick waited until Julie's voice faded down the hallway before stepping out from behind the curtain. If Ethan or Nick, or God forbid Terry, found out about this, he'd never live it down. He was a former marine for fuck's sake and he was hiding from Julie. What had he been thinking? Oh, that's right, he hadn't been. All he'd been able to do was stare at those big, brown eyes, begging him for help and he'd melted like ice cream in an oven. He tugged at the front of his pants. Well, not all of him had melted.

He glanced at the open door. He could close it and jerk off, but he wasn't in the mood. He wanted her—Annie. The name fit. She was warm and friendly. He grinned. She'd certainly been friendly with him. He'd have to talk to Ethan and make sure she didn't lose her job. She hadn't wanted him to say anything but she didn't understand that Ethan wouldn't have any problem with a sexy, little maid becoming one of the Club's pleasure associates. It happened all the time.

He strolled to the door, frowning a bit. Usually, Ethan broke the girls into club life. That wouldn't work this time. He wanted Annie and he wanted her before Ethan taught her about all the pleasures the Club had to offer. He'd pay Ethan whatever his friend wanted, but she was his little voyeur. He'd found her.

His dick hardened even more at the memory. She'd been so engrossed with watching the other couple she hadn't even heard him. He'd show her things she'd never even dreamed and then when she was panting for release, he'd tease her and finally fuck her. She'd been so tight and so receptive earlier. He'd barely touched her and she'd come all over his hand. He ran his fingers under his nose, inhaling her scent. She'd pay for making him hide behind the curtains but right now, he was late for his meeting with Ethan.

He headed down the hallway and stopped outside of Ethan's private office. He grinned. There she was—his little voyeur. Annie was sitting on the couch in the waiting room looking miserable. She was too cute to be that unhappy. With her long, black hair pulled up in a ponytail, her large brown eyes and hot, little body, his dick, which had been starting to relax, perked right back to attention. Soon, the two of them were going to finish what they'd started.

He plopped down next to her, making sure his thigh rested against hers. She glanced up at him as she scooted away, recognition flaring in her eyes as a pink blush rose to her cheeks. His gaze dropped to her breasts, hoping to discover if they were the same color as her cheeks when she got embarrassed, but unfortunately, her maid's uniform covered everything.

"Why are you here?" she asked.

Her tone wasn't friendly or amorous. She actually sounded like she wanted him to leave. He'd have to remedy that. He shifted closer as he leaned near her ear. "Did you miss me? I missed you."

"You need to go." She looked around him at the door to Ethan's office.

There were raised voices coming from inside. One was Julie's—raspy and brusque from years of heavy smoking and drinking.

"She's actually reporting you?" He shouldn't be surprised. Julie was a real bitch—unhappy in her own life so she took it out on everyone else.

"Yeah. I told you I'd get in trouble." She bit her lip.

He stifled a moan. Her mouth was lush, ripe and ready for his cock which stood up another few inches, agreeing with him.

"It's okay, though. She doesn't know you were there, so I'll only get a lecture." She glanced at the door again. "I think."

"Don't worry about Julie. Ethan seldom listens to her." He'd told Ethan to fire her a long time ago, but his friend refused. Ethan believed he owed Julie and Ethan was loyal to a fault.

"I'm not worried about Julie. She's a bitch and I don't care what she thinks about me but..."

Figures. She had a crush on Ethan. He leaned back against the couch. He'd been the one to finger her to orgasm and yet, she was worried about what Ethan thought of her. "Ethan's not going to care that I felt you up. If you haven't noticed, Ethan shares."

Her mouth dropped open.

That was too much. He had no idea how Ethan got all these girls to fall at his feet. It'd always been this way and usually, he was fine with taking seconds, but not today, not with her. "What? Did you think Ethan was going to take one look at you and fall in love, or maybe fuck you and fall in love?" He smiled, shaking his head. "Ethan's not the falling in love kind of guy." No, that was him. Every time he met a cute girl who needed him to save her, he was a goner. That was why the Club was perfect for him. He got to have great sex without the complications because he always fell too fast and too hard and that had scared away every woman he'd ever liked.

"I know Ethan's not going to fall in love with me. I don't want him to."

"Right." *Too late for that lie, honey.*

"Why are you here again?"

That smart little mouth of hers needed something to do. He grabbed her, pulling her onto his lap. She squeaked but then he was kissing her and she tasted just like he remembered—peppermint and something else, something sweet. At first, she froze in his arms but it only took a moment for her to fall into the kiss, and boy, could she kiss. She held his face as their tongues tangled. His hands ran down her back to her ass, pulling her against his dick.

"Let's go somewhere," he whispered as he kissed his way down her neck.

She moaned. "I can't. I want to, but I can't."

"Why?" He stood, lifting her and wrapping her legs around his waist. "We can make it fast this time."

"This time?" Her breath was hot against his ear.

A hot shiver ran through him. He needed to be inside of her now. "Yeah." He walked toward the door. There was a room down the hallway. It was an old office that Ethan used for storage but there was a chair in there and…Shit, he didn't need a chair the wall would do fine.

"So, we're going to do this more than once?" She tightened her legs around his waist, pressing herself against his cock. Her eyes lowered and she bit her bottom lip from the pleasure.

He almost took her right there in Ethan's office. Instead, he kissed her. It was hard and wild just like he felt. He pulled back, panting. "Fuck yeah. We're going to do this a lot." He wanted this little voyeur more than he understood. She was cute but there was something about her, something familiar and so fucking hot. She was curious, innocent and yet, sexy as hell. She'd keep him busy for quite a few weeks.

"I'd like that." She smiled at him and he felt his heart shift.

That wasn't good. He refused to, once again, fall for a girl he barely knew. It never led anywhere good.

She dropped her legs. "But it'll have to wait until after I meet with Ethan. I can't afford to lose my job."

"Ethan can wait." He grabbed her hand, dragging her out of the door and down the hallway. When she struggled, he turned and kissed her. This time, he made it slow and coaxing, letting his tongue delve into her mouth and play until she was clinging to him. "I'll talk to Ethan," he said against her lips.

"No." She pulled away from him, glancing over her shoulder as if Ethan were watching. "You can't. I'll get in trouble."

"No, you won't." He grabbed her hand again, pulling her closer. "Ethan won't care that you want to change positions." And man-oh-man, he had some positions in mind.

"I don't want to be a pleasure associate. I told you that."

"You meant it?" He ran his fingers down her cheek. Her skin was so soft and smooth. "You really don't want to be a courtesan?" Maybe, he should get to know her a little better.

"No. I really don't." She gave him a disgusted look.

"You just like to watch?" He kissed her cheek and then her neck, working his way up to her ear. "That's okay. I can show you a lot. Anything you want."

"You'd be okay with that?" She tipped her head, letting his lips explore.

"Absolutely." His hands trailed up her ribs. "I'll touch you. Fuck you. Eat you out. All while you watch other people fucking." He cupped her breasts as he kept kissing her neck and ear. Her tits were firm and large. Her nipples would probably be dark. "I'll take you to whatever show you want. They have all sorts here." He needed to feel her skin against his. He needed to taste her breasts. His one hand slipped to the buttons on her uniform.

"I can't visit the shows. I work here." Her hands were roaming his back and shoulders.

"It'll be okay. You can be my guest."

"I'm not allowed to be here unless I'm working." She grabbed his hands, stopping him from unbuttoning her shirt.

"I'll talk to Ethan." He hadn't realized Ethan had made that rule. It was stupid and it needed to be changed.

"No." Panic filled her voice. "You can't tell him anything about us. You can't." She pressed his hand more firmly on her breast. "Please."

He sighed. Her crush on Ethan was irritating but it was kind of perfect. It'd keep him from falling for her. He wasn't too savvy when it came to love, but even he knew not to fall for a woman who was hung up on Ethan. "Okay." He kissed her. "I promise. I won't say anything about you to Ethan, but you have to help me out with this." He pulled her flush against him, so she could feel exactly how much he wanted her.

She smiled. "Okay, but later. I have to get back. If Ethan comes out and can't find me...."

21

He grabbed her hand, stopping her from leaving. "When?"

"Later tonight?" She blushed.

"Perfect." He kissed her hand. "Ethan is leaving tonight." He kissed her neck. "I'm going to be watching the place in the evenings for him."

"You'll be managing the Club?" She was surprised. "Ethan's going away?"

"Yeah." She didn't seem disappointed and that was great. "I can show you around." He leaned down and whispered in her ear. "What would you like to see first? Bondage, spankings, whippings, ménage? Name it and I'll show you."

"Anything. You pick, but how are we going to do this. I have to leave when my shift is over and there are cameras at the front door." Her face was turning red.

He trailed his finger down the side of her neck toward her breast. He really wanted to see them, touch them. "There's a back door. I can meet you there."

"No cameras?"

"I'll make sure they're off. No one will ever know." He kissed her again. God, she was sweet. "It'll be our secret."

"Anabelle!" bellowed Ethan.

CHAPTER 3: PATRICK

Patrick stared at Annie's ass as she hurried down the hallway toward Ethan's office. It was firm but with a little jiggle. Oh yeah, he was going to tap that. Even though he'd caught her watching, she seemed somewhat innocent. He wouldn't be surprised if she'd never done anal. The thought of being her first made his dick press more firmly against his jeans, begging for release. He sighed as she stepped through the doorway and out of his sight.

"What were you doing out there?" asked Ethan. "I told you to wait here."

Patrick slipped into the storage room in case Ethan looked in the hallway. Once again, she had him hiding like a scared little boy. She was going to pay for this too. Maybe, he'd spank her ass before he fucked her, or while he fucked her. If he didn't stop thinking about this stuff he'd come in his pants, and he'd never live that down.

"I went to the bathroom," snapped Annie. "Is that okay?"

Damn, she was a spitfire. His little voyeur might lose her job after all, but he'd help her. He had money. He could pay her for their time together.

"There's a bathroom in my office." Ethan's voice moved farther away.

"I didn't want to use it. It might upset you."

"Why would that upset me?" Ethan sounded weary.

"Everything I do upsets you. Why would that be any different?"

Patrick stayed there a few moments longer. Ethan should be furious with her for speaking to him like that, but he wasn't. Instead, his friend seemed resigned. Something was going on and he didn't like it. He wanted Annie. He didn't want to share her with Ethan.

"If you'd behave," said Ethan.

"Behave! By whose standards?"

"Enough, Annie." Ethan almost groaned. "Nick, go find Patrick. He should be here by now."

Patrick slipped out of the supply room and jogged toward the elevator. Then, he turned and headed back toward the office.

Nick came into the hallway. "Ethan's looking for you and he's not in a good mood."

"I thought you were avoiding this place," he said.

Nick was one of his closest friends. He'd met him at La Petite Mort Club, and they'd had some great times, but now his friend was staying away from the Club because he was abstaining from sex.

"I'm not going into the actual Club," said Nick. "I thought I might be able to point out a few things to you. Ethan's been doing this so long he's forgotten what it's like for us when we step in."

"Thanks, but I'm pretty sure I can handle it."

"Earlier today, you were begging me to watch the Club." Nick sent him an odd look.

That was true. "You do usually manage the place for Ethan and—"

"You know, I can't. Not now. I'm six weeks in and ten to go. I can't chance being around here."

"Is Sarah worth it? Four months of celibacy." He'd fallen in love plenty of times, but he didn't think he could've stopped having sex for one hundred and twenty days.

"Fuck yeah, she's worth it. I mean, I wish Ethan would give me her phone number but you know him and his stupid, fucking rules." Nick ran his hand over his face. "It's not easy."

"But rules are rules."

La Petite Mort Club had a lot of rules. They were in place to ensure everyone's pleasure and safety. This rule wasn't any different. Nick and Sarah had been in a timed-contract. When it was over, they could've signed another contract but instead they opted to wait. According to the rules, they had to wait four months and then if they still wanted to see each other, Ethan would give their contact information to the other party. They didn't have to stay celibate for the four months and everyone had tried to explain that to Nick, but he'd insisted that he was going to return to Sarah with a clean conscience. Nick was head over heels for this girl and Patrick knew from experience that feeling like that always ended in heartbreak.

Nick smiled, his eyes gleaming. "And day one hundred and twenty one is going to be fucking fabulous. We won't come up for air for months." He slapped Patrick on the shoulder. "Come on before Ethan gets more pissed. He should be done with his little maid problem by now."

"What happened?" It was time to play dumb.

"Julie caught Annie getting off while watching a couple have sex."

"Who's Annie?" It wasn't good that Nick sounded like he knew her. "And this is a sex club with shows."

"The problem is with who's Annie." Nick walked into the outer office and knocked on the door.

"Come in," bellowed Ethan.

Annie stood in the center of the room, her dark eyes spitting fire at Ethan.

"That is Annie," said Nick. "Annie Argotos."

"No." It was like a punch in the gut.

"Yep," Nick grinned. "The little voyeur is Victor Argotos' baby sister."

"I'm not a child any more but no one seems to see that," she said.

"I'm not allowed to see that." Nick sat on the couch. "It's forbidden."

Patrick stood in the doorway, unable to move. Vic had been in the marines with him and Ethan. They'd gone on many missions together. Too many. They were like brothers. The three of them had watched out for each other until Vic and Ethan had gone on a mission that'd ended badly. Vic hadn't come back the same and a few years later, he'd disappeared. Vic may be gone but Patrick was honor bound to protect his friend's family, not fuck his baby sister.

CHAPTER 4: PATRICK

Annie's beautiful, brown eyes widened when she looked at him and a slight blush covered her cheeks. Patrick couldn't look away. This was little Annie, Vic's baby sister. It couldn't be. She'd been around thirteen or fourteen in the picture he'd seen and in his mind she'd stayed that age, but this woman before him was not thirteen. She had great tits - large and firm -, a tiny waist and an ass and hips that he wanted to explore in every way possible.

"You're late." Ethan snapped at him. "Get in here and close the door. I'll be done in a minute."

"We're done now." Annie turned to leave, but Ethan grabbed her arm.

"We are not done."

"Yes, we are." She jerked free. "You've lectured me. Now, I have to go back to work."

"Oh, no." Ethan grinned, but it wasn't friendly. "You aren't going back to work."

"Are you firing me?" Her eyes narrowed. "You said you weren't going to fire me."

Patrick held his breath. Ethan needed to fire her. Vic's baby sister shouldn't be working here.

"No, but I am suspending you."

"What?" Her voice was shrill.

"You are not"—Ethan walked up to her until he was so close that she had to tip back her head to look at him— "going to run around here watching people have sex and pretend you're working."

Her face heated and she glanced at Patrick. He looked away, his eyes landing on Nick who raised a brow at him and then nodded at Annie.

"I'm getting a drink. Does anyone else want one?" He moved to the bar. He had to do something to keep his eyes off of Annie. Nick being suspicious he could handle but if Ethan even suspected he'd touched her, the other man would kill him—literally.

"I didn't mean to do it, Ethan." Her voice was soft and repentant. "I told you that. I went in there to clean and…and saw them. I only watched for a minute. I was going to close the curtains when Julie found me." Her eyes pleaded with Ethan to believe her.

Liar. Patrick poured himself a hefty drink. She was pretty convincing though.

"Julie said she called you and—"

"She did. I was so scared. I thought the couple"—
her face heated even more—"might've heard the phone but
I don't think they did. I grabbed the curtains—"

Patrick bit back a snort. Yeah, she grabbed the
curtains to shove him behind them. She sent him a quick
glare.

"To close them but Julie—"

"Julie swears there'd been someone in that room
with you?" Ethan's eyes narrowed. "Who was it?"

Patrick's throat tightened. He was a dead man.

"No one. I was alone. I swear." She crossed her
heart.

Patrick almost choked on his whiskey. Nick's dark
eyes bore into him, so he took another sip and tried to look
innocent.

"Julie's been in this business a long time," said
Ethan. "She knows—"

"She hates me. She's always looking for a reason to
yell at me. She wants you to fire me." She took Ethan's
hand. "I swear. I was alone. I work hard. I do a good job."

"I know you do." Ethan's tone was softening. He
was actually buying the little liar's tale.

"Julie is a bitch," said Nick. "You should fire her."

Annie turned and smiled at Nick. Patrick tossed
back the rest of his drink and refilled it. Nick got a smile
for saying something bad about Julie. He'd given Annie an
orgasm and had gotten nothing. Nick was once again
watching him and he almost walked across the room and
wiped the smirk from Nick's face with his fist.

"I'm not firing anyone," said Ethan. "Julie is just doing her job."

"I know she is," said Annie. "I'll try and do better, but it's hard with her always checking up on us every minute and it isn't only me who feels like this. Ask any of the maids."

"I'll talk to Julie," said Ethan.

"Thank you." Annie smiled and hugged him.

Patrick took a large gulp of the whiskey. He hadn't gotten a hug either. He'd had to work for every kiss and every touch. He deserved at least a smile.

"What am I going to do with you?" Ethan squeezed her tight and then let her go. "I need to know you'll be safe when I'm gone."

"Gone? Where are you going?" asked Annie.

Patrick watched her over his glass. She should be a fucking actor.

"Take her with you," said Nick.

"To the wedding?" There was disbelief in Ethan's tone.

"Yeah. She can be your guest, your date." As soon as Ethan looked at Annie, Nick turned toward Patrick and grinned.

He was going to kick Nick's ass as soon as Ethan left. Until then, he had to pretend that the idea of Annie spending two weeks alone with Ethan didn't make him want to kill someone.

"Hmm." Ethan studied her. "I could bring her along."

He took another sip of his drink. Ethan wouldn't touch her. She was Vic's baby sister, but…Ethan was only a man and Annie was too cute to ignore.

"I'm not going to a wedding as your pretend date." She crossed her arms over her chest which made her breasts strain against the fabric of her uniform.

God, he wanted her to do that when she was wearing only a bra or naked. Yeah, naked would be better.

"Stop staring at her," growled Ethan.

Patrick jumped but Ethan's death glare was directed at Nick. Women loved Nick almost as much as they loved Ethan and Nick was the wrong kind of guy for Annie. "I thought you were staying celibate for Sarah."

"I am." Nick grinned. "But I can still look as long as my only date is…" He raised his right hand.

If Nick weren't careful, he'd break his friend's hand. He may not be allowed to touch Annie, but she was his to dream about not Nick's.

Ethan stepped in front of Annie, blocking Nick's view. "This girl is like my sister. You will not look at her."

Nick rolled his eyes. "Fine. I promise. I'll look the other way whenever I see her."

"Stop it." Annie shoved Ethan. "Stop acting like this."

Ethan turned to face her. "I can't."

"Ethan, I love you like my brother and I appreciate everything you've done for me and my family, but I'm not a little girl anymore."

"You are to me," said Ethan. "I still remember your pigtails and missing teeth." He tugged on her ponytail.

"Men!" She shoved him again. "I'm a grown woman"—her eyes darted around Ethan to Patrick—"with wants and needs and desires."

"Shut up. Don't talk like that." Ethan clamped his hand over her mouth.

She pulled away. "You need to hear this." She stepped out of his reach. "I'm not a virgin, Ethan. I haven't been for a long time." Once again she glanced at Patrick.

He shifted closer to the bar to hide his hardening cock. If Nick or Ethan saw how her words were affecting him, he'd be teased to death by one and tortured and killed by the other.

"Right now, I don't have a boyfriend or a lover but I'd like to have one."

"Stop." Ethan took two steps forward and clapped his hand over her mouth again, holding her tight this time. "I don't want to hear that. None of it." He glanced behind him at his two friends. "And you can't say things like that in a room full of men." He glared at Nick. "Especially, men like him."

"Hey! I'm not going to touch her and you know it," said Nick.

Patrick's mouth dropped open. Men like Nick? He was a man and he'd had his fair share of women—so what if he wasn't into threesomes or orgies like the other two. He was still a man and a dangerous one to young, pretty females. Ethan should ask Annie about that. God, what was he thinking? That'd be a disaster.

Annie struggled in Ethan's hold and he finally dropped his hand.

"Don't do that again. Ever." She was almost spitting mad. Her eyes were snapping and her face was heated.

Patrick's cock grew harder. He'd love to use that anger, that fire, in other more pleasurable ways.

"Then stop talking like that," said Ethan.

"I'm going back to work." She turned in a huff.

"Your shift is over."

She spun around. "I still have two hours left."

"No. You're done for today and you're done for the next two weeks."

"What? You can't do that." Fear was replacing her anger.

"Consider it a vacation." Ethan strode to the bar. "While I'm gone you're not to be here." He poured himself a drink.

"But…but, I need the money."

"It's a paid vacation." Ethan took a sip of his drink.

"I won't take your charity."

"It isn't charity. It's never been charity." Ethan turned toward her, his tone pleading. "Why can't you understand that?"

"Because it is charity and I won't accept it. I'll earn my money either here or somewhere else."

"It's a fucking vacation, Annie. Say thank you and go rest, study, do something. Anything but come here."

"I haven't worked here long enough to earn two weeks paid vacation. It isn't fair to the other maids."

"I don't give a shit about the other maids." Ethan's knuckles were white as he gripped his glass.

"Why don't you have Patrick keep an eye on her?" suggested Nick.

Patrick choked on his drink. "What?"

"Actually, that's a good idea," said Ethan.

"No. No, it's not." That was the worst idea ever. His mind scrambled for a reason he could tell Ethan while Nick struggled not to laugh and Annie's dark eyes were glaring a hole right through his skull.

"It's perfect because I don't know what else to do with her." Ethan sent Annie a disgusted look. "She's as stubborn as her brother, maybe more. As soon as her dad died she stopped taking my money and no matter what I try, she keeps refusing."

"Dad shouldn't have taken it either."

"He was like a father to me. I was honored to help." Ethan's tone was hurt. He turned back to Patrick. "You're the only one I trust to watch out for her. You love Vic as much as I do."

He grabbed onto the bar as guilt jabbed him in the gut like a knife. Vic would kill him–should kill him–for what he'd done to Annie. He glanced at her and she was watching him closely, wariness in her eyes. His hands itched to pull her close and calm her worries. There was no way he could watch over her. "I can't be here both day and night." There. That was the perfect excuse. "She works days. I can only be here at night."

Her jaw jutted out. He didn't know her well but he recognized that as a bad sign.

"I'll change her schedule." Ethan's hand waved through the air as if wiping the problem aside. "Actually, that's even better. I don't want her taking the bus."

"Now, you want me to pick her up and take her home too?" This was unbelievable. It'd be bad enough being in the Club with her, but alone in the car. Alone at her house. He'd never survive.

"Yeah. Mike usually picks her up and takes her home, but I've given him the two weeks off too. I was going to hire someone,"—Ethan's eyes darted to Annie— "a female, to fill in for him, but I haven't had time." He slapped Patrick on the shoulder. "Now, I don't have to do that. Plus, she has a few items that need fixing around her house. Things I haven't gotten around to doing."

"I'm going to be her handyman too." This kept getting better and better.

Nick choked on a laugh, hitting his chest as all eyes fell on him. "Sorry." He raised his glass. "Went down the wrong pipe."

Patrick mouthed, "Fuck you, asshole" behind Ethan's back and Nick snorted on another laugh.

"Don't worry, Patrick. I don't need you for anything." Annie's brown eyes were filled with hurt.

Nick sobered and Patrick wanted to bash his head against the wall. She'd seen their exchange.

"You have three choices, Annie." Ethan was done playing around. "You can come with me to the wedding, stay home with pay or Patrick will pick you up, watch over you here and take you home. If you don't want him helping around your house, fine." His eyes landed on Patrick. "Although, he should want to do all those things and more."

That was the problem. He wanted to do a lot more for her, with her, to her.

"Vic would've done everything he could've for either of our families," said Ethan.

"You're right. I'm sorry." He was being an ass. Vic was his friend. He owed the other man his life. He could contain his lust for two weeks. She was only a woman. The Club was filled with women. He'd fuck several of them, numerous times a day and forget all about Annie except as Vic's little sister.

"Annie?" Ethan turned to her. "What's your decision?'

"You're an ass."

"Insulting me wasn't one of your choices."

"You didn't give me choices. I need the money and there's only one way I can earn it."

"Good. Change out of your uniform and Patrick will take you home."

"Tonight? I can't." He needed a woman before he went anywhere alone with her. He could still taste her on his lips. He rubbed his hand across his chin, inhaling her scent that still lingered on his fingers. His dick which had softened during the conversation, perked up again like the pesky fellow it was.

"Why? You're here to take over for me. This is your first job."

"Don't bother. I'll take the bus." Annie stormed from the room, slamming the door behind her.

"She has a temper," said Nick.

He glared at his friend who only grinned at him. This was all Nick's fault. "Go fuck yourself." If it weren't for Nick, Ethan would've never thought to make Annie his responsibility.

"Oh, I'm sure I'll do that later"—Nick stood—"but right now I'm taking Ethan to the airport."

"What about your driver?"

"Mike started his vacation already." Ethan grabbed a carry-on bag from the closet. "Sorry, we didn't have time to go over everything. I'll call you from the airport."

"We went over it last week. It's fine." There wasn't much to do except be here. Ethan's staff was well trained, well paid and completely competent.

"Keep the office door locked unless you're in here." Ethan tossed Patrick a set of keys.

"Don't forget to tell him about the cameras." Nick opened the door.

"Oh, yeah." Ethan motioned to a door in the back of the office. "There's a couch, shower and fridge back there."

"You sleep here?"

"Sometimes. The nights aren't as exciting when you're the boss."

"Cameras," prodded Nick.

"There's a TV back there and two boxes. They look like cable boxes. One of them is but the other is a surveillance system."

"You have a security team for that." He'd hired that team for Ethan.

"Yes, but someone needs to watch them and I like to keep my eye on things without wandering around the Club." Ethan headed toward the door. "When you're in charge people tend to ask for favors. Telling them no doesn't lend itself to happy customers, so I stay in my office."

He'd never thought about it, but he didn't see Ethan in the actual business part of the Club often. They usually met here.

"And these cameras are everywhere." Nick's tone seemed to hold a warning.

Patrick started sweating. He had to calm down. If Ethan had seen him and Annie, he'd be dead. "You film the couples?"

"Yeah, but I don't watch everything."

"What about the couples who don't want to be filmed or watched." Like him and Annie. God, he didn't want that on tape. His dick didn't agree. It really wanted to get a look at that video.

"We have to know for sure nothing bad is happening," said Ethan.

"So someone is watching everything?" He was going to have to bribe somebody.

"No. The security staff monitors the harder core activities. The cameras in the hallways and the other rooms are filming all the time but they only notify me if there's a sound of distress." Ethan laughed. "That took a while to get right. At first, I was getting a text every time someone came."

He chuckled as his mind raced. He needed to erase that part of the tape. Right after he watched it. "So, do you keep the footage? It could be confiscated—"

"Terry informed me of the liabilities as soon as I hired him as the Club's lawyer. The footage is erased after twelve hours. That gives me enough time if something happens but probably not enough time for the police to get involved."

"Oh. You need me to watch—"

"I need you to keep an eye on things, that's all. However you want to do it."

"I like to roam the floors and get to know everyone," said Nick.

"All the girls, you mean," said Ethan. "I swear the first time he watched the place he fucked more than he worked."

"Hey, the place was still standing when you came back."

"But some of the girls weren't." Ethan laughed and then turned back to Patrick. "You'll do fine. You can text me or talk to Julie. I know you don't like her, but she can help if you need something."

He'd fumble through on his own before he asked her for help.

"We gotta go," said Nick.

"Patrick," Ethan's face was serious. "Keep Annie out of trouble. We owe Vic that much."

"Why in the hell is she even here?"

"We have to leave," said Nick.

"One minute." Ethan turned back to Patrick. "After Vic's mom died, he disappeared."

"I know that. I had Hunter search for him. Shit, I looked for him." He'd spent months and a fortune trying to find his friend.

"Well, I'm sure you didn't know that his dad fell apart. Started drinking and gambling. Between the medical bills for Vic's mom and his dad's…habits, they almost lost everything. I found out about it and talked to Mr. Argotos. I convinced him to take some money–for his kids. He didn't want to but he agreed. I kept their accounts full–not full enough for him to gamble too much, but full enough so they wouldn't lose the house."

"Why didn't you buy the house?"

"I did and he mortgaged it again. This seemed safer."

"And once he died?"

"I continued with the arrangement, inputting money in the account until a few months ago. Annie insisted on sitting down with the accountant, who of course, worked for me. She figured out what I'd been doing."

"And she wasn't okay with it?" Most people didn't care where free money came from as long as it didn't stop coming.

"She was furious. I tried everything but she insisted on paying her own way. It was when I caught her waitressing at a strip club that I hired her."

"She was working at a strip club?" He'd paddle her ass when he saw her. His cock twitched at the idea of her lying over his legs, her ass bare for his slap and his caress.

"As a waitress, not a stripper."

"Yeah, we all know it wouldn't have been long before she was dancing."

"That's why she's here."

"You're going to miss your flight," mumbled Nick.

"Watch her Patrick." Ethan turned and followed Nick out of the door.

Oh, he'd watch her all right. He'd make sure she learned how stupid she was being. Waitressing at a strip club, watching a couple have sex when anyone could've come up behind her and coaxed her into doing...anything, like he'd almost done. She had to learn to be more careful, especially, in these kinds of places. These next two weeks wouldn't be so bad. He'd spend them teaching her to navigate the dangerous world of men and sex, but he'd keep his hands to himself. It wouldn't be that hard. She was one woman in a club full of women. Plus, she was Vic's sister. That meant she was his sister...like his sister. He'd watch her and make sure she didn't get into trouble, but that was all he'd do.

Book 2

Watching The Voyeur

CHAPTER 1: ANNIE

Annie changed out of her uniform and into her T-shirt and jeans. This sucked. She wanted to kill Ethan and Patrick. She grabbed her purse from her locker and pulled out the picture Vic had sent to her his first year as a marine. She ran her finger over her brother's face. He was so young and full of life and hope. Her heart broke all over again for the loss—her brother's and hers.

She touched Ethan's face. He was to Vic's right and he was so handsome. He still was, but she'd never been attracted to him—her crush when she was ten didn't count. Her gaze drifted to the third man in the photo—Patrick.

Even as a teenager, she'd been drawn to him, this stranger in a photo. There was something about his smile and his eyes that made her feel safe. He looked like the kind of guy a girl could count on. She touched his face. He'd been the star of so many of her fantasies and for one moment, one brief, lovely moment, she'd thought she'd get to live her dreams for a few weeks. However, as soon as he'd discovered who she was, the lust in his eyes had disappeared and he'd looked at her as if she'd had two heads. It was high school all over again.

Growing up, Vic had been her favorite of her five brothers. She'd been the baby, the last child and the only girl. Her parents had spoiled her but not her brothers, except Vic. Her two oldest brothers hadn't paid much attention to her and the two brothers closest to her age had been her tormentors. Being six years older than her, Vic had been old enough not to fight with her and young enough to still play with her. He'd been her everything— her confidant and her protector. She'd adored him and his friends, until she'd started liking boys.

By then, Vic had already been a marine and had been stationed thousands of miles away, but that hadn't stopped him from keeping her safe, and to him that meant keeping all boys away from her. The threat of Victor Argotos followed her around like an unwanted shadow. If Vic heard about any boy paying attention to her, he'd send one of her younger brothers or one of his friends' brothers to kick the boy's ass. It'd only taken a couple of times for all the boys in the area to realize that Annie Argotos, although cute and friendly, wasn't worth the risk. She'd thought she'd gotten used to the look of horror on their faces when they heard her last name, but seeing it on Patrick had almost made her burst into tears.

She stuffed the picture back in her purse. She was done crying. She'd cried too many nights over boys who didn't like her enough to risk a confrontation with one of her brothers. She didn't need a guy like that in her life. She wouldn't let a guy like that in her life.

When she left the locker room, she was glad that Patrick wasn't waiting for her. He wasn't going to change his mind about wanting to be with her, so the best thing she could do was to get him out of her head and that meant staying as far away from him as possible.

She hurried down the hallway. She had no doubt he'd come to take her home. He was a former marine and Ethan had ordered him to do it. Everyone did what Ethan commanded. She'd probably be like that too if he hadn't basically lived with them since she was seven. Ethan's home life hadn't been good and her parents had practically adopted him. She loved him like a brother. Unfortunately, he could be just as overbearing and she was done with that. She'd had a taste of freedom when she'd gone away to college and she liked it.

She slipped out the back door and headed down the street. She had two weeks without Ethan or Julie watching her every move and she was going to take advantage of it. More than likely, Patrick would stay away from her. He'd barely looked at her once he'd found out who she was and that was great. Really, it was because tomorrow night she'd be on her own in a sex club. She'd get her job done as fast as possible and then she'd find someone to fill her nights. There were a couple of guys who worked in the kitchen that had flirted with her, until Ethan had noticed, but Ethan wasn't going to be around and...

"Annie, stop!" yelled Patrick.

She couldn't help it. Her legs froze. She was not his puppet, but she knew better than to run. He'd only catch her. She was fast but he'd be faster—her brothers always had been. She spun around. He strode toward her, his handsome face taut with anger. She knew that look. She'd seen it on all her brothers' faces and her father's. She was getting a lecture.

"Where do you think you're going?"

She smiled up at him, putting on her most innocent expression. It worked with her brothers—sometimes. His eyes darkened and dropped to her breasts for a quick second. That was interesting. Perhaps, he wasn't as immune to her as she'd thought.

"Ethan's gone. We don't need to obey him. He isn't God."

Patrick's eyes dropped to her breasts again and she inhaled making the shirt stretch across them. Maybe, she could have her two weeks of fantasy-come-to-life. She stepped closer, tipping back her head and letting her mouth drop open a tiny bit. She ran her tongue across her lips and fought a smile as a soft groan escaped him.

"You didn't seem thrilled with this arrangement so I figured I'd take the bus...unless you want to come home with me." This time she bit her bottom lip, just a little. They had a lot of unfinished business and she couldn't wait to tear his clothes off.

"I'll escort you home." His voice was strained.

She wanted to jump for joy. The star of her amorous dreams was coming home with her—in the flesh.

He cleared his throat and moved away. "Even though Ethan's gone, I'll follow his orders." His eyes dropped to her chest again and his face tightened even more. "All of them. It's his club."

"But I'm not his—"

"No, you're Vic's baby sister." He grabbed her wrist and headed for the garage, his long legs making her run to keep up.

"I'm not a baby or a little girl."

"You are to me." He dropped her hand and opened a car door.

It was a Mustang—an old one, '67 or '69, metallic blue, big, strong and beautiful. She climbed inside, looking up at him her face heating at what she was about to say. She wasn't usually this forward, but she wanted him and he wanted her. Obeying Ethan was stupid. "That's funny. I'm pretty sure you knew I was a woman a few hours ago."

He slammed the door in her face. A moment later he climbed into the driver's seat and started the car, pulling out of the garage.

"Earlier, never happened," he said.

"You can't undo the past." She should've known better than to hope he was different.

"You can forget about it."

She crossed her arms over her chest. He was attracted to her—by the bulge in his pants, he was very attracted to her—but she knew that look. With five older brothers, she could write a book about that look—stupid, male pride. He wouldn't do anything to her or with her again, no matter how much he wanted to. "Fine. We'll both forget about it."

"Good." The tension eased from his shoulders.

"It wasn't that great anyway," she mumbled. With five brothers, she'd learned at an early age to aim for their pride when striking back.

"What?" His head snapped in her direction. "I seem to recall you coming so hard you about broke my fingers."

"Hmm. I don't think that happened." She stared straight ahead, trying not to blush.

He almost growled and then took a deep breath. "You're right. It didn't." He glanced at her as he ran his fingers under his nose and inhaled before sliding them into his mouth. "Mmm." He pulled them out, wiping them on his shirt. "Never happened at all."

She wanted that mouth on her—her lips, her neck, her breasts and between her thighs. She squeezed her legs together to try and ease the ache as she shifted on her seat.

"You okay?" He smirked. "You seem uncomfortable."

"I'm fine." She was going to make him pay for that—big time.

CHAPTER 2: PATRICK

Finally, silence. Patrick didn't want to talk about what he'd done with Vic's baby sister, but he sure as shit wasn't going to let her forget that he'd made her come and he'd only used his hand. He would've made her scream, maybe even pass out, if he'd used his tongue or his dick. He glanced at her and his mouth went dry, as the smug smile slipped from his face.

With one hand she was pulling her T-shirt tight across her glorious chest while the other hand brushed her breasts as if there was something caught on the cloth. He couldn't pull his eyes away from the subtle movement of those lush tits as they shimmied and bounced with each passing stroke of her fingers. He wanted to push her hand aside, raise that T-shirt and squeeze those breasts. The skin would be soft and smooth. He'd pop one of them out of her bra and…

"Patrick, look out!"

His eyes flew to the windshield and he stomped on the brake, barely stopping before they hit the car in front of them.

"What the hell! Are you trying to kill us," she yelled.

"It was your…." He slammed his mouth shut at her raised eyebrow.

"It was my what?" she asked innocently.

"Nothing." The light changed and he followed the other cars.

"You were going to blame me, weren't you?"

He started to say yes but the superior look she was giving him made him stuff those words back down his throat. She'd played with her tits to get a reaction out of him, but there was no way he was going to accuse her of that. He'd been in a lot of relationships, not that this was a relationship, but he knew when to keep his mouth shut. "No. I was going to ask where your street was."

"You said, *It was your*, how is that asking for directions to my house? Plus, if you don't have them, how did you know to head this way?"

Now, she had a smug expression and he really wanted to remove it, by kissing her or turning her over his knee and paddling her beautiful, round ass until she moaned. "First, I said, *is this your* not *it was your* and second, Ethan told me where you live so I have a general idea but I'm not sure of the exact street." He glanced at her and her eyes were narrowed–smug expression gone. She didn't quite believe him but she didn't have any proof. He'd won that round and he wanted to cheer and beat his chest but decided gloating in silence was a wiser choice.

"Hmm. You don't need to turn for a while yet."

He drove in silence for several minutes, shifting to take the pressure off his stiff cock—just being near her made him hard. She wore a soft floral scent that made him want to locate those spots on her skin and kiss them. Did she dab some behind her ears? Probably. What about between her tits? His gaze darted to them but he forced himself to look at the road. He wasn't doing that again, not while driving.

"Do you mind stopping at Home Depot and the grocery store?"

"What? Why?" He wanted her gone so he could go back to the Club and get laid.

"Never mind."

"What do you need? I can pick it up for you tomorrow." Unfortunately, they'd be spending twice a day alone in his car.

"You can't drop it off tomorrow. You'll be picking me up at school. Didn't Ethan tell you?"

"No, he didn't." He was going to kill Ethan for this. No, he'd kill Nick. This was all his fault.

"Don't worry about it. I'll have my friend drop me off at work after class."

He almost asked if her friend was male or female but stopped himself. That wasn't important, although it sure felt important. "I'll pick you up after class."

"You don't have to."

"But I do."

"Right, because Ethan told you." She sighed. "You need to grow up and stop doing everything Ethan commands."

He slammed on his brakes, swerving off the road. A man could only take so much. He turned toward her. "I am grown up. Very grown as I'm sure you remember."

"I have no idea what you're talking about." Her eyes widened in false innocence.

His eyes dropped to her mouth and then her chest. He was going to remind her in explicit detail just how grown he was. He reached out and stopped—his hand only inches away from her. He couldn't remind her of anything. She was off limits. He dropped his arm. "I'm not doing this for Ethan. I'm doing this for your brother."

"That's worse. Vic isn't even around anymore."

"He'd want us to look out for you and I'm going to do that whether you like it or not." He pulled the car back onto the road.

"If Vic were so worried about me, he wouldn't have left."

"He's sick."

"He needs help but he refuses to get it."

"You don't understand what it's like." No one outside of the military did. It'd been hard for him to

53

readjust and he hadn't gone through what Vic had, although, he should've.

"No, I don't." She was silent for a moment. "Two streets up take a right."

"Where's the grocery store and Home Depot?" He was going to look out for her and that included making sure she had food and repairing whatever was broken at her house.

"Forget it. I don't want to inconvenience you."

"It's not an inconvenience." It was inconveniently keeping him from finding someone to fuck, but he'd do this for Vic.

"Pleeease." She obviously didn't believe him.

"I don't mind but I do need to get back to the Club. I've never watched it for Ethan before and I don't want something to happen while I'm in charge."

"I said don't worry about it."

"Do you have something to eat for tonight?" He couldn't let her go hungry.

"Stop, okay? You don't want to do this and I don't want you to do this, but we're stuck because you're too much of a child to do what you want instead of what you were told."

"That's the most ass-backward definition of child and man I've ever heard." He'd had about enough of her. "A child does what he wants to do no matter what. A man does what he has to do because it's the right thing, even if he doesn't want to do it."

She turned and stared out the window. God, he hoped she wasn't crying. He shouldn't have admitted that he didn't want to do this. She'd accused him of it, but he shouldn't have admitted it.

The orange Home Depot sign loomed up ahead.

"What do you need at Home Depot?"

"It doesn't matter." Her voice was rough as if she were fighting back tears.

He felt like a heel. "If you need something done at the house, I can help. I'm pretty good with my hands." He wanted to kick himself at her sharp intake of breath. "I didn't mean it like that."

"Please, just take me home, then you can leave and we can both be happy."

Happy? Leaving her wouldn't make him happy. Fucking her would make him happy, but he couldn't do that. However, he could help her. He pulled into the Home Depot parking lot.

"What are you doing?"

"You need something. We're going to get it." He parked the car.

"I said forget it."

"Stop being a baby. You don't have a car, and you need something from here. Let's get it and be done."

"I don't need your help."

He got out of the car, walked around to her side and opened her door. "Are you coming or am I going to have to drag you out of there?"

She looked up at him. "You wouldn't."

He leaned down, skimming his fingers over her hip that was farthest from the door. Her breathing increased as she watched his hand. He rested it on her tight, little thigh. Her leg was so tiny if he moved his thumb just a little he'd brush across her pussy. His hand trembled slightly as he unlatched her seatbelt and stepped away from temptation. "Don't try me."

He turned and headed toward the building, afraid to drag her out of the car because if she struggled even a little, and she would, he'd shove her down across the seat and fuck her. He glanced over his shoulder and she was still in the car. Part of him wanted to go back and show her he meant what he said, but touching her again would be too much. So, he'd take the coward's way out. "I'm not leaving until you get whatever it is you need."

She got out of the car, frowning as she followed him. He slowed his pace until she caught up.

"I'm not your dog. You can't give me orders and expect me to obey." She elbowed him in the side.

"Apparently, I can," he mumbled.

"I'm going to pretend I didn't hear that." She grabbed a cart and went into the building.

He chuckled as he followed her. He could think of worse ways to spend the evening. Her jeans hugged her tight, little ass and watching that jiggle had become one of his favorite things to do. God, he wanted to see it bare, in his bed, bent over a table, her kneeling on the floor chest down and ass up, offering herself to him. He bit down on the inside of his mouth. If anyone glanced at his pants they'd get an eye full.

She turned down the plumbing aisle and stopped. She pulled a paper from her purse and began searching the rows of materials.

"Let me see the list," he said.

"I don't need your help." She moved farther away.

"Okay, but I'll be waiting right here when you give up." He positioned himself behind the cart to hide his erection.

"Need any help?" A clerk appeared from the other aisle. The guy was young and his eyes roamed all over her.

"Yes, please." She turned and smiled.

Patrick's heart slammed against his chest. Those lush, stick-a-cock-between-me lips and her sparkling, brown eyes sent a spike of pain through his heart. Oh, she was dangerous. The clerk moved closer to her, his arm brushing against her shoulder as he studied her list. That guy was a dead man if he didn't step away from her.

"We don't need any help." He moved between her and the clerk, grabbing her list.

"Yes, I do." She snatched the paper back.

"No. You don't." He glared at the clerk over her head. "I've got this."

"I'll be over here if you need anything." The guy almost ran to the other end of the aisle.

"Great. Thanks a lot." She bent at the waist and began searching for pipe fittings and mumbled, "Asshole."

His hand hovered above her butt, not sure if he should crack it or caress it but he definitely needed to touch it. He settled on a soft slap.

"Hey," she straightened and tried to glare at him but her cheeks were flushed and her eyes had darkened with desire.

"Oh, shit." He should've known she'd like it. He'd caught her watching a couple have sex. She was into kinky.

"Don't ever do that again." This time she managed to look angry but there was a challenge in her tone.

"And what if I do?" He moved closer, never one to back down from a dare.

"You'll be sorry."

He laughed. She was half his size. "I'll risk it." He snatched the paper from her again.

"Give me that." She tried to grab it, but he held it out of her reach.

"What's leaking?" His eyes dropped to the V between her legs. She'd been so wet before, she was probably wet now.

Her lips thinned but a slight blush covered her cheeks. "Kitchen sink."

"You measured?"

"Yes, so give me the paper so I can get what I need to fix it."

"You'll fix it?" Sure, women were capable of doing this kind of work as well as men but he'd never met one who actually did.

"Yes. I've been fixing things around the house for years. Dad…he stopped doing that kind of stuff." She glanced away.

"Sorry about your father."

"Thanks. Me too. Can we get the stuff and go? I'm tired."

"Sure." He began gathering the pieces she needed.

"Give me half." Her hand was out and her foot was tapping the floor. "I know what I'm doing."

He sighed before tearing the paper in two and handing a section to her.

CHAPTER 3: PATRICK

"Next stop, the grocery store," Patrick said as he opened the car door for Annie before loading her items into the trunk.

"You don't have to," she said when he got into the car.

"You gotta eat." He started the car. She'd been quiet ever since she'd mentioned her father.

"I have food at home."

"Would you rather we stop tomorrow?" He didn't like sad Annie. Annoying Annie was…annoying but sad Annie broke his heart.

"Yes." She stared out the window.

He wanted to hold her and make her feel better. It wasn't sexual. He adjusted his pants. Okay, it was a little sexual, but mostly, right now, he wanted to comfort her. The last few years couldn't have been easy.

"Where are your other brothers?"

"My oldest brother is in California. Tommy, the next oldest, is in Germany and my other two brothers are still in the service."

"So, it's only you here?" That had to be hard. He also came from a big family and he saw his siblings at least once a month.

"Me and Vic."

"Is that why you're still here? Why you're not living near one of your brothers?" He knew the answer but wanted to hear her say it.

"Yes."

"Vic may not still be in this area." All leads on Vic had dried up when he'd disappeared into the streets with the homeless.

"I know, but"—she turned and looked at him—"I think he is. I got a card from him after Dad died."

"You got a card from him?" He almost slammed on the brakes.

"Yeah." Her eyes were wide now. "Why? Is that important? There was no return address."

"Did you tell Ethan? I need to see it? Do you have the envelope?"

"No."

"You don't have the envelope?" He was going to wring her pretty, little neck.

"Yes, I have the envelope but no, I didn't tell Ethan. I didn't think it mattered."

"Shit. Good. Okay." He had to calm down. "I need to see it. I can send it to the lab to make sure it was from him. We may get a lead."

"You...you'd do that?"

"Yes." He pulled the car into the grocery store parking lot. "I'd do anything for your brother."

"You know people who can look into this?"

He laughed. "I am the people who look into these kinds of things." He got out of the car and walked to her side, frowning at her as she opened the door. "I was coming to get the door." He took her hand and helped her step out of the car.

"I can open my own door."

"I never said you couldn't." He wanted to intertwine his fingers with hers and keep her by his side. She was so small and alone. Every fiber in his body screamed for him to protect her, to take care of her and that wasn't good. He dropped her hand and headed for the building.

He had to stop this. She was Vic's sister. He wouldn't fuck Vic's sister and leave her, and he couldn't get involved in another relationship. They never ended well for him. He always picked the wrong women and a girl who liked to watch other people have sex, wasn't the kind of girl who wanted a one man-one woman relationship. Although he had experimented with multiple partners, it wasn't his thing. He preferred one woman at a time and he insisted on monogamy in his relationships.

"What do you do? Are you a private investigator or something?" She was trailing a little behind him, so he slowed his pace.

"Or something." He grinned when she made a frustrated noise. "I run a consulting firm. We offer security, mercenary work, background checks and stuff like that."

"Cool."

"Not really. Most of the jobs are tedious." And sad. The men and women who worked for him usually lived alone. This kind of life didn't lend itself to families. Plus, most of the people they investigated were cheating or lying about something, just like the women he dated.

CHAPTER 4: ANNIE

Annie had planned on teasing Patrick in the grocery store too—bending over, displaying her ass, pretending to flirt with the produce manager—but when he'd gotten so excited about finding Vic, she'd lost interest in tormenting him. He was a nice guy—a sexy, hot, hunky, nice guy and if he felt she were off limits she'd back away. She didn't want to, but she would.

She grabbed a cart and headed for the produce section. She'd make some Pico de Gallo, a salad and a nice chicken breast. Patrick trailed after her as she moved from display to display collecting her vegetables.

His phone rang and he answered it, holding up his finger for her to wait. She ignored him. He wasn't her bodyguard; he was her ride home. Too bad he wasn't her ride. Her eyes trailed down his long, strong legs. He wasn't aroused any longer but she could still make out a faint outline of his cock and he looked pretty large. It'd been too long since she'd been with a man. She'd hooked up with a guy she'd met at a party almost a year ago, but that had been a drunken mistake and she hadn't even enjoyed herself. Her last good sexual experience had been years ago in college before she'd quit school and come home to help care for her mother. Her boyfriend had tried to stick it out, but they'd broken up six months later. She didn't blame him. He'd signed up for going out, partying and having sex, not a long distance relationship with no sex and her constant sadness. Then, Vic had come home—damaged was the best word for it—and it'd been the final straw for her father. He'd aged before her eyes and his spirit had died along with her mother. Dad hadn't physically disappeared like Vic, but he'd left her alone all the same.

"Annie." Greg, the produce manager, hurried to her side. "I didn't expect to see you tonight."

"Hi," she smiled and accepted his quick hug. They'd gone to high school together. "How are Sheila and the kids?"

"Great. We're pregnant again." He grinned like he'd accomplished a miracle.

"You dog you." She hugged him again. "Congratulations."

"Who's your friend?" Patrick loomed over her.

Greg backed away, his eyes widening at the sight of Patrick.

"Greg,"—she ignored Patrick's glare—"this is Patrick a friend of Ethan's."

"A friend of yours," Patrick corrected.

She shook her head. He was a lot of things but friend wasn't one of them.

"Nice to meet you." Greg held out his hand and Patrick hesitated before shaking it.

When they were done, she stepped forward, blocking Patrick. "I'm going to need a delivery later this week." She dug in her purse for her list.

"Sure thing," said Greg. "Billy will bring it by—"

"Why do you need a delivery?" asked Patrick. "Get everything now."

"I don't have time."

"The Club will be fine for another thirty minutes or so."

"That's nice of you." It actually was. "But, I have class tonight and I get my staples every other week."

"You let this Billy guy come to your house every other week?" His tone was incredulous like it was the stupidest thing in the world.

"Yes." She shot Greg an apologetic look.

"We'll stop whenever you need to." He looked over her head at Greg. "Cancel the delivery."

"No, Greg, don't." She turned to Patrick. "You're only driving me for two weeks. When it's over—"

"I'll talk to Ethan. His driver will stop—"

"I don't want to bother Mike with this."

"It won't be a bother."

"It will be. He shouldn't have to drive me as it is." She handed the list to Greg. "Call me before Billy comes by."

Patrick snatched the list from Greg.

"Hey, give that back to him."

"No. We'll stop whenever you want and pick this up."

She reached for the paper but he stuffed it into his pants pocket. Her eyes followed his hand, her fingers itching to dig it out.

"Don't even think about it." His voice was a whispered growl.

"Annie, not in the store." Greg touched her shoulder.

She slowly raised her eyes to Patrick's face, letting her gaze take in his burgeoning cock, his sculpted chest, his perfect mouth, and by the time she reached his eyes, they were dark with desire and warning. "If you don't give it back, I'll do more than think about it."

"Annie, not here." Greg nudged her and she glanced around.

There was an elderly woman by the tomatoes and a mother with two kids by the bananas. Unfortunately, this wasn't the time to dig in Patrick's pants.

She turned around. "It was good seeing you, Greg. I'll call you later with the list of items I need."

"Over my dead body," mumbled Patrick.

She ignored him and hugged Greg who was a bit reserved in his embrace.

"I'll see you later." She grabbed the cart and walked away.

"Over my dead body," muttered Patrick again as he trailed after her.

She greeted the butcher, another high school classmate, and he was also reserved due to Patrick's glaring presence. By the time she'd picked up everything she needed she was ready to strangle the hulking, sexy giant who followed her like a dark shadow. He was even worse than her brother. At least Vic had been friendly with the guys. They'd known he'd kill them if they touched her, so they'd flirted harmlessly and Vic was fine with that. Patrick wasn't.

"So, is this where you find your boyfriends?" he asked as he held the car door open for her.

She glared at him and tugged on the door but he wouldn't let it go.

"You should pay more attention. All of those guys are married."

She faced the windshield. She wasn't going to discuss this with him.

"Did you even notice that?" When she refused to answer he slammed the door and got into the driver's seat. "You know, I'm glad you're keeping your mouth shut for once."

She bit her lip to keep from speaking. This was getting to him, so she'd keep doing it.

"You should listen for a change. Those guys won't leave their wives for you no matter what they say."

She snorted. She'd gone to high school with their wives too. She had been and still was friends with them, but there was no way she was telling him any of this—the arrogant jerk.

"They just want to fuck you. That's it."

"At least someone does," she mumbled, unable to keep that to herself.

He swerved the car and parked on the side of the road. He was only one house away from hers but he didn't know that. "Is that what you want? Just someone who wants to fuck you?"

"It's a start."

He was gripping the steering wheel so hard his knuckles were white. "Figures." He took a deep breath. "Well, you're not going to find it on my watch. I'll make sure of that."

That was it. She opened the door and got out. If she stayed in that car one more minute, she'd either hit him or kiss him and right now, she didn't know which would be worse.

"Where the hell do you think you're going?" he yelled after her.

"Home." She quickened her pace as his footsteps got closer.

"Get back in the car." He grabbed her arm.

"No." She was in her driveway. "Go away."

"One way or another, you're getting in that car."

"No. I'm not."

The next thing she knew she was in the air and over his shoulder. He strode toward his car, his large hand on her ass.

"Put me down." She flung her legs, hitting him in the stomach with her feet.

He squeezed her butt, his thumb caressing her cheek. She couldn't believe she was getting turned on by this Neanderthal. She needed him to put her down before she moaned and gave herself away.

"This is my house."

"What?" He stopped mid-stride.

"I'm home." She leaned up on his shoulder. "I live here."

His large hand skimmed down to her thigh, his fingers resting between them. If he moved just a fraction north, he'd be touching her where she throbbed. She needed to get down before she tried to wiggle her body against his fingers and embarrassed herself.

"I'll get the car." He eased her off his shoulder, letting her body slide down his.

"Annie," yelled Mr. Johnsbrick, her elderly neighbor. "Are you okay?"

"Yes, Mr. Johnsbrick." She hurried to her house. "I'm fine." She grabbed her keys out of her purse. By the time she'd opened her door Patrick was getting out of his car in her driveway.

"You forgot your groceries." He came up behind her, standing way too close.

"Thanks." She reached for the bags.

"Who is that with you?" Mr. Johnsbrick leaned farther out his door. "Is that man bothering you? Should I call the police?"

She looked up at Patrick a smirk on her face.

"Don't you dare," he said.

"No, Mr. Johnsbrick. It's okay. He's leaving."

"I'm Patrick." He turned and smiled at the elderly man. "I'm a friend of her brother Vic."

"Oh Vic. Such a shame. He was a good boy."

"Yes, he was."

"Goodbye, Mr. Johnsbrick." She grabbed her groceries.

"I'll carry them inside for you." Patrick kept a hold of the bags.

"Let the young man help you, dear," said Mr. Johnsbrick.

"You're not coming inside." She'd been turned down and lectured enough for one night. A quick jab of guilt hit her gut when an expression of hurt crossed his features before he hid it.

"You promised to show me Vic's letter," he said.

"Oh. Right." She'd forgotten about that. More guilt stabbed at her. She'd forgotten about her brother. "You can put the food in the kitchen. I'll be right back with the letter."

CHAPTER 5: PATRICK

Patrick put the groceries on the table and grabbed the items that needed to stay cold. He opened the door to her refrigerator. The inside looked a lot like his, almost empty. His had some beer, hers some wine. They both had eggs, butter, bottled water and not much else. It was sad.

"Here's the card."

He put the items inside, closed the door and turned around. She was staring at the envelope in her hand as if it was worth a fortune and to her, him and Ethan, it was. It was proof Vic was alive, in the area and cognizant enough to care about his father's death.

She handed it to him and moved to the fridge. "Would you like something to drink?"

"No thanks." He didn't care for wine and wasn't taking one of her waters. Even though it'd kill him to watch those married men flirt with her again, they'd stop at the grocery store tomorrow so she could get her staple items.

She poured herself a glass of wine and moved to stand next to him. He pulled the card from the envelope and opened it. The words "Love Dad. Miss him." were scrawled across the paper.

"I told you there's not much there." She was right but she sounded so sad and so lost he found himself lying.

"It's something." It wasn't. He looked at the outside of the envelope. "The fact that there's no postmark helps."

"How does that help? We don't even know where he was when he mailed it."

"That's because he didn't. He was here, outside your house, at least long enough to slip the card inside your mailbox. When did you get this?"

"Three weeks after Dad died." Her hand shook as she took a sip of her wine. "So, he was outside my house."

"That was about five months ago, right?" He slid the card back into the envelope.

"Yeah." Her face had taken on an ashen hue.

"May I take this? I want to get Hunter working on it as soon as possible."

"You can keep it." She downed her drink and walked to the fridge and refilled her glass.

"Don't you have class tonight?" He stuffed the card in his pocket.

"Damn." She stopped drinking, staring at her glass. "You know what? I'll skip." She pulled out her phone.

"What are you doing?"

"Texting my friend, Chelsea, and telling her I'm not going to class."

"This note is good news." He had no idea why she was upset. "Five months ago Vic was here. He's probably still in the area." There was a nearby section of the city where the homeless lived. He'd bet a million dollars that Vic was there somewhere.

"Do you think he watched me?"

He couldn't place the emotion that swirled in her gaze but his instincts screamed for him to tread carefully. "I don't know. It's possible." He hesitated. "He'd never hurt you."

"I'm not scared of him. I'm pissed." She gulped her wine and this time, grabbed the bottle. "Two weeks after Dad died, everyone had gone home. I was alone and sad and he…he stood outside and watched. He didn't care enough to come in and talk to me." She tipped the bottle and took a drink.

"He's sick and you know that." He moved to her side, taking the bottle.

"I hate him." Tears formed in her big, brown eyes and one slid down her cheek. "I don't care if he's sick. He knew dad had died. The card proves that. He didn't give a shit about how the rest of us were feeling. He's so damn selfish."

"That man sacrificed everything for his country." Too many veterans came back broken and he was tired of everyone expecting them to just get better.

"Yes, and then he quit. He quit on us all." She tried to grab the bottle but he held it out of her reach.

"He needs help."

"He's not getting it on the streets. He's not even trying to get better." She shoved him. "Give me my wine."

"No. Drinking isn't going to help."

"Yes. It will."

"No. It won't." He wrapped his arm around her and pulled her to his chest. "I'm sorry Vic hurt you. He didn't mean it. He loves you more than anything."

"That's not true." She struggled, almost breaking free.

"It is true and you know it." He put the bottle on top of the fridge and wrapped his other arm around her.

"God, I hate him right now and I hate myself for feeling that way." She sobbed against his chest.

"I know." He skimmed his hands up and down her back as he rested his cheek against her hair. She smelled so damn good and it felt so right holding her.

"I hate you too."

He laughed. "No you don't. No one hates me. I'm a good guy."

"You are a good guy." She looked up at him.

"It's the bane of my existence."

She pressed against him but the sadness in her eyes was getting pushed aside by something else, something darker. Her hands ran up his chest as his hands slid down her back to her ass, pulling her closer. His erection, which had been an almost constant since seeing her watching the couple fuck, pressed against her.

"Please, Patrick." She stood on tip-toes her lips brushing softly against his as her hands tangled in his hair, pulling his head down.

That was it. He was only a man and he'd wanted her since the moment he saw her. He kissed her, hard and demanding. She opened for him, more than willing and he thrust his tongue inside, tangling with hers as he tasted her. With the hint of wine on her lips, she was sweeter than before and he was starved for her. She moaned as they kissed and he lifted her, holding her closer but it wouldn't be close enough until he was inside her. He took a step to the side, pushing her against the refrigerator as his hands, grudgingly left her ass for her thighs. He pulled them apart, wrapping them around his waist and he rocked against her.

"Oh, please, Patrick, yes." She whispered in his ear as his lips trailed to her neck.

Now, that she was secure—held between the fridge and his body—he shoved her shirt up and over her head. Her tits were fabulous, better than he'd imagined. They were large and spilling from the top of her light blue bra. He reached inside, his fingers delving under the warm, soft flesh and popped first one and then the other out. Her nipples were hard and brown, like ripe, little berries that he couldn't wait to taste. So, he didn't.

"Yes," she moaned as he sucked her breast and flicked her nipple with his tongue.

He rubbed against her pussy but they had too many clothes on. "Drop your legs." He pushed against her thighs but she clung to him. "We have to get rid of your jeans."

"Oh, right," she blushed.

He kissed her again, she was too adorable not to. Her legs dropped to the floor and she unbuttoned her jeans, pushing them and her matching blue panties down her slim hips.

"God, I want to eat your pussy," he said.

"You can do whatever you want." She reached for him.

The images of what he was going to do to her—all the ways and positions he was going to take her flipped through his mind like a very naughty slide show. Her hands went to his pants, unbuttoning them and slipping inside. She wrapped her fingers around his cock.

He moaned as she stroked him. Having been semi-aroused for hours, it wasn't going to take much for him to come. "Keep that up and you'll have to wait to be properly fucked."

"Maybe, I want to be improperly fucked." She bent her head toward his dick. Her tongue ran over the top of his cock like she was licking a lollipop.

He helped her push his pants and underwear down his hips. Something fell from his pocket—Vic's note. She tightened her grip on his dick as her lips opened wide, prepared to take him inside. This was Vic's little sister and she was going to suck his dick. His cock got harder, not caring who sucked it, but he did.

"Stop." He grabbed her face, pushing her away from him.

She looked up confused. "You don't want me to—"

"No. God, no. We can't." He let go of her, pulling up his pants as he stumbled backward. "You're Vic's little sister."

"You bastard." She shoved his chest.

Her tits were still out of her bra and they bounced and jiggled. He couldn't take his eyes from them. She noticed and moved closer. He backed up a step.

"Forget who I am, just for tonight." She took off her bra. "Please. I want you." She ran her hand down her stomach and between her legs.

His gaze followed her descent. He should look away, but he couldn't. Her fingers slid through her inner folds.

"I'm so wet for you. So hot. I need you. Please." She stepped closer, offering her hand to him. Her fingers glistened with her desire. Her other hand touched his chest and slid down to his dick, wrapping it in her grasp.

He opened his mouth and sucked her fingers, he had to taste her. He'd die if he didn't. She tasted perfect, so fucking sweet, but it wasn't enough not near enough. No. He couldn't do this. He had to get out of there now. "I can't."

He grabbed Vic's letter and fled, shoving his dick back into his pants. This was the third time today he'd acted like a coward, not a marine, and he'd only been around her for a few hours.

CHAPTER 6: ANNIE

Class was over and all Annie wanted was a drink but it'd have to wait. She still had work to do.

"I'll make the drinks." Chelsea followed her into the house.

"Wait on mine. I have to fix the sink." She headed into the kitchen and stopped mid-stride. "Shit. That son-of-a-bitch still has my stuff." She grabbed her phone. As much as she didn't want to see Patrick—ever again—she needed her Home Depot bag. She texted him.

ANNIE: I need my plumbing supplies.

PATRICK: I'll come by after work and fix the leak.

ANNIE: I don't need you to fix the sink. I just want my stuff.

She waited but he didn't reply.

Chelsea came into the living room, glass of wine in hand. "Is he coming over?"

"I don't know. Will you take me to the Club so I can get my stuff if he won't bring it here?"

"Sure."

She texted him again.

ANNIE: Should I come and pick it up?

PATRICK: I'll be there in a few minutes.

"Never mind. He's bringing it over."

"Good. I can't wait to see this guy."

"He's gorgeous but a jerk." She went into her bedroom and changed into a pair of old shorts and the T-shirt she used when working around the house. She refused to freshen up her makeup. She wasn't going to try and look nice for him. She didn't even want to see him. She left her bedroom. "When he knocks, will you answer the door?"

"Wow! You're really pissed at him." Chelsea sipped her wine.

"Wouldn't you be?" She'd been so horny and frustrated when he'd left she'd almost screamed.

"Yeah, but..."

"But what?"

"It's kind of romantic." Chelsea's eyes were wide and dreamy. "He's the honorable hero. Like Lancelot."

"Please. I'm not married. The only reason he's avoiding me is because of my brother and trust me, there's nothing romantic about that." She was so done with guys like him.

The doorbell rang.

"He's here." Chelsea hurried to the door and opened it.

"Is Annie here?" he asked.

Annie went into the kitchen. She didn't want to see him, but unfortunately she could still hear him. His deep voice brought back memories of him whispering in her ear, how much he needed to be inside of her. Her traitorous body softened.

"Yeah," said Chelsea.

"May I come in?"

"Ah…"

"No." She yelled from the kitchen. "Just give her the bag."

"I said I was going to fix the sink."

She jumped and spun around. He was standing in the kitchen doorway.

"Damn it, Chelsea."

"Sorry." Chelsea smiled around his back and mouthed, "He's hot."

She ignored her friend and held out her hand. "Give me the bag."

"No." His eyes raked down her body and she shivered. He smirked. "Where's the leak?"

"I don't need your help." She wanted to slap that grin right off his handsome face.

"That one." Chelsea moved into the kitchen and pointed at the sink. She poured another glass of wine and handed it to Annie. "If he fixes it, you can drink."

"Listen to your friend." He moved to the sink, squatted and opened the cabinet, removing the dish soap, cleaners, her toolbox and finally the pan that was catching the water. He opened the toolbox and pulled out the tools he'd need.

"I don't want your help." She moved over by him.

"Too bad." He slid the top half of his body under the sink.

She kicked his hip, not hard, but it made her feel better.

"Don't do that again."

She bent down by him and said, "This isn't going to change anything."

"I didn't figure it would." He started unscrewing the pipes.

"I still hate you."

His green eyes met hers. "I'm sorry to hear that." He looked back at the pipes.

"Please leave."

"As soon as I'm done."

She walked over to Chelsea who was staring at Patrick's long legs and slim hips.

Chelsea took a sip of her wine, licking her lips. "Delicious." She wasn't talking about her beverage.

She elbowed her friend and grabbed the glass Chelsea had filled for her. "Are you staying for dinner?"

Patrick paused.

"Chelsea. Are you staying for dinner, Chelsea?" She emphasized her friend's name. There was no way she was cooking for him.

He started working again.

"Sure." Chelsea whispered, "Are you going to invite him?"

"No." She pulled the chicken and vegetables from the fridge and she and Chelsea started cooking.

CHAPTER 7: PATRICK

Patrick's stomach growled as he put the tools away and slid the toolbox under the sink. The job was done and the food smelled delicious, but it wasn't for him. Annie had made that clear and he couldn't blame her. He'd handled the earlier situation poorly, but he didn't like her being mad at him. He stood. "All done. Don't use it for at least twelve hours."

"Goodbye." Annie pulled the chicken out of the oven and separated it onto two plates.

Chelsea nudged her.

Annie shot her friend a glare, but said, "Thank you for fixing the sink."

"You're welcome." At least someone was on his side. He smiled at Chelsea. She was a cute, little red-head but his eyes kept drifting back to Annie.

"Oh, crap." Chelsea pulled her phone from her pocket.

"What's wrong?" Annie carried the plates to the table.

"Nothing. I have to go."

"Why?" asked Annie.

"Ah…Bobby texted me. He needs me to pick him up from the bar."

"Bobby is at home sick."

"Oh." Chelsea's face heated. "That's right. I have to go see him."

"What about dinner?" Annie crossed her arms over her chest and Patrick's mouth watered.

"Patrick can have mine." Chelsea winked at him and then disappeared into the living room and out the front door.

"Traitor," she yelled after her friend.

He stood there, not sure what to do. He wanted to stay, but it was clear Annie didn't want him around.

"Don't you have to get back to the Club?" she asked.

"Yeah, but I have a little time." He really wanted to try that food. "Hunter is watching the place for me."

"Hunter? Is that the guy who'll look for Vic?"

"Yeah. He's the best there is at finding people." His eyes kept darting to the table.

"Thanks again for trying to find Vic. I do appreciate that." She emphasized the last word.

"I owe your brother a lot." More than he was willing to share.

She sat at the table. "You might as well eat."

"Thanks." He sat across from her. "It smells delicious."

"Thank you," she mumbled.

He dug into the food and groaned. "This is terrific."

"Thanks." This time she sounded like she meant it.

"You have real talent." He took another bite, glancing at the stove to see if there was more. The plate had been made for Chelsea who was probably one-hundred pounds. He was more than double that.

"Thanks," she said again.

Her one word comments were getting on his nerves. "Why aren't you working in Ethan's kitchen?"

"Too many guys around." Her eyes met his and they weren't happy.

"Oh." He understood Ethan's concern. Annie was too cute to be around a bunch of guys all day and she was quite eager to experiment sexually. His dick began to stiffen again and he wanted to scream. He'd eased his frustrations as soon as he'd gotten back to the Club. He could handle a dinner with Annie.

"How much more schooling do you have?" It was a safe topic.

"Depends on whether I want to go on for my Master's or not."

While they ate, they talked about school, cooking and his work. He told her tales of some of the funnier situations, leaving out the sad ones. She'd had enough sadness in her life.

He finished his dinner and helped her load the dishwasher. It'd been a nice evening. He could imagine a lot of evenings like this. She was sexy as hell, smart and funny. If they were together, they could go and watch TV or read and then later go to bed—to hell with later. If she were his, he'd take her to bed right now and not come up for air until the morning or afternoon.

"I should be going." He stayed near her by the sink. He didn't want to leave.

"Patrick…about earlier…"

"I'm sorry about that. I shouldn't have touched you."

"Why? I don't get it."

He started to speak but she moved closer, putting her hand on his chest.

"Do you think Vic wants me to be alone my entire life?"

"No. He'd want you to be happy."

"Being with you would make me happy."

He put his hand over hers, keeping it close to his heart. God, he wanted her and she was making a compelling argument.

"Are you worried because you aren't the marrying kind?" She stepped closer and her perfume, light and subtle, filled his senses. "I don't care. I'm not looking to get married. I just want to have some fun."

"I'm sorry. I can't." He stepped away from her. He'd been ready to agree to try and have a relationship with her, but that wasn't what she wanted. She wanted to watch people fuck at the Club. She wanted to experiment and he wasn't going to do that to Vic's sister. "Goodnight. I'll pick you up after class tomorrow."

CHAPTER 8: ANNIE

"Are you coming with us to Lost Souls? It's two-for-one margaritas," asked Chelsea as soon as class was over.

"Can't. I have to work, remember." Annie walked out of the classroom with Chelsea, Dave and Bobby.

"Call in sick." Dave put his arm around her shoulders.

"I can see she's not sick." Patrick leaned against the wall in the hallway.

"Oh, who is this?" Bobby's eyes roamed up and down Patrick's long, strong frame.

"Her boss." Patrick grabbed Annie's hand, pulling her away from Dave.

She yanked free from his grasp. She wasn't in the mood for his overbearing, protective attitude. He didn't want her, so he shouldn't care who did—not that Dave really did. He was a harmless flirt. "Why are you here?" The last two nights he'd waited for her outside.

"I'm taking you to work. Remember?" He grabbed her hand again, and began dragging her down the hallway.

"Have fun at the sex club, you two," called out Chelsea.

She sent her friend a glare over her shoulder. She'd told Chelsea almost everything that'd happened. Chelsea was positive Annie could get Patrick to give it up, but honestly, she didn't know if it was worth the effort. She wanted someone so crazy-hot to have her that he'd risk facing her brother or Ethan or at least, risk fooling around until Ethan came back into town.

Patrick opened the car door and waited for her to climb inside. She didn't move, instead she stared up at him and her heart, the traitor, skipped a beat. "Why were you waiting inside?"

"I don't like you walking out here by yourself." He nudged her shoulder.

She got into the car and he shut her door, walked around to the other side and climbed into the driver's seat.

"I don't walk out here by myself." Usually, she and Chelsea walked out together, sometimes accompanied by a couple of the guys from class.

"Might as well be by yourself." He pulled out of the parking lot. "Does Ethan's driver wait for you out here?"

"Yeah. It's not a big deal. This is a decent part of town. The area is well lit and there are plenty of other students around."

"It's not safe. I'll talk to Ethan."

"About what? About you being an overprotective jerk? I'm fine coming out here with my friends."

"Right. Your friends." He snorted.

"So, now you don't like my friends?"

"Not particularly."

"Really? You seemed to like Chelsea the other night."

"Jealous." He glanced at her, a slight smile playing about his lips.

"Hardly."

"So, you'd be okay if I asked her out?"

She'd kill him. "No, but that's because she deserves better than you."

"Ouch." He touched his chest but he was grinning.

"You're an ass."

"Won't argue about that."

"What's wrong with my friends?" She didn't care what he thought but she never could resist arguing with an overbearing male. It reminded her of her childhood.

"Chelsea's okay. I guess."

"You guess?" She didn't want him to date Chelsea but she wasn't going to let him say anything bad about her friend either.

"She's a flirt."

He was right about that, but so what? "You don't know her."

"Don't have to. I know her type, and the guys"—he continued before she could speak—"that Bobby guy is okay, but Dave…Nope."

"Why is Bobby okay but not Dave?" She'd have guessed Patrick would've been the other way on that one. Bobby was flamboyant, proud and obviously gay. Dave was shy and straight.

"You know." He glanced at her.

"I truly don't."

He stopped the car at a light and stared at her. "You're going to make me say it?"

"I'm not making you do anything. You're the one who has a problem with my friends, not that I care what you think."

"You'd better care."

"Why? You're no one to me." She wanted to clap her hand over her big mouth.

Surprise and perhaps a little pain flashed through his eyes before he faced the road. The light changed and he took off, driving a little faster than before as if in a hurry to get away from her.

She started to apologize but stopped herself. It was the truth. They'd fooled around a little but other than that, he was a stranger and he was doing everything he could to keep it that way. Besides for the drive to and from work, he avoided her. This was the first time he'd actually spoken more than a few words to her since their dinner.

"What's wrong with Dave?" she asked, hoping to resume their argument because the silence was oppressive.

He ignored her. She wanted to scream or slap him and she might have done both but he pulled into the garage at the Club and hurried around to her door. Her anger slipped away, just a little. It was so sweet that he insisted on opening the door for her.

He followed her to the elevator, putting his hand against the side to hold the door while she entered. He stepped in behind her and pushed the button. His jaw was clenched and his hands fisted at his sides. She almost caved and said something, anything to break the tension she'd caused but the doors opened and he put his hand on the side again and waited for her to exit.

"I'll see you at six." He walked down the hall, his back stiff with anger.

She watched him until he disappeared around the corner. She'd been unnecessarily unkind and she was going to have to apologize but he was going to have to back off, because he wasn't her brother or even Ethan. He could be so much more than either of them, but instead he pushed her away. She didn't like it, but she'd accepted it.

Last night, she'd gone by the kitchen on her break and had found Jake. He was cute and funny and in the same business as her. He didn't turn her on as much as Patrick did, but she was kind of attracted to him. She was having lunch with him today and would see where it went. Perhaps, he'd be open to a few weeks of fooling around and maybe, it'd turn into something more permanent.

She hurried to the maid's changing area and pulled on her uniform. She'd worked out a deal with Stacy, one of the day maids. Stacy would do some of her work, so she'd have time to wander around without Julie and Ethan watching her every move. She'd clean the orgy room the next five times it was assigned to Stacy. It was a disgusting trade but hopefully, it'd be worth it.

CHAPTER 9: PATRICK

Patrick slammed the door to Ethan's office. He was no one to her? No one? God, those words had hurt. It was bad enough he couldn't get her out of his mind. For the last two days he'd fucked every woman here who'd reminded him in any way of Annie, but every night he dreamt of her.

He poured himself a drink. Yesterday, he'd watched her flirt with one of the sous-chefs and one of the dishwashers. A dishwasher, for shit's sake. What kind of life did she expect to have with a guy like that? Oh, that's right, she didn't. She was only looking for a good fuck.

He wandered into the back room and sat on the couch, grabbing the remote. He shouldn't. It wasn't right, watching her while she worked and flirted, but his finger pressed the button and then tapped until he saw her on the screen. She was bending over one of the beds, changing the sheets. Her maid's uniform pulled across her bottom, accentuating her tight, full ass. God, his hand itched to give it a slap, not hard, but enough to make it jiggle. Then he'd taste her. Kiss first one cheek and then the other as his hand traveled between her thighs. Fuck, she'd be dripping for him.

She straightened and he sighed in disappointment. Her ass was one of her finest qualities. She grabbed the soiled bedding off the floor and stuffed it into the cart.

There was a knock on the office door and Nick called out, "Patrick?"

"Back here."

Nick strolled into the room, a drink in hand.

"I thought you were avoiding this place?" He pressed the button to move the camera to another room.

"I thought I'd check up on you. See how things are going?" Nick plopped onto the couch next to him. "First time I watched the Club, I could barely contain myself. I tried everything with every female. It was a veritable orgy in here."

"I'm not much of an orgy guy."

"No, you're not are you?" Nick studied him. "Have you been prowling the Club as the new boss-man?"

"Some." He couldn't follow Annie to the next room with Nick here, so he started to scan through the different rooms. "Like Ethan, I prefer to stay back here."

"Oh, so you like to watch just like that little maid you have the hots for."

"I do not have the hots for Vic's sister." He really was going to punch Nick in the mouth one of these days.

"Please. You were watching her when I came in the room."

"I was not—"

Nick snatched the remote from him and clicked back a few times. "Ah, there she is—your hot, little maid."

"Give me that." He grabbed the remote and clicked to the first floor. "I've been watching the Club. All areas." It was true, kind of. He did force himself to scan through the building a couple of times a night.

"Is that all you've been doing? Watching the little maid."

"No. Yes. I'm not watching her. I'm looking out for her like Ethan asked. That's all." He perused the first floor, finishing his drink. Everything was calm. People mingled and drank, and some were involved in spanking scenes. Nothing unusual. "Want another drink?" He dropped the remote on the couch and went to the bar.

"Bring the bottle," said Nick.

He came back with Nick's scotch and his bourbon. Nick had changed the channel to the basement—the BDSM rooms. Everyone looked happy—either punishing or being punished.

"You should show this to your little maid," said Nick. "I'm sure she'd like to watch this scene."

"She's not mine." But he couldn't tear his eyes away from the screen. A woman was tied to the bed while two men took turns whipping her and pleasuring her. Annie would be squirming in her panties watching something like this. It wouldn't take him much to make her come, maybe only a brush of his fingers across….He finished his second drink. "I'm going to walk the floor."

"Patrick, wait."

He stopped in the doorway between the rooms.

"You like this girl."

"No, I don't." If he kept repeating it enough, maybe it'd be true.

"You're a fucking liar. That day in Ethan's office you looked at her like you wanted to devour her, like perhaps you'd already had a taste but…"

"She's cute. I noticed her. That's all."

"Bullshit."

"She's Vic's little sister. She's off limits."

"Says who? Ethan? He's not here."

"She's like a sister to him."

"But not to you."

"You don't understand." He owed Vic his life.

Nick roared with laughter. "I have three sisters. I understand."

"Yeah, and you want your friend to fuck them?"

"I didn't want anyone to fuck them." Nick leaned forward. "But it didn't matter. They wanted someone to fuck them and they were going to find someone to fuck them, no matter what I did."

Nick had a point. She was already flirting with two guys.

"She's not a child. She's a woman with wants and desires." Nick tossed back his drink. "Think of it this way. Someone's going to be banging her brains out. It may as well be you."

"I can't. I won't fuck her." He wanted to, more than he wanted to breathe, but he couldn't.

"Then don't. There are a plenty of things two people can do that don't involve a dick in a cunt."

CHAPTER 10: PATRICK

Patrick strolled the main part of the club, chatting with clients and acquaintances. He checked with the bouncers, and everything was good. It was a quiet night. He forced himself to stay out there for hours. He couldn't sit and watch Annie all night. That was probably why he was so horny and hard for her. She was like his private movie star.

He flirted with a few of the ladies but wasn't interested in doing anything else. He headed back to the office. She should be almost ready for lunch. Maybe, he'd join her. No, he was no one to her. He poured himself a drink and turned on the monitor. She couldn't keep him from watching her while she ate. It was kind of like being together. *Yeah, in a creepy, stalker way.* Even that didn't stop him from clicking through to the lunch room, but she wasn't there.

He checked the schedule of where she was assigned to clean. He went forward from the room he'd last seen her in a few hours ago, but he couldn't find her. Maybe, she was in the rest room or the locker room. There were no cameras in either of those places.

He waited, clicking between the bathroom and the locker room. This was ridiculous. He was a grown man, a former marine. He wasn't going to hunt her down so he could watch her eat. He flipped to the second floor rooms before he changed his mind. He was here to watch the Club not Annie.

There was a small orgy going on and everyone seemed to be enjoying themselves. He clicked to the next room. Empty. In the next one, three girls and a guy were having some fun. The next, had two guys and a woman. His finger froze on the button. The curtains in the connecting room moved. He clicked the remote until he could see in the adjoining room. "Son of a bitch."

Annie stood in the window, peeking through the curtains. The little voyeur was at it again.

CHAPTER 11: ANNIE

Annie glanced around before entering the room. Jake was supposed to meet her here for lunch. She'd wanted some privacy. Maybe, they'd make out a bit and she could quit thinking about Patrick. He wasn't available, not to her anyway. Her phone beeped and she pulled it from her pants pocket. She wasn't supposed to carry her personal one when working, but Julie wasn't around and the nighttime supervisor didn't care. She may have to convince Ethan to let her work evenings all the time. It was much nicer without Julie's constant harping.

JAKE: Sorry. Can't make it today. Tomorrow?
ANNIE: Maybe.

There was no reason to seem too available. She shoved her phone in her pocket and dropped her bag on the table by the couch as she sat down. She'd eat alone, again.

She pulled out her sandwich. It was chicken with an avocado sauce, tomato and lettuce. She took a bite and stared at the wall. There were curtains in front of the couch. Her heart beat faster. The drapes in the other room had covered a viewing room. She put her sandwich down and crept to the curtain, pulling it aside and froze.

There was a woman and two men in the adjoining room. The men were kissing and undressing her. She looked happy—more than happy. One man uncovered her breasts. They were large and her nipples were already hard. He leaned down, taking the tip in his mouth. The woman's head rolled back in ecstasy as her hands went to his head, holding him in place. The other man wasn't just watching. He pushed the woman's pants down, his large hand going between her legs as he kissed her neck.

Annie's fist tightened in the curtains. She should close them, walk away, but she couldn't tear her eyes from the scene in front of her. The men were easing the woman onto the bed. Annie's nipples tightened and she ran her fingers across them, imagining it was a man's hand on her—Patrick's hand. Wetness pooled between her thighs. She was so fucking horny. She let go of the curtain and unbuttoned her pants. It'd only take a moment for her to find release.

"I can't believe you haven't learned to shut the goddamn door before you do this shit."

She jumped at the sound of Patrick's voice and spun around. She was an idiot. She should've locked the door. She opened her mouth to make an excuse but the words froze as his hungry eyes raked over her, pausing on her breasts. Her nipples tightened even more. His gaze lowered to her pants and his tongue came out wetting his lips. She gasped, almost feeling that caress on her skin. God, she wanted this man, but he'd never agree. He'd lecture her and run away.

"I'm on lunch." She pointed to the sandwich on the table. "Lock the door behind you." She turned around.

CHAPTER 12: PATRICK

The little tease was dismissing him. Him! Patrick stepped into the room, closing and locking the door. A soft sigh escaped her lips but she didn't turn around. She moved toward the curtain, pulling it aside so she could continue watching the show.

He stood, torn between what he should do and what he wanted—so fucking badly—to do.

Her phone beeped and she pulled her it from her pocket. She smiled and texted someone. He moved closer and she looked up at him, surprised.

"I thought you left." Her eyes were huge in her face as if she'd been caught doing something wrong, which she had.

When he saw the name Jake on her screen, jealousy rushed through him. "You were meeting someone here?"

"What?" She tucked her phone into her pocket. "No. I mean, it's none of your business."

"None of my business?" He was going to throttle her.

"Who I see and what I do on my time is none of your business." She poked his chest. "So, go away."

"I was told to look out for you."

"I'm not a child. I'm a woman and I will date—"

"Date? Is that what you call this?"

She flushed as she glanced at the threesome in the other room. They were all undressed and everyone was in the bed making a naked-woman-sandwich. "I didn't know"—she waved her hand at the curtains—"about that."

"I bet this Jake-guy did. He told you where to meet him, didn't he?"

"No. I picked the room."

"Liar." He moved closer. She was bound and determined to fuck someone. She was so ripe and ready. Jake or some other slob would have no trouble taking what she offered and then breaking her heart. He couldn't let that happen. He was supposed to protect her. He brushed a strand of hair off her cheek. "You're not going to behave are you?"

"I'm not misbehaving."

"Sneaking off on your lunch hour to watch people fuck, while being fucked is a pretty good definition of misbehaving."

"I wasn't…That hadn't been my plan."

He skimmed his fingers across her shoulders, but he really wanted to touch her magnificent breasts. "When Jake didn't show up, why didn't you leave?"

"I remembered the other room, and I wondered. Then I saw them and…" She blushed.

His eyes darted to her shirt, wanting to unbutton it to discover if her flush trailed over her tits. "And your pussy got wet"—he leaned down to whisper in her ear—"and needy, didn't it?"

She shivered and nodded.

He ran his hands downs her arms and she trembled. He entwined his fingers with hers. "I can't have you creeping around like this. Anyone could catch you." He tugged her toward him. "And you're not even smart enough to shut the door and lock it."

"Hey!" She struggled, but he had her now and wasn't letting go.

"Oh no. You wanted this." He leaned down and kissed her ear. "You need this." He pulled her to the couch. "Sit." He smiled when she sat without hesitation. She had no trouble obeying when it was what she wanted. "Stay."

"I'm not your dog."

"If you don't do what I say, I leave."

Her eyes narrowed but she didn't move. She wanted him as much as he wanted her. Nick was right. If he didn't do this, she'd find someone else.

"I'll take care of you. Make sure you're safe."

"I don't need you—"

He bent and kissed her. It was deep and commanding. It was time to show her who was in charge. He dipped his tongue into her mouth and she was sweeter than he'd remembered. Her fingers tangled in his hair and his hand moved up her waist to cup her breast. It was soft and firm—perfect. She whimpered as she tried to pull him to her on the couch. It took every ounce of control he had, but he stopped the kiss and moved away.

"Promise you'll do what I say." He couldn't go any further until he had that promise. Her breath hitched in her chest and his eyes followed those tits. He needed to get that shirt off her now. "Exactly, what I say."

She nodded.

He turned and opened the curtains.

Candy and the two guys were stretched out on the bed. Oh, his little voyeur was in for a show. Candy was a regular, an insatiable regular.

"They're done." Annie's voice was sad.

"Hardly." He couldn't help it. He grinned. She was such an eager, little voyeur.

"But..." She stared at the people on the bed, the men obviously no longer aroused.

"You don't know Candy." He sat down next to her. "She's never done until she passes out."

"But she..." Her eyes darted between the scene and him. "Already. With two guys."

The way she emphasized "two" made him burst out laughing. "And here come two more."

Her head snapped around so fast he almost heard it.

"Oh, my God," she whispered as two shirtless males strolled into the room.

The two men from earlier moved to a loveseat near the bed. Candy pushed her blonde hair from her face and leaned up on her elbows, smiling as she opened her arms.

"She's going to....Again?" Annie glanced at him— horror and arousal waged war in her eyes.

"Oh yeah." He took her hand. "And we're going to watch."

"You don't think I'm...I mean, I've never actually watched before the other day."

"Shhh. You don't have to explain yourself to me." He tugged on her hand. "Come here."

She moved closer, but her back was stiff. His little voyeur was nervous. It was adorable and making him as hard as concrete.

"Watch the show. They're starting."

She turned toward the window and he shifted his leg around her so she was caught between his thighs. He pulled her hair out of her ponytail, running his fingers through it and massaging her scalp.

"Relax." He kissed her neck, just a soft touch of his lips and she shivered.

His arms shook with his need to pull her to him, under him and shove himself inside of her, but he couldn't. He would not fuck Vic's baby sister. He'd protect her and give her pleasure, but that was all.

CHAPTER 13: ANNIE

There was so much going on that Annie could barely breathe. In front of her was the woman Patrick called Candy. The lady was petite and cute with big breasts that had to be fake. Of course, none of the guys seemed to care that they weren't real.

The one man, who she'd nicknamed Curly because he had curly black hair, was kissing Candy's neck while he squeezed her nipples, which were red and long. The other man was behind Candy kissing his way down her back.

"Do you like what they're doing to her?" Patrick whispered in her ear.

She shivered. He was so close and he smelled so good—something musky and clean, male through and through.

"Answer me." He gave the outside of her thigh a soft smack.

"Yes." She jumped. It hadn't hurt, but it had surprised her.

"What part?" He kissed her neck as his hands drifted down her front unbuttoning her blouse.

"I...I don't know."

"You do know." When he got to the bottom, he untucked her shirt from her pants and pulled it off her shoulders. He tossed it aside as she turned to face him. His eyes were dark with passion and she leaned toward him.

"Watch the show." He turned her head forward.

Curly was sucking Candy's breast while his hand played with her other one. Candy had one leg tossed over his thigh, but the other guy's head was buried in her crotch.

Patrick unclasped her bra and removed it from her arms, tossing it by her shirt. "They're getting ahead of us." His lips trailed across her neck to her ear. "We better hurry."

His hands skimmed up her stomach to her breasts, playing with her nipples as he kissed her neck—sucking and nipping, sending pleasure shooting through her body and straight to her pussy. She moaned leaning against him. His erection pressed against her back and she turned kissing his cheek.

"Watch the show." One of his hands left her breast, and traveled south, unbuttoning her pants.

She squeezed her thighs together. She wanted this but she didn't. She wanted him but not like this. It was dirty and wrong and God she was turned on.

"Lift up."

"I...I...I don't know." She wanted to kiss him, to hold him, not watch those other people.

"Look at Candy's husband."

"Her husband?" Her head snapped back to the scene. "Which one's her husband?"

"The older man on the couch."

Her eyes went to one of the first guys who'd been with Candy. His dick was hard again as he watched his wife get eaten out by another man while Curly sucked her breasts. The other guy on the couch was stroking Candy's husband's cock.

Annie was lifted in the air and then her pants and underwear were around her ankles. She kicked off her shoes and then the clothes. Patrick's fingers slipped between her thighs and her hips rocked forward, wanting more. His touch was too light. She needed something harder. She clamped her legs shut and he only chuckled in her ear, his breath hot against her skin.

"Don't worry, little voyeur. I'm not going anywhere." His finger skimmed back and forth, back and forth, getting farther between her pussy lips with each pass and with each trip upward, he brushed softly against her clit.

She closed her eyes, resting her head against his shoulder as her thighs drifted open, giving him more room to play.

"That's it baby, let me inside." He nipped her neck and she thrust her hips into his hand.

"Open your eyes and watch."

Candy was on her hands and knees now. Curly was at her back, his dick hard and thick and poised to enter her from behind. The other guy knelt in front of her, holding his cock like an offering. Candy opened her mouth and took him inside, her cheeks hollowing out with her suction. The guy's face tensed in ecstasy.

Patrick grabbed her knee with the hand that'd been on her breast and pulled her legs farther apart as his other hand cupped her pussy. He inserted two fingers into her in one thrust.

"Oh!" She froze at the intrusion, letting her body get used to him.

"Fuck baby, you're so tight." He held still for a moment and then began to pump into her.

She raised her arms over her head, wrapping them around his neck. "Oh…oh, Patrick."

"Watch the show, Annie."

He matched the thrusting of his fingers with the guy who was fucking Candy.

"Look at her husband."

The other guy who'd been on the couch with the husband was now on his knees sucking the man off. The husband's eyes were on his wife and Candy's eyes were locked with her husband's as she sucked a man's dick while another guy fucked her from behind.

"Is that what you want?" Patrick's strong arms surrounded her as his fingers stroked in and out, driving her to the edge. "Do you want some guy inside you while you suck another man's cock?" His words were hard and dirty and making her even wetter.

Her body tensed and she pushed back against him.

"That's it. Come for me, Annie." He nipped her ear and she shot over the edge, shaking and quivering against his hand. He kept finger fucking her until her body settled and then he slowed, finally, pulling his hand away.

He kissed her neck and lifted her from between his legs, laying her on the couch. She smiled up at him, her gaze dropping to his huge erection. His eyes devoured her and she spread her legs and opened her arms, welcoming him.

"Oh, fuck." He wiped his hand on his shirt. "Shit. Lunch is over. I've got to go."

"What?" She sat up, covering her breasts with her hands and crossing her legs. She had no idea what she'd done to make him want to leave, now, when he still hadn't found his release.

"Shit, shit, shit." He bent and kissed her hard, wrapping her in his arms and holding her close.

She grabbed his face, her tongue tangling with his. A throb started between her legs again. She wanted him inside her. She wrapped one leg around his pulling him down to her.

"This is…I can't."

She wrapped her other leg around his waist as he lowered himself between her thighs, his large body covering and protecting her.

He thrust against her as he buried his face in her neck. "You feel so fucking good." He pinched her nipple and her legs tightened around him, rubbing her aching pussy against his hard cock.

"Please." She needed him inside of her. She reached between them and started unbuttoning his pants.

"No." He grabbed her hand. "We can't."

"What?" They'd just…he'd just fingered her to completion but this he couldn't do.

"No sex."

"What?" she repeated, staring at his handsome face which was wracked with guilt, desire and pain. This was ridiculous. He was being ridiculous. "Why not?"

"I'm not going to fuck you." His hips kept thrusting against her, not listening to his words.

"Are you sure?" She tightened her legs around him, finding some pleasure from the friction but not enough.

"Yes. Fuck. Yes."

"Just undo your pants. I want to feel you. Touch you."

"I can't." He panted in her ear.

"You can leave your underwear on. You won't be fucking me, you'll only be…closer."

She reached between them again and he didn't stop her when she unbuttoned his pants. He didn't stop her when she unzipped him, but his hand grabbed hers as she shoved his pants and underwear down his slim hips.

"Underwear stays." He yanked them up, groaning as they hit his engorged cock.

"Suit yourself." She was done fighting with him. This wasn't perfect but it was better. She arched her back, rubbing herself against him. He felt so good, so hot and hard as she pressed her clit into him.

"Shit, Annie." He thrust harder and faster "This isn't going to…."

Her hand slipped inside his underwear, grabbing his dick. He hissed through his teeth.

"You like that." She stroked him in long, firm strokes, running her thumb over the head of his penis with each passing.

His breath came in pants and he buried his face in her neck.

"I'll take that as a yes." She kissed his cheek and kept stroking as she rocked against him.

He shoved his underwear out of the way and wrapped his hand around hers, tightening her grip and moving her faster. His knuckles brushed against her clit and she trembled, moaning her release. His dick lengthened in her grasp and she used her other hand to cup his balls, squeezing gently.

"Fuck! I'm coming." His body thrust and his dick jerked, shooting his cum all over her belly. He collapsed on top of her.

He weighed a ton but she wasn't going to say anything because he felt so right in her arms.

CHAPTER 14: PATRICK

It took all his will power, but Patrick forced himself to roll off Annie and sit up, tucking his misbehaving dick back into his underwear. He should've never done that. It hadn't been part of his plan. He was supposed to pleasure her and keep her out of trouble, not rub one off on her, but she'd felt so fucking good. Her hand drifted down his back. He wanted to lean into her touch but instead he stood.

"Take as much time as you need. There's a bathroom over there." He pointed across the room as he pulled up his pants and zipped them. "I'll see you at six." He walked to the door and hesitated. He was being an ass but if he stayed a moment longer, he'd be on her again and then he'd be inside her. "I'll…I'll lock the door." He left the room and hurried to Ethan's office.

He shut the door and leaned against it. "Fuck. What did I do?" He knocked his head against the door once, twice and then went to the bar and poured a drink. He took the glass and the bottle into the back room. He grabbed the remote and sat on the couch. She'd still be in there, all naked and rumpled. Shit, she'd looked so hot when she'd come—her eyes closed, her mouth slightly open and her cheeks flushed.

His dick started to rise again and he glared at his crotch. "You're not helping. She's off limits." Yeah, like touching her had been okay. He downed his drink and refilled his glass. That'd been the stupidest idea he'd ever had, but he hadn't fucked her. There'd been no penetration—not by his dick and that's what counted. Any other guy would've fucked her six ways to Sunday.

He finished his second drink. This was just like him, find a perfectly unsuitable girl and fall head-over heels, and it'd be easy to fall for Annie. She was smart, sexy as hell and she challenged him, but she also wanted to fool around at the Club. He'd never be enough for her because she wanted to experiment and he wasn't into sharing his women, not when he cared about them.

He'd keep her safe until Ethan came back and then, she was his friend's problem. He should check on her and make sure she hadn't moved to another scene. His dick twitched to life with hope. He glanced down. "Stop it. I'm sure she went back to work."

He turned on the remote. She wasn't in the room anymore. He clicked through the channels until he saw her heading down the hallway toward the maid's station. He stared at her ass. Shit, it was nice. It fit his hand nice too. She disappeared into the locker room. His show was over for the moment.

He flipped through the channels. The Club was quiet. He turned off the television, took a gulp from the bottle and stretched out on the couch. He'd take a little nap. His head was buzzing and even though he hadn't had sex, he had come and he needed sleep, especially, since he'd be taking Annie home later. He grinned and then sobered. He'd take her home and that was it. Keeping her safe from the other guys at the Club was one thing, but fooling around with her at her home was not acceptable. There were no guys at her home and the worse she could do was watch porn and masturbate. Images flashed through his mind and his dick hardened. "Fuck," he mumbled as he turned on his side and tried to think of something besides Annie touching herself.

CHAPTER 15: PATRICK

Patrick woke with a start. It took him a moment to realize he was at the Club in Ethan's office. He sat up, his head pounding. Damn, he should've eaten something before all that alcohol. Yeah, like Annie's pussy. He shook his head and went into the bathroom. He had to stop thinking about her.

He pissed and brushed his teeth, appreciating the fact that Ethan kept extra supplies around like toothbrushes, underwear, shirts and pants. Ethan habitually broke new girls into club life and it was nice to let them brush their teeth after a night of debauchery.

He splashed water on his face and glanced at his watch. "Shit. It was six-twenty." He'd slept for hours. Good sex did that to him and he'd come harder with only

Annie's hand than he'd ever come with any other woman. Damn it, he was in trouble.

He hurried out of the office and down to the maid's station but Annie wasn't in the hallway. He'd expected her to be frowning at him but with a hint of pleasure in her gaze, maybe even a little shy seeing him the first time after they'd fooled around.

He leaned against the wall and waited. A few minutes later, a maid came out of the locker room.

"Is Annie Argotos in there?" he asked.

"Annie? No, she works nights. I'm day shift." She started to walk away and he grabbed her arm.

"Is there anyone in there from night shift who might know where she went?"

The maid glanced at her watch. "I'm already late."

"I'll take care of Julie. Check for me, please." He gave her his best smile and she frowned.

"I don't want to get stuck cleaning the orgy room."

"You won't." He pulled out his cell phone. "What's your name?"

"Tina Struthmore."

He sent a text and showed her the phone. "See. You're covered. I told Julie you were assisting me. You'll be fine." She was reading the text. Unbelievable. She didn't trust him.

"Okay," she said after finishing. She went back into the locker room.

He paced in the hallway. Annie might have been pissed about what they'd done. If she'd gone to the bus stop he was going to spank her. His dick twitched in his pants, urging him to hurry to the bus stop and find her so he could put her over his knee, her bare ass sticking up, begging for his hand.

Tina came back into the hallway. "She's gone. She wasn't feeling well and signed out early."

"What? When?"

"Around two. Must've been something she had for lunch."

She'd had him for lunch and then she'd left and hadn't told him.

"Can I go or do you need me to do something else?"

"No. That's all. Thanks." He pulled out his phone as he hurried to the garage. He dialed her number and the phone rang. He jumped in his car. They were going to have a talk because if she were unhappy about what they'd done...No, she couldn't be upset about that. She'd come twice, but why hadn't she told him she was leaving? The phone went to voice mail. "Annie, call me back."

He pulled the car out of the garage and raced off down the street. She'd better be okay. He'd kill her if something had happened to her. He snorted. He hoped she was fine so he could kill her. He called her again—still, no answer. "Damn it Annie, answer the phone or call me back or text me. Something."

All kinds of horrible images raced through his head as he headed to her house. She could've gotten kidnapped on her way to the bus station. The Club wasn't in the best of neighborhoods. Or shit, she could've been raped or stabbed or hurt or the bus could've crashed. He called her again and again, but it always went to voice mail.

He flew into her driveway, slamming on his brakes. He jumped out of the car and ran to the door, pounding on it. "Annie, are you there?"

"Everything okay?" Mr. Johnsbrick came out onto his porch.

"Yeah." He hoped so. It'd better be okay. He hit the door again. "Annie."

The door opened and Chelsea stood there a bottle of wine in her hands. "It's Patrick." She hollered over her shoulder.

"Tell him to go away," yelled Annie from inside the house.

Chelsea smiled at him.

"I'm going inside." He raised his brow in challenge.

Chelsea stepped aside and he walked into the house.

"Annie, I'm going to crash in your guest room. See you later." Chelsea shut the door and stumbled down the hallway giggling.

"What? No. We're not done drinking and I haven't told you what else that asshole...." Annie's voice trailed off as she came around the corner and saw him.

"How did you get home?" He stalked toward her. She was fine. Safe. Perfect. He was going to kill her.

"Get out."

"How did you get home?" He continued forward.

"Get out of my house." The glass of wine in her hand trembled but she held her ground.

"No." He stopped a few inches away from her. He could smell the fruity scent of the wine and the soft fragrance of her perfume or her shampoo, or just her. His dick immediately rose. "I'm going to ask you one more time. How did you get home?"

"None of…"

"Wrong answer." He wrapped his arm around her and picked her up, her wine spilling down his pants.

"Hey! Put me down."

He sat on the couch and positioned her over his legs. "I shouldn't but I'm going to give you one last chance to answer my question. How did you get home?"

She struggled to get up but one of his hands was on the small of her back keeping her in place. "Let me go. I'm not telling you…"

His other hand came down hard on her ass.

"Ouch! Hey!" She stopped wiggling.

"You're going to tell me what I want to know or I'm going to spank you again. Is that what you want?" The sweatpants she wore hugged her tight little ass and he couldn't keep his hand from skimming over her butt cheeks. The cloth was soft but her skin would be softer. "Answer me or do you want another spanking?"

He prayed she said yes. By her breathing, she was as turned on as he was. She had to feel him, rock hard and throbbing against her side. He caressed her again, letting his fingers trail between her thighs.

"I called Chelsea and she picked me up."

His hand froze between her legs.

125

"Now, let me up." She squirmed and his dick grew harder as she wriggled against him.

"I'm not done asking you questions." The last thing he wanted to do was let her go. He swatted her again and she jumped but stopped struggling. "Why didn't you tell me you weren't feeling well?" She must not have been too sick since she was feeling good enough to drink. "I would've taken you home. Did you eat your lunch?" He ran his hand over her butt again. He couldn't stop touching her.

"Let me go." Her voice cracked.

"Answer my questions and I will." He prayed she wouldn't want him to by then. He was pretty sure by her rapid breathing that she didn't want him to stop now. There was one way to know for sure. He moved his hand up her leg again.

"I didn't want to talk to you. Still don't."

His hand froze. He could've sworn his heart actually stopped. "What?" His voice was soft, almost a whisper.

"I don't want to do this with you. Let me go."

He moved his arm and she surged off his lap and stumbled away.

She didn't want him. She'd already tired of him. He stood. "Okay. I...I..." He headed for the door and stopped with his hand on the handle. "I'll pick you up after class tomorrow." Right now, he didn't want to see her ever again but he had a job to do.

"Don't bother."

He spun around. "You may be done with me, but you aren't taking the bus. Do you hear me?"

"I'm off the next two nights and Chelsea will give me a ride to school and back."

"Oh. Okay." That was good. It'd give him some time to get over her. "I'll see you in two days."

"Whatever," she said.

He walked out of the house, having no idea how this could've gone so bad so fast.

CHAPTER 16: PATRICK

Patrick stared at the screen, watching Annie work. It'd been four days since she'd spoken to him. He'd picked her up from school two days ago and she'd remained quiet, only answering his direct questions. He shouldn't care. It was better this way, but it hurt. He'd once again fallen for a woman who didn't want him. No, she preferred the company of Jake. She chatted with the sous-chef on her breaks and had eaten lunch with him yesterday. He wanted to beat the other guy's face to a pulp, but he wouldn't—at least, not yet.

There was a knock on the door. Patrick clicked off the TV and went into the other room. Hunter had said he might stop by.

"Patrick," Nick called out as he stepped into the office.

"What are you doing here again?"

"Bored sitting at home. I thought I'd see how you were doing. Ethan's been gone a week." Nick headed for the bar, glancing around. "Have you scratched your itch with your little maid?"

"No." He took the drink Nick offered. "And I'm not going to." Because she didn't want anything to do with him.

"You're an idiot." Nick went into the back room.

He followed. If Nick realized he'd been watching Annie again, he'd never hear the end of it. "I thought you were trying to be celibate for Sarah?"

"I'm not trying. I am celibate." Nick flopped on the couch and grabbed the remote.

"Watching that isn't going to help."

"It's like watching porn, only live. As long as my only companion is my hand, I'll be fine."

"Well, don't jerk off in here."

Nick laughed. "I'd be the office's first. With so many willing females around, there's no reason to give your arm a workout." He pressed the button and the screen came to life.

Damn it, Annie was still in that room.

"Maybe, I wouldn't be the first." Nick glanced at him.

"It's not like that." It was and he had. He sat on the chair near the couch.

Annie bent making the bed.

"She's got a great ass," said Nick.

129

"She's off limits." He snatched the remote and turned off the TV.

"I can't believe you're still being such a douche about this."

"If you're so sure everything is going to be perfect with Sarah, why are you still a member here?"

Nick's mouth opened and shut. "Fuck. I don't know."

"Because it might not work, that's why and with you and Sarah it'll be a shame but that's it. With me, I'll be throwing away my friendship with Ethan and Vic."

"Vic already did that."

"Maybe, maybe not. Hunter is tracking down a lead. Annie got a card from him after their dad died."

"That's great." Nick frowned. "You know what? You're right. When Ethan comes back, I'm going to sign my membership over to Mattie. My little brother could use some high class ass."

"Your little brother gets more ass than he knows what to do with."

"That he does, but the Club is different." Nick finished his drink and stood. "Want another?"

"Yeah." He tossed back the rest of his bourbon and handed his friend his glass.

As soon as Nick left the room Patrick turned on the remote. Annie was gone. He clicked through the cameras. "You should wait and make sure it works out before you sign over your membership." His friend had a tendency to tire of women pretty quickly.

"No, I shouldn't and you shouldn't wait either," called out Nick from the other room.

"You're telling me to cancel my membership?" Playing dumb was his only recourse.

"No. I'm telling you to go after Annie."

He flipped to another room but she wasn't there either. He looked at his watch. It was lunch time. He clicked to the break room and sure enough she was having lunch with Jake. His hand almost crushed the remote.

"Uh-oh, you may be too late." Nick handed him his drink.

"He's just a sous-chef that she has lunch with sometimes." Like when she wanted to watch people have sex.

"Jake is not just a sous-chef. Women eat him up like candy."

"You know the asshole."

Nick laughed. "Jake's not an asshole and yeah. He's Mattie's friend."

That was not comforting. "What do you know about him?" He had Hunter looking into the guy, but Nick knew him. "Is he a player?" He'd end Annie's flirtation immediately if that were the case.

"Jake? No, not really. I mean he does sleep around but he was in a long term relationship for over a year. So, he can commit."

"What happened?"

"Not sure. They broke up. Jake was pretty upset about it for a while, but it looks like he's back in the game." Nick grinned. "His other relationship had been with a maid from here too. He must like those uniforms."

"Go to hell."

"If you want her, stop dicking around and go after her." Nick sat down on the couch.

He clicked off the remote. He had no desire to watch her laugh and talk with the other man. "It's not that simple."

"Because she's Vic's sister?"

"Yes and no." He took a drink. "She hates me."

"She didn't last time I saw her, so what did you do?"

"I listened to you."

"So, you and she—"

"No. Not exactly." They'd had fun and then she'd walked away.

"Tell me what you did."

He had nothing to lose, so he did. He didn't give a play-by-play but Nick got the gist of what'd happened.

"So, she really does like to watch. I'd wondered if she'd accidentally stumbled in on the scene the other week like she'd done with me."

"She watched you too?" He was going to kill her.

"During the interview with Sarah, she came into the room to clean it and interrupted us. It was accidental. She had no idea." Nick laughed. "I've never seen a face get so red." He grabbed the remote and turned on the camera, switching to one of the private rooms where a couple was going at it. "I do see the potential in watching with a willing female though." He shifted on the couch.

"Don't get fucking turned on." He'd punch the guy in the face.

"Sorry. Can't help it. It's kind of hot. I hadn't considered fucking Sarah while she watched another couple or couples but I'll have a talk with Ethan about a discounted membership. Voyeurs only."

"Stop. Okay." He tossed back his drink and walked to the bar, bringing back the bottle of bourbon.

"Fine. I'll think about it tonight." Nick grinned. "So, you truly don't know why she's mad at you?"

"No. I mean, I didn't fuck her but she came, twice. She definitely enjoyed it." He filled his glass and sat.

"How old are you?" Nick shook his head. "Never mind. Let me teach you about women. First, she may not be happy about not being fucked, especially since you didn't abstain because of her but because of her brother. Most women don't want their lover thinking about their brother when they're fooling around."

"I wasn't thinking about Vic." If he had been, he wouldn't have touched her at all.

"I think you were, at least subconsciously, because if you weren't you would've plowed that sweet pussy."

"Shut the fuck up."

Nick laughed at him. "Sorry. You're so fun to rile. Okay, so after you jerked off on her."

"It sounds worse than it was." He should've never done that, but her hand had felt so fucking good.

"Does it?"

"Are you going to tell me what you think the problem is or not?"

"I shouldn't have to. You should be smart enough to see for yourself but,"—he sighed—"I'm a nice guy so I'll help."

"Great. I can't wait."

"You ran."

"What?"

"Like a coward."

"I'm not a coward."

"You acted like one. You blew your wad and then ran, leaving her alone."

"Shit." He had done that. "I didn't run because I was finished. I ran because if I hadn't I would've fucked her."

"Does she know that?" Nick sipped his drink. "A lot of women feel very vulnerable after sex. That's why they like cuddling. You didn't hold her or even fall asleep next to her, you jumped and ran – wham, bam, thank you ma'am."

"Son-of-a bitch." He was an idiot.

There was a knock on the door.

"I'll get it," said Nick.

He turned on the television and watched Annie and Jake finishing their lunches. He had to tell her. He had to explain. He'd tried to protect her from guys like that and he'd become one.

Nick and Hunter came into the room.

"Hey." He nodded at Hunter as he flipped off the TV. "You have news?"

"Yeah," said Hunter.

"I'll leave you to your visit." Nick shook hands with Hunter. "Patrick, think about what I said. It's going to be someone. Just like with Sarah. If it hadn't been me, it would've been someone else." He smiled. "Maybe even you."

"Yeah, you cheated on that one. I didn't even get the interview." They'd laughed and joked about that for weeks.

"And every day, I'm thankful that I didn't let you have that interview and that I didn't sit that one out." Nick turned and left.

"He's got it bad for that woman," said Hunter.

"Yeah. I've never seen him like this."

"We all fall in love at least once." Hunter dropped his lanky form onto a chair. The man was tall and lean but damn the guy could fight. He could also blend in anywhere. With the right clothes and a different hair style, the man could look like a completely different person. He was a perfect private investigator.

"That's what I'm afraid of. I mean, this is Nick, so it'll probably be Sarah who ends up destroyed but I worry about him. He has no idea of the emasculation and pain that might be waiting for him down the road." Unlike him, who'd fallen in love several times and had always ended up hurt.

"Speaking of pain that's waiting…Do you want to talk Vic or Jake first?"

He already knew Jake was a good guy in Nick's book, and he wasn't ready to have it confirmed. "Vic."

"I found someone who remembered the lady who gave those cards to the homeless. I'm going to talk to her. She may remember Vic."

"That's great." Finally, some good news.

"It's a lead. I tracked her down at a local missionary but she's taken a few days off. I'm going back tomorrow."

"Okay. Let me know what you find."

"Of course. Now, on to Jake.'

"Nick knows him." He should've let Hunter update him on Jake first. Then, the hurt would be over because if Jake were as great as Nick said, he had no reason to stop Annie from being with the guy. She shouldn't be alone.

"I don't think he knows him as well as I do."

"What did you find out?" By the look on Hunter's face, the news wasn't good.

"Jake was in a relationship a few months back with a maid." Hunter's eyes met his. "Apparently, that's his type."

"Yeah, Nick said the same thing." His friends were assholes.

"Did Nick tell you his last girlfriend had an abortion right after they broke up?"

"No, he did not tell me that." He stood. "He would've if he'd known." They may fuck a lot of women but none of them would abandon their kid even if they left the woman.

"I still need to follow up on some things. I haven't spoken with the girlfriend yet.'

"I heard enough." There was no way Annie was going to date this guy. No way.

"There may be more to the story," said Hunter. "This is only the initial findings."

"It's enough for me." He turned on the television but the lunch room was empty. He clicked through until he found her in one of the rooms. "Let me know what you find out about Vic."

"I'll let you know what I find out about both of them." Hunter left the office.

He wanted to go to her right now and tell her she couldn't see Jake again—not on lunch, not on break, not ever—but she was already mad at him and with her temper that conversation wasn't going to go over well. Plus, he needed to explain why he'd left the other day and that wasn't a conversation they should have here. He'd have to wait to talk to her. She started vacuuming the room, bending and stretching. He sipped his drink, his eyes on her ass. Tonight they'd talk and tomorrow he'd show her a scene because he damn well wasn't going to let the Jakes of this world touch her.

Book 3

Touching The Voyeur

CHAPTER 1: PATRICK

Patrick waited in the hallway for Annie to come out of the maid's locker room. He was done with her silent treatment. Actually, her being silent would work perfectly because he needed her to listen, not talk.

She came out smelling fresh and clean after her shower. He clenched his hands to stop from pulling her close to inhale her flowery scent. His eyes wandered down to her chest, wondering if she dabbed a little perfume between her breasts like so many women did. It was one of his favorite spots. The skin was soft and warm, making the perfume, whatever it was, smell better – muskier and earthier.

She smiled and he couldn't help it, he smiled back. He'd missed this.

"Oh, Patrick." Her smiled slipped from her face.

It was like a punch in the gut. She'd been looking over his shoulder.

"Sorry, I forgot to text you. I don't need a ride home anymore." She looked around him and smiled again.

"He's not taking you home." He didn't need to turn around to know who was behind him. It was the guy she'd been spending all her time with—the guy who impregnated women and left them.

"What?" She frowned as her gaze went back to him.

"You heard me." He didn't care how mad she got. She was not dating this creep.

"Hey," said Jake as he walked over to Annie's side.

It took everything Patrick had not to beat the guy bloody just for standing near her. "You can leave. I'm taking her home tonight and every night."

Jake looked at Annie. Patrick prayed the guy would start something so he could kick his ass.

"Don't listen to him." She grabbed Jake's hand. "Come on."

"Don't push me on this, Annie." He stepped in front of them.

"Ethan didn't want me riding the bus and I'm not. Jake's going to take me home from work and Chelsea is going to bring me to work. So you"—she jabbed his chest—"are not needed."

"No."

"No? That's all you're going to say?"

He raised his brow. She was coming home with him even if he had to toss her over his shoulder.

"Well, that's not going to work for me," she said.

His gaze went to Jake. "Do you want to tell her about your last girlfriend or should I?" Breaking Jake's nose would mess up his handsome face. His fists clenched at his sides. It'd be a service to all women.

"Miranda? What about her?" Jake glanced at Annie and shrugged.

"Don't play dumb. I know. It's what I do for a living." He stepped closer to the younger man. "I dig and find people's dirty little secrets."

"I don't know what you're talking about. Annie knows I dated Miranda but we broke up ages ago."

"Yeah, right after she told you she was pregnant." He'd given the guy the chance to come clean or leave.

"What?" Annie shifted away from Jake and Patrick had to fight to keep the smirk from his lips.

"Miranda is pregnant?" Jake's face paled as he turned toward Annie. "I'm sorry. I have to talk to her." He looked at Patrick. "I didn't know. I swear. You'll make sure Annie gets home safe, right?"

He nodded, feeling a little guilty. He pulled his phone out of his pocket as Jake hurried down the hallway. He texted one of the bouncers, telling him to go to the employee entrance and delay Jake.

"Give me a minute." He moved a few steps away so Annie couldn't overhear him and called Nick. He explained the situation. He could let Miranda tell Jake that she'd aborted his kid, but if Jake did something stupid like hurt the girl or himself he'd feel pretty damn bad. He hung up the phone. Nick and Mattie were on their way to the Club to meet Jake. He walked back over to Annie and grabbed her arm. "Come on." He headed for the garage.

"This hasn't settled anything. Even if Jake gets back with Miranda, I'll find someone else to give me a ride home."

He opened the car door for her. "That's not going to happen." He slammed the door, silently apologizing to his car for the rough treatment. As soon as he got inside, she started harping at him.

"Why are you acting like this? You don't want to chauffeur—"

"I already told you I don't mind." He said through gritted teeth.

"Pleeease."

"Beg nicer and I might agree with you." He glanced at her but she wasn't smiling.

"I'll get Chelsea to pick me up."

"I'll bring you to work and take you home, like I said I would." Was it that hard for her to be around him? She'd like him well enough when he'd had his fingers in her pussy.

She crossed her arms over her chest but remained silent. He couldn't keep from taking quick peeks at her breasts which were being displayed so nicely. He pulled into her driveway and she jumped out of the car and hurried to her house.

"Damn it, I would've gotten your door." He followed her. "Why is it so difficult for you to let me get the door for you?"

She spun around key in hand. "You don't want to be near me. You don't want to be around me. So, don't." She shoved him. "Go away. I don't need you to babysit me. I don't need anything from you. I don't want anything from you." She shoved him again and then turned and opened the door, slipping inside and slamming it behind her.

He stared at the door. Each one of her words was like a dull knife cutting out chunks of his heart.

"You heard her. Get out of here before I call the cops," hollered Mr. Johnsbrick.

"I'm leaving."

As he drove down the street, her words echoed in his head—all of them, not only the ones that'd hurt. She thought he didn't want her. He had to explain. He turned the car around and went back. Fortunately, Mr. Johnsbrick was no longer on his porch. He hurried to her door and knocked.

No answer.

He knocked again. "Annie, we need to talk." He knocked harder. "Annie, let me in." He pounded. Let her neighbor call the cops. "I'll break down your fucking door."

"Go away."

"Not until we talk."

142

"I don't want to talk to you." She paused. "Ever."

He smiled slightly. She was a stubborn one, but so was he. "Too bad. I need to explain what happened, why I left. Please let me in."

"I don't want to hear your lies."

If he could get close to her, she'd forgive him. He had to get in that house even if it meant playing dirty. "Hunter has a lead on Vic."

The key turned in the lock and the door opened. Her eyes were red and swollen. His chest constricted. He'd done that to her. He was an ass.

"Annie...."

"Bastard." She turned and went into the living room. She sat in the corner of the couch, her knees tucked up to her chest. "What did he find?"

He closed and locked the door. Not that they were going to do anything. She was off limits except at the Club. He sat next to her. "I'm sorry about—"

"Tell me what Hunter found." She moved to the chair across from him.

He frowned. She'd had no reason to move away from him. "I will but first—"

"No, tell me about my brother."

"Okay, but only if you promise we can talk about the other day—about afterward." He leaned toward her. "Promise?"

"There's nothing to talk about."

"I need to explain why I left. I think you misunderstood."

She looked up at the ceiling, blinking back tears. "Tell me about Vic."

"And then we'll...I'll explain why I left." At her silence he prodded, "Okay?" He needed her to agree. She wouldn't go back on her word.

"Fine. Okay."

It was like a weight was off his shoulders. He could explain and then they could...nothing tonight, but tomorrow, they could explore the Club. His cock stiffened in anticipation.

"Vic?" She waved her hand to hurry him along.

"Yeah, right. Hunter found the woman who'd handed those cards out to some of the homeless, trying to get them to reach out to their families. He's going to meet with her and get back to me."

"So, she knows Vic? She's seen him?" She leaned toward him, her brown eyes dancing with excitement.

"Don't get too excited." He took her hands, amazed once again at how soft her skin was. "She may not remember Vic. Hunter still has to talk with her."

"Yeah, of course, but it's something."

"It is that." His gaze dropped to her mouth, her lips were parted as if waiting for his kiss.

"Thank you." She pulled her hands from his and stood. "Good night. Lock the door behind you."

"Wait." He grabbed her arm. "We still have to talk about the other day...about us."

Her breath hitched in her throat. "There is no us."

"You agreed." He was disappointed. He shouldn't be. Women broke their word all the time but like usual, he'd thought she was different.

"I agreed you could talk and you can." She pulled her arm from his grasp. "I'm going to bed but you can stay here as long as you like and explain everything."

"What?" He stared after her, their conversation replaying in his mind. Damn it. She hadn't agreed to listen. Her bedroom door shut and then the lock clicked. Like that was going to keep him out. He moved across the room. "Open the door."

"Good night," she said pleasantly. "Don't forget to lock up when you leave."

"This is your one warning."

Silence.

He slammed his shoulder against the door and couldn't help but feel some pride at her squeak of alarm. He hit the door again and it flew open.

Annie was on the bed, covers pulled up to her chin, her eyes wide, but not with fear, with surprise and something else...excitement.

His dick jump for joy as he strolled forward. "Now, I'm going to explain why I left the other day...after...after we..."

The excitement in her eyes dimmed.

He sat on the bed and took her hand. "I didn't leave because I wanted to."

"No one made you."

"I made me." His thumb caressed her knuckles.

145

"Yeah, because you were done. Like I said, this wasn't my first time."

"No, because I wasn't." He scooted closer. He shouldn't. It was dangerous but he did it anyway.

"But you…" She waved her hand toward his crotch and he wanted to grab it and put it on his hardening dick.

"And I wanted to again. I knew if I didn't leave, the next time, I'd be inside you." He kissed her hand. "You have no idea how hard…"

Her eyes dropped to his dick and he laughed.

"You have no idea how…difficult it was for me to not fuck you the first time. I never would've been able to stay out of you the next time." His eyes dropped to his hand, where he still caressed her skin. "Not when you were so soft and so satisfied and so fucking naked." His dick was beyond hard now. It was painful.

"I thought…"

He leaned toward her because he needed to be closer. "You thought what?"

"That you left because…you were done with me."

He couldn't help it. It was like a force of nature was calling him closer. He leaned forward and kissed her. It was soft and sweet. "Never," he said against her mouth.

Her hands came up around his neck and he kissed her again but this time it was dark and deep, his tongue thrusting into her mouth like he yearned to thrust into her eager, little body. She shifted downward and he followed. It was natural. She was a woman. They were in a bed. She wanted him and he wanted her. He kissed her neck and she tugged the covers from between them.

He lifted up, staring down at her. "There have to be rules."

She shook her head. "No. No rules." She ran her hands up under his shirt and he moaned at the scrape of her fingernails on his bare skin. "You and me." She kissed him. "Doing whatever we want to do."

He dropped his head to her neck and inhaled. "I want that. I do. But I can't fuck you. I can't do that to Vic and Ethan."

She shoved him and he rolled to the side.

"You're not doing it to Vic and Ethan. You're doing it to me. With me." She sat up and slapped his shoulder. "What do I have to do to make you see that?"

"You don't understand about baby sisters."

"God. You're so difficult." Her lips curved in a smile and he knew he was in trouble. Her hands drifted to the bottom of her shirt and lifted it upward.

He grabbed her wrists, stopping her before she could display her perfect tits. "Rules." He raised his head and sucked on a nipple, which was peaked and hard under her shirt. She grabbed his head, holding him closer.

He pulled her to the mattress as he moved to her other breast. His hand rubbed the wet T-shirt across her nipple. She spread her legs, wrapping one around his waist. Fuck, she felt good. Even through his jeans and the blanket she was hot and he knew she'd be fucking soaked for him.

He eased off her breasts. He had to control this scene or he'd lose it. "Rules. Agree or we stop." He thrust his cock against her, making him bite his lip. "Okay?"

"Yeah." She started unbuttoning his pants, so he grabbed her hands, holding them above her head.

"Say it." He nipped her ear and kissed his way to her mouth. "I don't trust you."

"Hey." She tugged on his lip with her teeth.

He kissed her quickly. "You have a way of manipulating your words."

"What do you want me to say?" She wrapped her other leg around his waist and his hips bucked against her making her moan. "Please, tell me your rules."

"From now until Ethan returns, I'll show you around the Club."

"Really?" Her eyes sparkled.

He almost groaned. He was in so much trouble. "Yeah, but I want to be clear on this. It'll end when Ethan comes back and then you'll behave."

"What do you mean by that?" There was a warning in her tone but he ignored it.

"No more sneaking around and watching people fuck. We're going to get that out of your system. Whatever you want to see, you tell me and I'll arrange it. If you don't know what you want to see, I'll decide. Understood?"

"Yes." She tugged on her arms and he let her go.

"So, you agree that this is done when Ethan returns. If you still want to watch people fuck, you'll buy porn." He ran his fingers down her cheek. "You'll break his heart if he finds out about this."

"He needs to treat me like an adult."

"He can't. He sees you as his little sister. He always has and always will." He caressed her lips with his thumb. He couldn't stop touching her. It'd been too long already.

"You expect me to become celibate again because Ethan can't understand that I'm a grown woman. I won't do it." She crossed her arms over her chest.

His mouth watered and he had to shake his head and force his eye to her face. "You don't have to be celibate. You only have to find a nice guy. A guy who'll treat you right–you know, marry you and have kids. And you're not going to meet a guy like that at the Club, especially not Jake."

"You can't tell me who to date."

"Don't start with me, Annie." He was in no mood to argue with her. He was rock hard and ready to go.

"I never said I was serious with Jake. We just talk a bit."

"Don't get serious with him because he won't be serious about you."

She frowned at him, but didn't say anything. He'd take that as consent and to be sure, he'd tell Ethan about Jake as soon as his friend returned. Right now, he had to get moving because otherwise, he was going to come in his jeans. "So, you agree that this ends when Ethan returns. All of it." They had a week. It wouldn't be enough but it'd be all he got.

"Yes. If that's what you want."

"It's what has to be." He ran his hands over her breasts and she reached for him. "One more thing." He kissed her as her hands slid under his shirt. "No sex."

"What?" Her hands stopped, resting against his stomach.

"We can't fuck." He said through gritted teeth. If he didn't move from this position soon, they would.

"I'm not agreeing to just this."

"You like this." He lowered his mouth to her neck and she shivered.

"Yes, but it's not enough." She shifted her hips upward, rubbing against him. "I want you inside of me."

God, he wanted that too, but he couldn't. "I'll make it enough for you." He kissed his way to his ear. "There's so much I can show you. So many things you haven't seen or done yet." He thrust against her. If she didn't agree soon, he was going to tear her clothes off and shove himself deep inside of her, principles be damned. "Please."

"Yes. Okay. I agree to your rules. No fucking."

"Thank, God," he said.

CHAPTER 2: ANNIE

Right now, Annie would agree to almost anything Patrick wanted, as long as he touched her. It'd been days since the last time and she couldn't stop thinking about him. Right now didn't count since he was in her home, on top of her in her bed.

He yanked her legs from around his waist and tossed the blankets aside. "Now, where were we?" He lowered himself onto her again.

She opened her legs for him and wrapped her arms around his broad back, sighing at the feel of his muscles and strength under her fingers.

"Mmm," he moaned a little as she lifted her hips, brushing against his dick. He was so hard for her. There was no way they wouldn't fuck. He'd never keep to that rule.

"Kiss me," she said and pulled his head toward hers.

He held himself above her, his lips only a few inches away. His green eyes were intense as he studied her, causing her stomach to flutter and more wetness to pool between her legs.

"Is something wrong?" If he stopped again, she'd kill him or die screaming with lust.

"I want to look at you."

"Oh." She wasn't sure what to do with that. It was sweet and frustrating at the same time. They were in her bed. She was wearing a thin T-shirt and loose shorts. She wasn't wearing a bra and he was between her legs, hard and very aroused. Never in her life had she had a man in this position just want to look at her.

"God, you're so beautiful." He skimmed his thumb over her lips.

"Patrick." Her tone was chiding. She had a good body but she was cute at best.

"Don't Patrick, me. You're beautiful."

"Kiss me." She tightened her legs around him, pulling his hips into hers.

"You fight dirty." He lowered his head and captured her mouth.

His kiss was everything she'd ever wanted. It was hot and deep and dark and commanding. He was in control and she loved it. He held her face as his tongue thrust into her mouth, slanting his lips for deeper access. He dropped his head to her neck, his hips thrusting against her.

"You're fucking addictive," he mumbled against her ear before his lips trailed down her neck and his hand ran up under her shirt.

She grabbed the bottom of his shirt and pulled it upward. "I want to feel your skin against mine."

He sat up, grabbed her ankles and lifted her legs before dropping them onto the bed. He straddled her thighs as he pulled his shirt over his head. Annie almost drooled. He was gorgeous. His muscular chest was wide and it tapered to his waist. There was a light dusting of hair on his skin that trailed down below his pants. She wanted to start at his nipples and follow that trail with her lips and tongue, but he was too far away. She couldn't wait another minute to touch him, so she ran her fingers over his pectorals, around his nipples and then downward.

He grabbed her hands when they got to his pants.

"I want to touch you." She wanted to taste him too. She licked her lips hoping he'd get the hint.

His gaze darkened but he shook his head. "Rules, Annie. You have to follow the rules."

"But that's…"

"My turn." In a flash he had her shirt up and over her head. His hands cupped her breasts and she arched her back, forgetting all about touching him. "You have the most gorgeous tits, I've ever seen," he said as he teased her nipples, plucking at them and making them harder.

"Please." She thrust her breasts into his hands. She wanted more. She wanted his lips on them, his tongue, and his mouth.

"Patience." He lightly pinched her nipple and she gasped. "You like that, don't you."

She shouldn't like it because it'd hurt, but she did. The pain and then pleasure had gone straight to her pussy making it clench and weep.

"Answer me, or I'll stop." He moved his hands away from her.

"Yes." She grabbed them, putting them back on her breasts.

"Do you want me to do it again?"

She felt her face heat, but she said, "Yes."

He grinned and began squeezing and teasing her breasts and nipples. This time when he pinched one of them, he immediately ran his tongue over it, replacing the sharp pain with a lick of pleasure. She bucked against him, but his legs on each side of her thighs kept her in place.

"You're almost there already, aren't you?" He continued playing with her nipples—his one hand teasing one breast while his tongue and mouth flicked and nibbled at her other.

"Yes. Oh, please, please." She grabbed his head, trying to force him to take her breast—to suck it.

"What do you want me to do?" he asked, against her chest. His mouth was so close to her nipple but so far away.

"Please…my…please…"

"What? Say it." He licked her nipple and then blew on it.

"My breast." She slapped his shoulder. "Take my breast.

"Like this." He grabbed it with his hand.

"Nooo," she moaned. "Your mouth. Suck my tits, please." She should be embarrassed but she was too far gone for that. She wanted, no needed, his mouth on her.

"That's my girl. Tell me what you like." He ran his tongue around her nipple and then brought his mouth down on it, sucking and licking.

The pressure from the suction zipped through her breasts and down her belly, becoming liquid heat between her thighs. She didn't want him to stop—ever, so she held his head in place, as she rocked her hips but he was still straddling her thighs. "Please, Patrick." She needed some pressure, some friction between her legs.

He laughed a little against her breast and then kissed his way to the other side. He took that tit in his mouth and suckled as his hand wandered beneath her shorts. He stilled. "No panties? What a naughty girl you are." His fingers grazed across her mound.

She shifted upward. She needed him to touch her, really touch her not this fleeting caress, but he easily avoided her thrusts.

"Patience, sweet." He blew on her nipple as his hand kept trailing up and down her pussy lips. "You're so fucking wet."

She grabbed his hair, yanking his head up so he met her eyes. "I need you. Please." She never begged but she was begging now, her body aching with the need for release.

His mouth came down hard on hers, as his fingers finally slipped between her lower lips. His thumb skimmed over her clit as he thrust two fingers inside her.

She grasped his arm, not sure if she wanted him to stop. His fingers were long and hard, stretching her.

"You like that?" He pumped them in and out

"Yes." Oh, she definitely didn't want him to stop. She rotated her hips matching his rhythm.

He kissed her again as he increased his pace, his thumb grazing over her clit with each inward thrust.

Her legs trembled as she lifted toward him, trying to get him deeper. "Harder, please, more." She rocked against his hand.

"Come for me, baby. Come for me." His mouth latched onto her breast, his teeth grazing her nipple as he thrust another finger inside her and pressed down on her clit with his thumb.

It was too much. Her body trembled and shook as she screamed and rode his hand. He kept thrusting, keeping the pressure on her clit and prolonging her orgasm. When she settled and finally came back to earth, he was lying next to her, leaning up on an elbow watching her.

She smiled, suddenly shy. This man's fingers had been knuckles deep inside of her.

"Welcome back." He brushed a strand of hair off her cheek. "You're so fucking amazing when you come.

It's the most beautiful thing I've ever seen." He kissed her gently.

She ran her hand up his chest and her eyes darted to his pants. He was still hard as a rock and didn't look too comfortable. "Let me." She grabbed the waistband of his pants and started to unbutton them.

"No." He pushed her hand away. "No sex, remember?"

"But you...you can't be comfortable."

"I'm fine." He rolled onto his back. "But I can't stay."

"Oh." This was just like the last time.

He turned his head, staring at her. "Don't be like that. It's not because I want to leave; it's because I have to."

"But you don't."

"Don't start this again." He sat up, flinging his legs off the bed. "You agreed. No sex. Don't try and change it now."

"But this"—her hand wandered around his waist— "is no different than what you did to me." Her fingers traced the outline of his erection.

"You're right." He grabbed her hand, stopping her. "Maybe, we shouldn't have..."

Damn, she may have ruined her chance of being with him again. She had to fix this. "It's not sex. It's assisted masturbation."

He looked at her over his shoulder, amusement in his green eyes. "Is that the technical term?"

"It should be." She sat up and touched his arm with her other hand. His skin was hot beneath her fingers. "Please, let me."

He shook his head, but his eyes kept dropping to her boobs. "No. I can't. It wouldn't be right."

She wanted to scream but she knew that never worked with guys like him. "Why did you...you know..." Now, she was embarrassed. He'd pleasured her, knowing he wouldn't get anything and she didn't understand that—at all.

"Do you want all the reasons?"

"Yes." Now, she was worried.

"You won't like some of them." He let go of her hand and grabbed his shirt from the floor.

"Tell me anyway and don't lie."

"I won't. Never to you." He turned so he was half-facing her. "I know you're...curious and"—his lips curled in a smile—"horny."

"I am n..."

"No lies." He touched her lips, silencing her. "I also know some guy will jump at the chance to be with you. You're hot and sexy and eager."

"But not you," she said. He should've punched her in the gut it would've hurt less.

He lifted her face, making her look at him. "Most especially me. I shouldn't be near you. I certainly shouldn't be sticking my fingers inside of you and making you come, but I can't stand the thought of someone else touching you. So, I'm going to keep you safe."

She wanted to ask for how long but he'd told her this would only be until Ethan returned.

"Now,"—he kissed her gently—"get some sleep. I'll see you after class." He stood and left.

She stared at the door long after he was gone. Tonight had been great, but she wanted more. She had a week and she was going to use every opportunity she had to push him further and further because she wanted more than his fingers inside of her.

CHAPTER 3: ANNIE

Annie and Chelsea had spent most of the previous night formulating their plan. Chelsea swore it'd work. According to her friend, a man could only handle blue balls for so long before he snapped. She wasn't so sure. Patrick was stubborn and honorable to a fault, but it was better than nothing. Even, if the plan failed, Patrick was going to show her around the Club. She ached just thinking about it.

"Good luck," said Chelsea as they stepped out of the classroom and into the hallway.

Annie's heart thudded when she saw Patrick leaning against the wall waiting for her. He was so delicious looking. He had on blue jeans and a button down white shirt. The simple clothes accentuated his maleness, and she couldn't stop her eyes from darting to the front of his pants.

The jeans were worn as if he'd had them a long time and had gotten hard in them many, many times.

He pushed off from the wall and headed toward her. She raised her gaze and met his. His eyes were darker than before and his face tenser. He must've noticed where her gaze had wandered. She smiled and he shook his head, smirking at her which made her grin even more.

"Ready?" he asked as he stopped in front of her.

"One minute." Making alpha males, like Patrick, jealous worked. She'd seen it time and time again with all the guys her brothers had filled her home with over the years. She turned and hugged Bobby. "I'll bring the recipe to class tomorrow."

Bobby let his hand wander down her back almost to her butt. She stiffened slightly. He was taking this a little further than they'd discussed.

"Relax," he whispered in her ear. "I should be the one worrying. Your boyfriend wants to kill me."

She kissed Bobby's cheek. "See you tomorrow."

She broke from his grasp, glancing at Patrick whose face was tight with anger. Maybe, making them jealous only work with teenage boys and not men. She turned and whispered to Chelsea, "I don't know if this is a good idea."

"Give us a minute." Chelsea pulled her back into the classroom. "Stick with the plan."

"I don't know." She leaned against the door. "He seems more mad than jealous."

"Oh, he's mad and jealous." Chelsea stood on tiptoe and peeked out the window at the top of the door. "I'm a little afraid to leave Bobby alone with him."

"Patrick isn't going to hurt him."

"I don't know. He looked ready to knock Bobby into next week when his hand went to your ass and I swear there was steam coming from Patrick's ears when you kissed Bobby." Chelsea grinned. "It was great." She hugged Annie. "Now, go and explore that club with your hot boyfriend."

"He's not my boyfriend." She wished he were but he wasn't. This was a week-long fling. That was it.

"Pleeease. That guy is crazy about you."

"If he were he'd be all over me and he's not."

"Stop it. You have to push him. He's trying to stay honorable." Chelsea sighed. "Like a hero in a romance novel."

"It's great to read about but not so great to experience."

"Stop complaining. You said that the sex….well, the not-sex, the fooling around is great."

"But I want more. I want him." Just seeing him made her throb with need.

"And you'll have him. A guy can only take so much temptation. I promise. Stick with the plan and you'll have him…exactly where you want every thick, pulsing inch of him." Chelsea opened the door. "Now, go and be naughty."

Chelsea shoved her and Annie stumbled into the hallway. Patrick grabbed her arm, steadying her.

"You okay." He kept a hold of her even when she was no longer in danger of falling.

"Yeah." She stared up at him and his eyes darkened.

"We need to go." He tugged on her arm, sending Bobby an angry look before pulling her down the hallway.

After holding the car door for her, Patrick got into the driver's seat and tore out of the parking lot. Annie tried hard not to smile. Step one accomplished. Now, she needed to ease him back a little.

"Are you okay?" she asked.

"I'm fine."

"You seem upset."

His fingers tightened on the steering wheel. "Your boyfriend isn't going to join us tonight or ever. So, don't even bother asking."

"My...boyfriend?" He was supposed to be jealous not crazy—her, him and Bobby...no, no way.

"Yeah. I'm not going to cheat Ethan by sneaking him into the Club and he doesn't look like he can afford a membership." He shot her a dirty look. "So, if you want a third person in our little tete-a-tete, you'll have to pick someone who's already a member. Member. Not employee."

"I don't...I don't want that." Did he want someone to join them?

His hands loosened on the wheel a little. "He's okay with this?"

"Who? Bobby?" Her mind was spinning. She'd never done a threesome, had never even thought about it, but if he wanted to…Would she?

"Yeah. Your little boyfriend."

"Bobby's not my boyfriend. We're just friends." This was better. It was the conversation she'd expected.

"You hug all your friends?"

"Ahh…yeah, sometimes."

"You shouldn't."

"Why not?"

"You're sending mixed signals." He pulled the car into the garage at the Club.

"By a simple hug?" Oh God, she'd done this to herself. She'd been warned all her life about the way guys took every touch and look as a sign that a girl wanted him.

"A hug isn't simple. You press your body against his. That means you want more." He got out of the car and slammed the door.

She almost opened her door and got out, but he was already pissed. There was no reason to antagonize him anymore. He opened the door and she stepped out.

"I hug Chelsea too." She stood close to him, staring up into his handsome face. God, she wanted to jump him right now.

"Her, I'd sneak into the Club."

She stiffened. He wanted Chelsea. She should've expected it. Chelsea was a flirt and all the guys liked her, but it still hurt. "I'm not into girls."

"Have you ever—"

"No, and I don't want to."

"You might like it." He stepped closer and closed the car door behind her.

"Not interested." Obviously he was, but she couldn't…wouldn't dwell on that. He'd made it clear that this was a few days of messing around and then they were done. It shouldn't matter that he wanted another woman or more than one woman, but it did.

"Good to know." He turned and headed for the elevator. When he noticed she wasn't following he stopped. "Problem?"

"I…I want to know what your plans are." That was vague and not at all what she'd been supposed to say.

"My plans? I'm going to go inside and watch the Club."

"I meant for us." She shouldn't have tried to make him jealous. Before she'd hugged Bobby, Patrick had been in a good mood and he'd looked at her with desire. Now, his face was a mask, except for the little bit of anger that peeked through.

"Us?" He sighed. "Maybe tonight isn't—"

"I want to watch another scene."

The breath whooshed from his chest.

"With you." She walked over to him and touched his arm. "Just the two of us. Watching others…" Initially this had been a way to get him alone with her, but now, she did want to watch. It was erotic and her panties were already wet with anticipation.

"What do you want to see?"

"Surprise me. I'll do…I'll watch anything you want."

"Annie…" His voice held a warning.

She stood on tiptoe and kissed him. It was supposed to be just a tease, but his arms wrapped around her and he lifted her off her feet. He strode across the garage, putting her down on the hood of his car. His hands cupped her ass and he pulled her against his erection.

"Closer." This was what she'd craved. Him right there where he belonged, between her thighs. She wrapped her legs around his waist.

He nipped her lip and then caressed the hurt with his tongue. He leaned into her, pushing her down until she was lying across the car. He pulled up her shirt, revealing her bra. She'd bought it for him. It was black lace and barely concealed her nipples which were already hard and pointing at him, begging for attention.

"Fuck. You're killing me." His lips claimed her nipple and he sucked her through the cloth, using his tongue and teeth.

His mouth felt so good—hot and strong. She writhed against him. "Please, Patrick." She needed more.

He unbuttoned her jeans and pushed the zipper down, sliding his hand inside and cupping her through her underwear.

"You're so wet, baby." He kissed her neck. "That's so fucking hot."

"Please." She couldn't form any other word, so she used her hand. She reached between them and grasped him through his pants. He was so big and hard and all hers. More wetness pooled between her legs. She wanted him inside her. She ran her hand up and down his length, squeezing.

"Fuck." He thrust against her hand and then grabbed her wrist, pulling her away from him. He grabbed her other hand and raised her arms over her head.

"I want to touch you." She arched her back, trying to get loose, but he held her firmly in place.

"No."

"No?" She squirmed harder. She was tired of him telling her no, but then his finger found its way under her panties and he skimmed it across her little nub. She stopped struggling as a moan escaped her lips.

"You like that?" He did it again.

"Yes." She did. She really, really did.

"You'd better behave or I'll stop." He ran his fingers along one side of her pussy and then the other.

"No, please." She shifted upward, trying to get his finger on her clit.

He grinned and he was like every erotic dream she'd ever had—sinfully handsome and in control. He ran his finger over her again and again. She rocked against him. She needed him inside her, if not his dick than his finger, anything. He trailed hot, open mouth kisses up her neck to her ear as he stroked her. Pleasure was zipping through her, but she needed a little more—more pressure, him inside her, his mouth on her breast, something…anything…more.

"Time for work." His hot breath in her ear made her shiver and then he straightened, stepping away from the car and her.

She leaned up on her elbows panting. "What?" Her mind was a fog of passion.

"Time to go to work." He stared at her tits.

"You're...you're going to leave me like this?" She was a bundle of frustrated nerves. She'd kill him if he didn't get back over here and finish this.

"Yep." He smirked.

"You're kidding, right?" Please, please, he had to be kidding.

"Nope. It's time to go to work." He held out his hand, his eyes still on her breasts.

She pulled her shirt down, covering his view. He didn't get to look, not if he was going to be such a jerk. She ignored his hand and jumped down, her legs wobbly beneath her. He grabbed her elbow to steady her, a look of pure masculine satisfaction on his face. She wanted to scratch it off. Instead, she jerked free from his hand but he grabbed her arm again.

"'Let go of me. I don't need your help."

"Never." He pulled her close, anger marring his handsome features. "You need some lessons in obedience." He slapped her butt and she squeaked.

Her heart raced. Suddenly, she wanted to finish the spanking scene they'd started the other night. She'd masturbated several times imagining what he'd done to her. What more he would've done if she'd let him.

He grasped her ass and pulled her up and against him. "Keep your phone with you."

He let her go. The slide down his body almost made her come. He stepped back and walked to the elevator. She stared after him, trembling. Afraid if she moved, she'd either fall to the floor at his feet, begging him to take her or jump him and make him give her release. Both would be embarrassing. He held the elevator door and watched her with a smug expression on his face. She wobbled toward him, wanting to slap him, kiss him and drop to her knees and suck him off all at once.

He followed her inside and pushed the button for their floor. She could smell his cologne and the underlying scent of him. It made her mouth water. She glanced down at his pants. He was straining against his jeans. It looked uncomfortable. She could help him with that. She started to turn toward him when the elevator stopped. She almost screamed.

The doors opened. He put his hand on the side, making sure it didn't close. "After you."

She stepped out of the elevator and headed for the maid's locker room. If she didn't get away from him soon, she'd jump him.

"Annie," he said, stopping her in her tracks. "You'd better come when I tell you."

She stared at him as he walked away, not sure if he was talking about her showing up when he called or her coming when he commanded.

CHAPTER 4: PATRICK

Patrick closed the door to Ethan's office and leaned against it, catching his breath. She was going to kill him. He'd die of blue balls and frustration. He poured himself a drink, grabbed a towel from behind the bar and went to the TV. He quickly skimmed through the Club to ensure that everything was fine and then he found Annie.

She was already pushing her cart toward her first assignment—her legs now steady under her. If he could fuck her like he wanted, she wouldn't walk for a week. He sipped his drink as he watched her work. She bent over a bed, pulling the sheets off. He unzipped his pants and stroked his cock as she worked. If it were anyone else, he'd call in one of the girls and have her suck him off while he watched Annie clean the rooms. His lips curled in a snarl.

If it were anyone else, he'd be in that room fucking her until she screamed.

He stroked faster, in no mood to delay his release. He was so hard it wouldn't be long. She stuffed the sheets in the dirty laundry bin and moved to the next room. His body stiffened and he groaned, catching his load in the towel. "Fuck." This wasn't at all what he wanted. His hand was no substitute for a hot, wet pussy.

He tossed back his drink and went into the other room to check the Club schedule. He had to find a scene for Annie, for them. His dick twitched at the thought. His right arm was going to get a workout the next few days because now that he'd touched her again, crossed that line, he wasn't going back. He wouldn't fuck her, but he'd give her pleasure. He'd make sure that when Ethan returned and their time was over, she'd compare every lover to him. His mind screeched to a halt. She wouldn't compare him to her future lovers. She couldn't. He'd never be her lover. He'd only be the man that got her off with his fingers. The thought soured in his skull. He may win in the foreplay department but some little-dick loser would be the one who'd get to come inside of her. He couldn't think about that because there was nothing he could do about it. He couldn't fuck her. He couldn't.

CHAPTER 5: ANNIE

Annie entered the unlit room on the second floor and jumped as Patrick moved from the shadows.

"Sorry. I didn't mean to scare you." His voice was smooth and seductive in the darkness. "Lock the door."

Her heart raced but it wasn't from fear as she closed the door. The click of the lock echoed through the room.

"Come here."

She moved toward him, her legs heavy with nerves and desire. They were going to do this. They were actually going to do this—planned not by accident.

He handed her a drink.

"I can't. I have to go back to work."

"No, you don't." He took her hand, clasping it around the glass.

"I do. I need the money and I—"

"Don't take charity, I know. But, I'm the boss and—"

"No." She pulled away from him. She didn't want to go back to work, but if she gave in on this he'd push her to quit just like Ethan and she wasn't going to take their money.

He grabbed her arm, yanking her to his hard frame. "No, isn't allowed in this room."

"What if I don't want to do something?" She trembled against him. He was so warm and strong.

"Then tell me that." His hand cupped her ass, pulling her closer. "We won't do anything you don't want to do."

His dick, already aroused, pressed against her stomach. There wasn't anything sexual she wouldn't do with him, but she wouldn't take his money.

"I don't want a drink."

"That's fine, but you aren't going back to work"— he kissed her quickly, stopping her protest—"because I told your supervisor that I needed you to clean Ethan's offices. That'll be your assignment for the second part of everyday until Ethan returns."

"They'll suspect that we're…"

"Do you care?" His hand trailed down her butt cheeks and between her thighs, his long fingers teasing with their nearness.

She didn't, not right now with his hand on her ass, but she would later when the girls whispered behind her back about her failed attempt to snag a rich benefactor. "I will."

"Okay." His word was whisper soft. "I'll make sure they see me on the floor. They won't suspect anything." He pushed the glass into her hand. "Please have a drink. It'll help you relax."

He moved away from her and she missed his warmth.

She sipped her drink. It was good - fruity and sweet. "Are you mad?" There was something about the way he stood, all stiff and formal, as if she'd disappointed him.

"Not at all." He poured himself an inch of some liquor and tossed it back.

When he turned to face her, there was only desire in his eyes. He glanced at his watch. "Finish your drink. The show is about to start."

"What are we watching?"

"You'll see." He opened the curtains.

She moved toward the two-way glass. There was a bed in the room. She'd cleaned it numerous times over the last few months. The bedding was pristine white and she knew the bed was soft. She glanced at Patrick and couldn't stop a slight shiver from racing through her. His eyes were hooded and his face tense with desire. She bit her lip and his gaze dropped to her mouth.

Someone entered the room in front of her and she turned to watch the scene. It was a man and woman. They looked normal. Everyone always looked normal, but their appetites weren't. The man was handsome—older, distinguished with graying hair. The woman was young, one of the girls who worked here. She wore a sexy black dress, longer than most, but with a slit up the side.

"Do you want to hear them?" asked Patrick.

"Ah...I don't know." She was too nervous and excited to know what she wanted.

"We'll leave it off for now." He moved behind her, placing the remote for the speakers on a nearby table.

The man in the other room was saying something. He looked agitated—pacing back and forth, his hands gesturing.

"What's going on?" She glanced at Patrick over her shoulder. She didn't want to see people fight.

"Finish your drink." He nudged her arm.

She gulped it down, the alcohol forging a warm trail to her belly. He took the glass from her and went to the bar.

"I don't want another one."

"Are you sure? It might make this easier."

She stared at the man and woman in front of her. "What's he going to do to her?" She'd cleaned enough blood from the different rooms to know that some of the scenes got rough. "I don't want to watch anyone get hurt." She should've specified that when he'd asked her what she wanted to see, but she'd never imagined he'd want to show her this.

He grabbed two full glasses and carried them over to her. He handed her one. "Pain and pleasure can go together."

"I…I find that hard to believe." She took a drink. She might need this.

He leaned down and whispered in her ear. "Don't knock it until you try it."

She shivered and took another drink. "I don't know if I can watch someone hurting someone else even if she likes it."

"If you don't want to watch, all you have to do is tell me and I'll close the curtains." He kissed her ear. "You don't have to do anything you don't want to do. Ever. But I think you'll like it." His lips trailed down her neck in soft kisses, his tongue darting out for quick tastes of her skin.

"Okay. I trust you." The alcohol and his kisses made her limbs heavy, so she leaned against his strong body.

"You shouldn't." He nipped her neck.

"Too bad, because I do." She closed her eyes and tipped her head giving him better access.

"You need to watch." He moved away from her, not far but enough that there was coldness and air between them.

She opened her eyes and desire sparked in her gut and pooled between her legs. The man was on the bed and the woman was raising her dress, exposing her long, long legs. The man's eyes devoured her and he licked his lips.

Patrick's hands came around her waist, stroking her stomach through her shirt.

The older man motioned. The woman moved toward him and knelt on the bed. She bent, lying over his legs, her ass in the air. She wore a thong but that didn't cover anything. The man's hand caressed her butt cheeks.

Patrick unbuttoned and unzipped her pants, pushing them down her hips. "Step out of your pants." His voice was a rough whisper in her ear and his hands stroked along the outside of her bare thighs.

She kicked off her shoes and shoved them and her pants aside as the older man slapped the woman's ass hard enough to make the woman jerk upward.

Annie flinched. That had to hurt. There was a red mark on the woman's butt.

"Look at her face." Patrick's hands skimmed along her stomach, caressing the line where her underwear met her skin.

The older man caressed the woman's ass again and the woman's face was sharp with desire.

Patrick pushed her underwear down and she stepped out of them without being told. His hand teased along her pussy, cupping her but nothing else. She squirmed against him wanting him to touch her, stroke her.

"Watch the scene." His voice was rougher.

The older man alternately swatted and caressed the woman. She'd jump and then squirm as the man's fingers delved between her ass crack and then journeyed toward her pussy.

"See how wet she is." Patrick's fingers slipped between Annie's folds. "How wet you are from watching. Imagine how much wetter you'd be if that were you, stretched out over my lap. My hand slapping you and then touching you, gently, softly, wiping away the pain."

She spread her legs wanting him to do all of it, even the spanking.

"Finish your drink"—he nipped her ear—"before you drop it."

She gulped down the alcohol and he took the glass, setting it on the table as his one hand continued to caresses her folds. She moaned as one, long finger dipped inside her.

The older man was doing the same thing to the woman, his fingers thrusting gently between her thighs. Patrick matched his every move. She leaned back, wrapping her arms around his neck. He rubbed his erection against her ass.

"What's he going to do next?" asked Patrick. "Will he fuck her or hit her with his fingers buried deep inside her pussy? Imagine how that'd feel."

The older man unzipped his pants and his huge dick popped out. The woman's mouth opened on a silent scream as he continued to stroke her. The woman was coming. Annie was coming. Patrick's fingers worked inside of her faster and faster. She squirmed against his hand, her breath coming in pants as her body tightened.

"Bend over." He withdrew his fingers and pressed on her back.

"What? No, please." She didn't want to move. She wanted him inside her. She wanted to come. She needed to come.

"You'll come when I say," he said, as if reading her mind. "And it's not time."

"But…" It was time. She was more than ready.

He pushed her forward, grabbing her hand and putting it on the back of one of the chairs. She moved her other hand next to it. He grabbed her upper thighs and spread her legs. He was going to fuck her. Chelsea had been right. He couldn't take any more. A surge of wetness flooded her, waiting for him. He ran his fingers up and down her inner thighs, as if painting her with her own fluids.

"That was for me, wasn't it?" He leaned over her, whispering in her ear as he continued to caresses her, his fingers slipping into her pussy with each upward stroke. "You're wet because of me." His voice was hard, demanding. "Not Jake and not your little, limp dick friend."

He grabbed her hair and yanked a little. It hurt but not bad and the feelings got all tangled with the pleasure from his fingers stroking inside of her.

"I'm going to punish you for teasing me. For flirting with those guys." He wrapped her hair around his hand, pulling her head back and making her look at him. "For teasing them with something that's mine. You're mine. This"—he shoved two more fingers inside her—"is mine."

The force and tightness of his three long fingers pushed her over the edge. She screamed as she came, her body bucking against his hand. She collapsed, his arm around her waist the only thing keeping her upright.

CHAPTER 6: PATRICK

Patrick gritted his teeth as Annie came on his hand. Fuck, he wanted to be inside her. He was raw, on edge and furious. She'd done nothing but tease and challenge him. He pulled his fingers from her and lifted her up, spinning her around.

Her face was relaxed from her orgasm but her sleepy eyes sharpened as she watched him lick his fingers.

"You taste fucking delicious"—he pulled her to him—"but I didn't give you permission to come."

"I...I couldn't help it."

"You'd better learn." He lifted her in his arms and walked to the front of the chair and sat down. He turned her head to the scene before them.

The spanking was over and the fucking had commenced. The woman was bent over the bed and the man was taking her from behind, his ass tightening as he thrust into her, his hands gripping her hips and holding her in place.

"Have you ever been fucked like that?"

She shook her head, squirming on his lap.

He could be her first in that position—in many positions. She wasn't a virgin but she was inexperienced. There was so much he could show her, teach her…but she was Vic's sister. *Someone's going to fuck her like that one day.* But it couldn't be him. Anger coursed through him. This was her fault. If she'd never been watching people fuck, he never would've touched her and then he wouldn't be dreaming of her, fantasizing about her.

The man in front of them collapsed with his orgasm.

"It's time for your punishment."

"My punishment." She sat up straight, pulling away from him.

His hands tightened on her waist. "Yes, your punishment for coming early." He lifted her and put her over his knees.

"Patrick…" She looked up at him.

The excitement with a hint of fear in her voice made his dick harden even more which was a feat because he was already harder than he'd ever been. He was going to come in his pants before they were done. He slapped his hand down hard on her ass and she yelped.

"Shhh." He caressed her butt, soothing the skin. He loved her ass. It was firm and yet there was plenty of it to touch and squeeze and worship. He bent, kissing her cheek where he'd slapped it, letting his tongue sooth the sting.

"Ohh," she moaned.

A shiver ran through her and he licked her again, letting his tongue dip between her cheeks before sitting back up. He slapped her again and this yelp was half groan. He stroked her ass, letting his fingers trail between the cheeks and down to her pussy.

"You're fucking soaked again." He couldn't resist, he licked his fingers and then rubbed them between her thighs. "You like this don't you?"

"No." She shook her head but arched her back, pushing her ass toward him.

"Liar." He slapped her again. "Tell me the truth."

"No."

"I'm going to have to punish you for lying." He slipped two fingers inside of her.

"I'm...not lying." She was almost panting with desire.

"But you are. Your body is telling the truth." He thrust his fingers in and out of her and she rocked with his rhythm. "If you don't like this, I'll stop."

"No, please." She glanced up at him and her face was taut with passion. She was close. "Faster."

She was so gorgeous –hair tousled and her face heated with desire.

"Please." Her pussy tightened around his hand.

He should stop, make her wait to come. Punish her for making him want her, but he couldn't deny her any longer. She was his weakness. He shoved a third finger inside of her as his other hand slapped her ass. She screamed and bucked against his hand, coming again. He kept thrusting into her, sustaining her orgasm until she lay limp across his legs. His dick throbbed, needing release. He removed his hand from her and skimmed his fingers along the crack of her ass, teasing around her tight hole.

"Have you ever been fucked here?"

"No," she whispered, her body tensing slightly.

"Would that be sex?" His question was more to himself. If he fucked someone in the ass, he didn't say, I fucked them. He always clarified it with in the ass so it wouldn't actually be fucking.

"Patrick." She wiggled, trying to get up, so he let her go.

Guess it didn't matter if it were sex because she wasn't interested.

She knelt before him and his breath froze in his chest. He had to stop her because if she touched him it'd be over.

"Annie, don't."

"This isn't sex." Her small hands unbuttoned his jeans

That little bit of looseness was a blessing to his engorged cock and he hissed through his teeth. She unzipped his pants.

"Annie, we can't." He should stop her but he didn't move.

"This isn't sex," she said again as she tugged his pants and underwear as far down as she could without his help. "You said no fucking. This isn't fucking."

She had a point. He lifted and she shoved his clothes out of her way before wrapping her hand around his dick. She felt so good, touching him, stroking him. He shivered and bit down on the side of his mouth. If he didn't do something quick he'd come before she even got her lips around his cock and he couldn't let that happen. He needed her mouth on him, had dreamed about her mouth on him.

She moved closer and licked the head of his shaft— her tongue wet, hot and rough against the sensitive tip. It was heaven.

"Fuck" His head dropped against the back of the chair. He wanted to watch her suck him but he'd never last and he needed this to last.

Her hot mouth came down on him, sucking as she lowered, taking him deeper. She was so tight and the pressure was exquisite. His hand went to her hair, pushing her farther down as he thrust up. One of her hands caressed his stomach, sending tremors straight to his dick, while her other hand gripped him, stroking in rhythm with her mouth. His balls tightened and his cock got even harder, stretching. He gritted his teeth but it didn't matter. It felt too good. He was too close. He wrapped his hand in her hair and tugged, looking down at her. Her cheeks were hollowed out with her effort and when her eyes met his he almost lost it.

"I'm gonna come," he panted, trying to hold back until she moved but she sucked harder, her hand working faster and he blew, filling her mouth with his cum.

CHAPTER 7: ANNIE

Annie swallowed Patrick's sperm, trying not to gag. She'd never done that before.

"Are you okay?" He stroked her hair.

She nodded, staring up at him. She was glad she'd done it for him. He'd given her so much pleasure.

He touched her cheek and her face heated when she realized some of his sperm had leaked from her mouth. She wiped at it with her hands.

"Don't." He pulled up his pants and then bent and picked her up, lifting her onto his lap. "Don't be embarrassed." He kissed the side of her head.

"Was it okay?" She'd given blow jobs before but never to a man as experienced as him.

"It was great." He kissed her on the lips. It was slow and sexy and he stopped way too soon. "Have you ever swallowed before?"

She shook her head. "I haven't done much, obviously."

"I'm glad." He stood, carrying her to the couch behind them. He stretched out on his back, tucking one arm around her and pulling her to his chest.

His heart was steady under her ear. "I'd like to though."

He groaned as he pulled her closer. "You're killing me, Annie."

She kissed his chest, letting her tongue rasp over his skin and he moaned.

"If you keep that up, I'll punish you again."

That sounded good to her. She scraped her teeth gently over his nipple. He rolled to his side, pulling her underneath him. His pants were on but unzipped. Maybe, she could get him to cave on the sex part.

"I'm not kidding. We…I have to take a break."

She reached between them and grabbed his hardening cock. "You don't seem to need much of a break."

"Fuck, Annie." His mouth came down on hers and his tongue thrust inside of her. He kissed her hard and deep and then stopped pushing off her and standing.

"Patrick?" She sat up.

"I've got to go. I can't." He ran his hand through his hair. "I can't be near you right now."

She gasped. This was the other day all over again.

"No. Don't think like that." He knelt before her and took her hands. "I want you. I want you too much and if I stay…I'll take you."

"So." They'd been over this before.

"I can't, Annie. I just can't. Please try and understand."

She didn't understand, not at all, but he looked so sad and earnest that she nodded. His shoulders almost sank with relief and she wasn't sure if she wanted to cry or laugh. This big, strong, alpha male was, like most of them, nothing but a softie inside. She leaned forward and kissed him. He stiffened at first and then his mouth softened under hers. For one moment, he was kissing her back with fierce desire and the next he was gone. He hopped to his feet, his breathing labored.

"I've got to go." His eyes raked over her once more before he strode to the door. "I'll lock it. Stay as long as you like." He smiled at her over his shoulder. "There's lunch in the fridge. I'll see you when you get off work."

As the door closed behind him she covered her eyes and moaned. He'd brought her lunch. Boy, she was in trouble. She wanted him more than anything right now and he was running away as fast as he could. She sat up and walked to the refrigerator. She should get dressed but she liked walking around half naked. It was risqué and sexy and damn it, she wanted that in her life. She was tired of doing the right thing, being the good little sister and daughter. It was time she was a woman first. She smiled to herself. That was the ticket. She'd acted like a woman earlier and had taken the lead and Patrick had been putty in her hands. Well, not soft like putty, he'd been rock hard and delicious and he'd let her blow him. Now, all she had to do was convince him that other things weren't sex or didn't count as sex.

CHAPTER 8: ANNIE

When Annie came out of the locker room, Patrick was waiting for her. She couldn't help it. She blushed. His eyes darkened as they roamed down her body, lingering on her chest. Her nipples hardened and he must've seen it through her T-shirt because he almost growled.

"Come on." He hurried down the hallway toward the garage.

She followed, staring at his ass. It was tight and firm and she was going to touch it. She was going to touch all of him. He waited at the elevator, his hand on the side, keeping the door open for her. Her pussy throbbed with need. He was so old fashioned and gentlemanly. She'd

never met anyone like him. She glanced up at the corner—
too bad there were cameras in here.

The elevator stopped and he followed her to the car,
his heat warming her back and making her wetter. He held
the door open for her.

As soon as he got behind the steering wheel she
said, "Thank you for lunch."

"You're welcome. I wasn't sure what you liked."
He pulled out of the garage.

"It was delicious." It'd been a half-sandwich and
salad from somewhere. "Where'd you get it?"

"A small mom and pop deli that Nick told me
about."

"It's very good."

"Is that what you want to do? Have your own
restaurant?"

"Yeah, maybe, but it'll take years. I need
experience first."

"Hmm."

"What does that mean?"

"Nothing. Just thinking. When do you finish
school?"

"A few months. Why?"

"Then you can quit the Club."

There was a pinch near her heart. He was that eager
to get her out of his sight. "Maybe. I like working here." At
least, she did now.

"You like cleaning those rooms?" He pulled into
her driveway.

"No."

He hopped out of the car and moved around to open the door for her. "Then why would you want to stay at the Club?"

She stepped out and he was close. Usually, he moved back but there was a challenge in his words and his stance. It wasn't his lucky day, because she didn't back down from challenges.

"I like the people I meet." She ran her hands up his chest and around his neck. "And I like to watch. You know that."

"Annie, what are you doing?" His hands went to her ass and squeezed as if he couldn't stop himself.

"I think it's obvious." She kissed him.

He kissed her back for a moment and stepped away. "You need to go inside." His voice was raspy with need.

"Come with me." She took his hand and tugged.

"I can't."

"We'll talk." At first.

"You're killing me," he said as he followed her into her house.

She pulled him toward the bedroom but he stopped, refusing to go another step.

She felt her temper rise but fighting with him didn't work. "I'm going to change. There's beer and wine in the fridge. Will you pour me a glass?"

"Where'd you get the beer? If you had that delivery—"

"Chelsea picked it up for me." She struggled not to grin like an idiot. He was jealous and she loved it.

"Oh. Okay."

"Pour me a glass of the zinfandel, please."

"Sure." He watched her cautiously as if not sure what this mature Annie would do.

She went into her bedroom, closing the door and then opening it. If he wanted to watch her change that was fine with her. She dug in her drawer and pulled out a negligee. She'd bought it years ago but it hadn't seen much use. She stripped and then stopped before putting it on. If she walked out there in this, he'd run. That wouldn't help her pride and it wouldn't do anything to assuage the hunger between her thighs. She dropped the nightgown and pulled out the tiniest pair of shorts she had. They were old and worn and she only kept them to sleep in because they were so comfortable. She then grabbed a tank top that was slightly too big and kept slipping off her shoulder.

When she walked into the living room, Patrick was sitting on the couch a beer in his hand.

The breath left his chest in a whoosh as his eyes narrowed. "What in the hell are you wearing?"

"Pajamas." She hurried to the couch and sat next to him.

"I can't stay here." He jumped up.

"Come on. Finish your beer."

"Change."

"What? Why?" She put on her best innocent expression.

"Because you're tempting me and you know it."

"In this?" She glanced down at her clothes. They were perfect. The shorts were so little and tight, they showed more than they hid and the shirt gaped, exposing most of one breast. "These are just some old clothes I wear to sleep." She grabbed his hand and pulled. "I promise. I won't bite."

"What if I want you to?" He shook his head. "No, forget I said that."

She tugged on his hand again. If he left, she'd probably rant and rave and go crazy from frustration.

"Promise you won't touch me," he said.

She laughed. "Now, you sound like a girl."

"I'm serious. You said we'd talk and that's it."

"And I'm not doing anything." She patted the couch next to her and then grabbed her wine glass, taking a sip.

CHAPTER 9: PATRICK

It was a bad idea but Patrick sat. He should go but he didn't want to. He wanted to wrap his mouth around her luscious tits and suck her through her shirt—the damn thing was indecent and he loved it. It was almost see through and it hugged her breasts, accentuating her hardened nipples. And those shorts…He didn't know where to start with those shorts. Her ass hung out on each side and her pussy lips were outlined in exquisite detail. If she spread her legs just a little, he could probably see her clit.

"So, you own a security company."

It wasn't a question but he latched onto the topic like a lifeline because he had to get his mind off all the things he wanted to do to her. "Yeah. Started it after I left the military."

"Tell me about some of the cases you've worked." She leaned forward and his eyes dipped to her chest. "You have to have some sordid tales."

He could see everything and it was glorious. He had to touch them. They'd be soft and warm. His hand lifted, as if pulled by a string, but she shifted and leaned against the back of the couch. He coughed to clear his throat. "Some. Most are kind of sad. End of marriages and stuff like that, but there were a few that were kind of funny."

He rambled on about his company as his eyes roved over her. She actually seemed interested in what he was saying and she asked smart questions. Her nipples lost some of their tenseness and he wanted to flick them to make them perk up. He liked seeing her hard and waiting for his mouth. His eyes dropped to her crotch. That was waiting for his mouth too. Would she taste sweet or tart or perhaps, a little of both?

He took a swallow of his beer and she took a sip of her wine, licking her lips. Those lips had felt great around his cock and that tongue...Damn, she was good with that tongue.

"Patrick...Patrick..." She ducked her head to capture his gaze.

He blinked a couple of times, coming out of his sensual fog.

"Do you want another beer?" She stood and her pussy was eye level but too far away.

He sat the beer down on the coffee table and then ran the tip of one finger over her hip bone, where her skin showed. Her breath hitched but she didn't move.

"Come here." He slipped his finger into the waistband of those fabulous shorts and pulled her forward. She shivered as his hand skimmed across her stomach. "These shorts are indecent."

"They're one of my favorites."

"Mine too." He forced his eyes to her. "But they have to go." In one quick tug her shorts were down around her ankles. He moaned as his dick tried to burst from his pants. She wasn't wearing any underwear. He leaned forward and kissed her stomach right above her pussy, inhaling her arousal. He opened his mouth and trailed wet kisses across her abdomen.

Her hands went into his hair. He kissed his way down her thigh and she trembled, her hands moving to grip his shoulders. He hadn't even touched her pussy yet and she was already dripping down her thighs and shaking with desire. He couldn't risk her falling, so he picked her up and put her on the couch, slipping onto the floor and kneeling between her legs.

"Patrick." She rested on her elbows, staring at him.

"This isn't sex." He couldn't take his eyes from her. She was luscious.

"No. It's not."

"I'm not going to fuck you."

"Of course not."

"But I am going to taste you." He yanked her forward, lifting her legs and putting one on each of his shoulders. He kissed her thighs and lowered his head. He couldn't wait any longer. Next time he'd use more finesse, but this time, he had to taste her. He licked her sides, letting his tongue dip into her. She was delicious. He had to have more, so he did.

She gasped her hips tipping upward. He grabbed her ass, holding her still. He was in charge and she'd move when he said she could. He licked her again before thrusting his tongue inside of her.

"Oh…Oh…please." She tried to twist and shift but he held her still.

He kept licking and thrusting. Her hands clenched the couch. She was panting. She was close but he wasn't ready to let her come yet. He eased off her and blew across her soaked pussy. "Not yet, Annie."

"Oh God, don't stop."

He kissed her thigh, sucking it hard to give her a little pinch. "I didn't give you permission to come."

"Please." Her head thrashed to the side as she arched her back to get closer to him.

"Not yet." He blew across her pussy again and she shivered.

"You're a monster."

He laughed and nuzzled where her leg met her hip. He eased her down to the couch and used his fingers to stroke her. He dipped one finger inside and then up and down the sides of her cunt. Soon, she was thrusting to meet his rhythm.

"Don't come, baby. Not yet." He lifted her off the couch again, his hands squeezing her ass.

"Please, Patrick. Put me down."

"No, baby. You'll come too soon just like earlier today." He lowered his faced and licked her cunt. She tasted fabulous—like tart peaches—and he couldn't get enough.

"Oh, God," she moaned.

She was so close, almost in pain, but he'd show her the pleasure in that later. He brought his lips down over her clit and sucked, using his teeth a little and she screamed. Her back arched and her body trembled in his hands. He licked her slow and steady, until all the tension fled. Then he gently eased her back down on the couch.

He lifted her legs, stretching them out along the cushions. His gaze landed on her tits. The nipples were soft now with her release. He'd been so busy tasting her he'd completely forgotten about them. Next time, he'd pay them the homage they deserved.

Her hand come up and caressed his face.

"All right?" He kissed her palm.

"Perfect." She scooted over. "Lay by me."

He shouldn't but right now he couldn't deny her. He stretched out next to her, rolling her to her side and pulling her close. She stiffened as she felt his erection pressing against her butt.

"You—"

"I'm fine."

She turned toward him, her hand going to his pants. "You're not fine."

"Annie." He grabbed her hand.

"Not sex. Just touching."

"It's too dangerous. You're naked."

"I'll get dressed." She leaned over him and his hand caressed her ass.

God he loved her ass. She rolled back and lifted up, putting her pussy on display as she slid those sexy shorts up her body. His mouth watered. He wanted to bury his face between her thighs again but then she was covered and her hands were on his chest, under his shirt and her mouth was on his.

She ran her tongue over his lips and he opened, letting her taste herself. She leaned more heavily against him as her hands unbuttoned his pants. He grabbed her face, holding her in place for his mouth to ravage. She unzipped him and he groaned as her tiny hand wrapped around his cock.

"Fuck, Annie." It felt so fucking good when she touched him.

"You like that?" She stroked him in long, strong strokes, running her thumb over the head of his cock with each ascent.

"Yeah." He kissed her harder, more fervently as she increased her rhythm. He thrust his tongue into her mouth like he wanted to thrust his dick into her pussy.

She leaned away and took off her shirt, freeing her gorgeous tits.

"Come here." He grabbed her breast.

She slapped his hand away. "Not this time. These"—she pressed her tits together—"aren't for your mouth."

"Oh, God." His dick grew another few inches. "Hurry up. I'm gonna come just thinking about it."

She laughed and moved down his body. She licked and sucked his cock making it nice and wet and then squeezed her tits around it. His hips thrust upward, out of his control. He grabbed her hands, holding her soft tits tighter against his dick.

"Oh, fuck. You feel so fucking good."

Her tongue darted out licking his cock and she moved her hand, letting him hold her breasts in place as she cupped his balls, squeezing gently. He rocked against her, the warm, soft skin of her breasts making a fabulous friction.

"I'm gonna come." He should be embarrassed. He couldn't last five minutes once she started touching him, but right now, he didn't care.

She kept moving, stroking against him, around him and he exploded, his sperm shooting onto her tits and face. She stuck out her tongue, licking it off his cock. With her wide, dark eyes and her innocent face, it was the most erotic thing he'd ever seen and he came again.

CHAPTER 10: PATRICK

"Fuck, baby. That was hot," said Patrick.

"You liked it then?" She was staring at him with uncertainty.

"Yeah." His dick started to rise again at the sight of her big eyes and his cum on her cheek and body. He forced his gaze away from her breasts and pulled her to him, kissing her gently.

"I should probably clean up." She gestured at her chest as she sat up.

His eyes dropped to her tits. They were fabulous on any day but right now, branded with his sperm, they were making him hard again. "Leave it." He grabbed her, pulling her down and rolling on top of her. He groaned as she widened her legs, making room for him between her thighs. "I want to look at you." He brushed a strand of hair away from her face before his gaze dropped to her chest again. "God, you're beautiful."

"I'm…covered in…"

"Yeah, me and it's hot." He wiped the sperm off her cheek.

Her eyes darkened as she grabbed his hand, bringing his cum soaked finger to her mouth and sucking.

That was all it took for his dick to be locked and loaded again. "Fuck, Annie, you're gonna kill me." He kissed her again, thrusting his tongue into her mouth over and over. He couldn't get enough of her—her taste, the feel of her under him.

Her legs wrapped around him, pulling him closer to where he wanted to be but couldn't. "Stop. Let me look at you." He rolled off her and sat up. Her large, full breasts glistened with his sperm, her shorts were indecently short and the crotch was wet with her own juices, her hair was rumpled and her lips swollen. "You are the sexiest thing I've ever seen."

"Really?" Her eyes sparkled. "What if I do this?"

He should run but he couldn't move as she raised her hand to her breast and began massaging his cum into her skin with her long fingers. His nostrils flared, taking in the scent of her arousal. His dick hardened to the point of pain. If he didn't do something fast he was going to fuck her right now. "I'll get you a towel." He jumped from the couch and fled into the kitchen.

He grabbed a towel from the counter and hit his head against the cabinet—once, twice. He couldn't fuck her. He couldn't but his body disagreed. He turned on the water and splashed some onto his face. That wasn't where he needed it. He threw some on his misbehaving cock and then inhaled deeply. By the time the water was warm, he was in control, at least a little. He crammed his semi-erect penis into his pants and zipped them before wetting the towel and going back into the living room.

He hesitated in the doorway. The gleam was gone from her eyes, replaced with hurt. He'd done that to her. Again. He'd hurt the one person he was trying so damn hard to protect. He moved to the couch and sat down next to her, wiping her face and then chest. "I'm sorry."

"For what?" There was a challenge in her tone.

"For hurting you." He tossed the towel on the coffee table. "I had to leave to get it together. You drive me wild. Make me lose control."

"You do that to me too. I thought maybe you were...maybe, I'd gone too far." She glanced down and then back up to his face.

"No. Never." He kissed her. "Nothing you do is too much. Nothing. If you like it, it's good. Don't apologize for your kink."

"Is that what I have, a kink?"

"Yeah." He grinned. This was better. She was happy again. "You like to watch and that's cool."

"I also like to do." She grabbed his hand.

"Annie…" Uh-oh, back into dangerous territory. His dick perked right up, ready to dive in and conquer. Obviously, it was still a marine whereas he'd become some eunuch uncle.

"Stay with me for a bit. Hold me. That's all."

With her big, brown eyes pleading with him and her tits still wet from wiping off his sperm, he couldn't say no. He couldn't refuse her anything and that was a problem. "If you try and take advantage of me, I'm leaving."

"Never, I promise." She laughed as she moved to the side, making room for him.

"You lie." He stretched out next to her, pulling her close so her back rested against his front. His dick hardened again, but it was all locked up in his pants now so he was safe.

"I promise. I won't try anything, I swear, besides this." She grabbed his hand, placing it on her breast.

He gave her a squeeze. "I was going to do that anyway." He buried his head in her neck, inhaling her scent. "Where'd you learn about titty fucks? Watch someone else at the Club?" She could've been watching for weeks before he'd caught her. He was glad he'd been the one to discover her and not someone else.

"No. Video."

"You watch porn? You dirty girl." He swatted her backside a little.

"It was…Vic's and I was a lot younger then. It was before he joined the marines. The house was always full of his friends. I used to spy on them. I had crushes on most of them at one point." She laughed.

"On Ethan?" He tried to keep his tone neutral but he was jealous. All women loved Ethan.

"Definitely." She ran her hand up and down his arm. "But that was when I was a child and it was a child's crush. Nothing more." She pressed his hand against her breast.

"Good." He kissed her neck.

She shifted so she was looking at him. "What are you going to show me tomorrow?"

"It's a surprise, but I think you'll like it." He rocked his hips, rubbing his dick against her ass.

CHAPTER 11: ANNIE

Annie's panties were already damp when she entered the room where she and Patrick were meeting for lunch. She wanted him and today she'd make her move. They'd done so much already but she wanted him inside her—not his fingers or his tongue but his dick. The others were great and she wanted those too, but as foreplay not the main event.

"Lock the door."

"Oh." She jumped. "You scared me. Again"

"Sorry. I don't ever want to frighten you." He flipped a switch and a soft light highlighted the room. He was sitting on the couch. There was a glass and a bottle of alcohol of some type on the table next him. In front of the couch was a closed curtain, concealing a mirror into another room. He looked delicious—his hair slightly rumpled as if he'd run his hands through it, his eyes hungry and a slight bulge already forming in his pants.

"It's okay. I just hadn't realized you were here." She closed and locked the door, before strolling toward him. Her legs were wobbly with anticipation and the juncture between her thighs throbbed for his touch.

"I couldn't wait to see you."

"You could've stayed last night." His confession made her heart soften and her resolve to convince him to make love to her harden. They liked each other—a lot. They wanted each other—a lot. Doing everything but having sex was foolish.

His eyes moved up her body, devouring her and she responded. Her nipples hardened and her pussy wept for him.

"No, I couldn't have."

"Why?" Her fingers went to the buttons on her blouse. He really liked her breasts and she wanted to give him everything he liked.

"You know why." His eyes darkened as they stared at her fingers.

She wanted to push the issue but this wasn't the time. He was horny but in control. "We could've done something else." She shrugged out of her shirt and let her eye drop to the growing bulge in his pants. She licked her lips slowly and he inhaled sharply.

"We wouldn't have." His eyes darted to hers for a quick moment and he smiled. "Well, we would have but we wouldn't have stopped there."

She shimmied out of her pants, leaving only her matching pink bra and panties. She bit her lip and started to kneel. She wanted to lick him and taste him until he lost control.

"Not yet." He took her hand and pulled her onto his lap. "This first." He handed her a drink.

"Thanks." She sipped it and coughed. "It's strong."

"Drink. You'll need it."

Her heartbeat picked up a notch. "What are we going to do?" She was nervous and excited at the same time.

"Trust me?"

She turned, staring into his eyes for a long moment. He was an extremely attractive man but there was more to him than looks. He was honorable, kind, funny and he'd never hurt her—not physically. He was going to break her heart when this ended but that wasn't his fault. "Yes."

He kissed her. His lips warm and teasing, his tongue darting into her mouth for a quick taste and then he broke it off and tapped her glass. "Drink."

She wrinkled her nose and took a big gulp. "What about you?"

"I don't need one."

"I don't want to be the only one drunk." She tipped the glass to his mouth. Having him a little tipsy might help her convince him to make love to her.

He took a drink and then refilled the glass, taking another sip before handing it back to her. She drank as his hands started running up and down her legs, skimming along between her thighs and almost brushing against her pussy, but not quite. She wanted to grab him and make him touch her, make him assuage the ache he was building inside of her, but she drank a little more as she watched his hands teasing her. She was soaking wet and ready for him. She turned her head to look at his face as she let her thighs fall apart. Their gazes locked and held as his hands ran between her thighs, up and down but never touching where they met.

"Your skin is so soft here." His fingers played along the very inside of her legs. "You're soft everywhere, but especially here."

"Where else am I soft?" Her words were a raw whisper. She needed him to touch her.

"Here." He dipped his head and kissed the tops of her breasts, his mouth open and the kiss hot and wet just like her.

She started to put the glass down so she could unhook her bra but he stopped her.

"Finish it."

She frowned but chugged the last two swallows. He took the glass and refilled it.

"You drink some." Her body was already warm from the liquor and him. She didn't need more to drink. She needed more of him. She reached behind her and his eyes lowered as he waited for her to remove her bra. "Drink or I won't take it off."

He raised his eyes to hers. His gaze was amused as he took a sip, looking back at her chest.

"More."

He took a large gulp and she unhooked her bra but moved her hands to the front to hold it in place. It dipped forward, revealing some but not all.

"More." She liked ordering him around.

He drank again, it was half empty now. "The rest is yours." He held it to her lips.

She swallowed, finishing the drink. Her limbs already felt heavy and not just from desire.

He took the glass and filled it again, but left it on the table. "Now, show me your breasts."

"Kiss me first."

He dragged his eyes from her chest to her face. "No."

She leaned toward him. "Yes." Her lips dropped to his but she lost her balance and ended up kissing more of his cheek. She laughed. "I think I'm a little drunk."

His hand caressed her ass. "Good." His other hand came up and tugged on her bra as his lips found hers.

She sat up, breaking their kiss. "Stop. I'll do it." She waited for his eyes to go to her chest again and then she slowly let the bra fall forward and pulled it off her arms.

He lowered his face to her chest, rubbing his cheek against her breast. "You're very soft here."

He turned his head and trailed hot, open mouth kisses across the tops of her breasts. She grabbed his head, holding him to her as the electricity from his mouth surged through her body. He kissed lower until his breath teased her hard nipple. His other hand was between her legs teasing again, coming close but never quite touching her pussy. She was done playing.

"Patrick, please." She shifted, trying to bump into his fingers but he avoided her. She was getting desperate. She clenched her legs together, trapping his hand between them.

"Trying to force me won't work," he whispered against the side of her breast. "You've got me, but not where you want me."

It was true. His hand was between her legs but not high enough.

"Ask nice, Annie." He ran his tongue over her nipple. Her back arched and she moaned. He blew across it. "I'll give you what you want, but you have to ask for it."

"Touch me." She relaxed her thighs, freeing his hand.

He moved his hand to her knee. "I am touching you."

"Not there," she almost groaned.

"Where then?"

She grabbed his wrist and he let her drag his hand up her thigh to the juncture between her legs. "Here."

He didn't move his hand—at all. She wriggled her hips but he held still.

"Say it, Annie. I want to hear you say the words."

"Touch my pussy. Stroke me, Patrick. Please."
There. She'd said it. Her face was on fire but she'd said it.

He moved his thumb, caressing her clit as his fingers stroked along her labia. "Hold your tits together for me." His voice was rough with desire.

She squeezed her breasts together.

"Offer them to me." His eyes were like fire heating her with his gaze as his fingers stroked her through her panties.

She twisted, pushing her breasts toward his mouth. He licked his lips and it was like he'd licked her. She shivered as his other hand moved from her ass to her back, pushing her closer and then his lips came down on her nipple as his fingers slipped underneath her panties.

"You're so wet and hot." He kissed his way to her other breast. "You taste so good." He suckled her and her thighs fell apart while her hips thrust toward his hand.

He slipped two fingers inside her as he continued to suckle her breasts. He shifted his hand and curled his fingers as he shoved into her.

"Oh...oh...God!" That spot felt so good, like a current of pleasure strumming through her body. She needed to get closer, let his fingers touch her more.

He leaned her back on the couch. His mouth continued to lick and tease her nipples while he finger fucked her. His other hand moved to her abdomen and pushed downward, making each stroke of his fingers inside of her hit her g-spot with more strength and intensity. She moaned. She was so close, her body coiling as he stroked her over and over. She needed to move with him. She wiggled but his body kept her in place, keeping him in complete control.

"Come for me, baby." He bit down gently on her nipple as his fingers shoved deeper, pressing into her g-spot and thrusting in short, hard pumps.

She screamed and bucked against his hand, squeezing the fingers that kept stroking her.

Several minutes later, when she stopped trembling he brushed the hair from her face and kissed her gently. He grabbed the glass and helped her lean up. "Drink."

"Water." She turned her head away from the alcohol.

He kissed her and rolled over to get off the couch, moaning as his dick pressed against her for one sweet second. He came back a moment later with a bottle of water. She started to get up but he knelt on the floor next to the couch.

"No. Stay like that." His hand went behind her back helping her to lean up enough to drink the water. When she was done, he held the glass of alcohol back to her lips. "Now this."

"I…"

"Please, for me."

She'd do anything for him. She took another couple of sips. "You too." When he hesitated she said, "For me."

"You don't play fair." His eyes darkened as he took a large swallow. He put the glass down and glanced at his watch. "The show's about to start." He leaned down and kissed her. It started out soft and warm but quickly heated, his tongue thrusting into her mouth and exploring.

She tugged at his shirt and he broke their kiss to take it off. She ran her hands across his wide chest and he kissed her again. Her hands drifted down his abdomen but he stopped them.

"Please, I want to touch you." She kissed him, sucking on his lower lip and he moaned.

"Annie, you're playing with fire."

"Burn me." Her hand ran over the hard length of him and his hips rocked against her. She unbuttoned his pants, her fingers slipping beneath the waistband but he stood before she could touch him.

"The show." He kissed her neck. "I'll be right back." He walked away and opened the curtain.

The mirror into the other room was positioned right in front of the couch. She rolled over for a better view. In the other room was a large bed—a large, empty bed in a large, empty room.

He walked back to the couch. "Get on your knees and rest your arms on the side of the couch."

The heat in her belly, just soothed, warmed again as she quickly got into position. Not quite doggie style but close. She looked up at him.

"Watch the show."

A man and a woman entered the other room. The woman wore assless chaps and her breasts were encased in leather except for her nipples. Annie giggled. The woman looked ridiculous.

The couch dipped. She glanced over her shoulder. Patrick was kneeling behind her, his eyes dark and focused on her ass. She shivered, waiting for his touch, and hopefully his cock in her pussy.

"Watch the show, Annie." He didn't bother to look at her.

She turned toward the mirror. The man and woman were kissing now. The man's hands held the woman's ass, pulling her into his erection. Patrick's hands skimmed over her butt, his fingers slipping under the waistband of her panties and pulling them down.

The man and woman moved to the bed. The woman was on her back as the man kissed and suckled her breasts. Patrick kissed her ass as he removed her panties and threw them on the floor. His hands, hot and rough, skimmed up her thighs, pushing them apart.

The man's hands were playing with the woman's pussy now. The chaps weren't just assless they were crotchless too. The woman was glistening with her desire. Annie wiggled her ass, hoping Patrick would touch her like the man was touching the woman. She was so wet and ready for him. Patrick's hot mouth kissed its way up her thigh. Her breathing froze, waiting for him to kiss her there but his fingers got there first, spreading her wide and then his tongue followed with a long lick. A groan rumbled through her body at the rough strength of his kiss.

"Tell me what they're doing," he said against her pussy. "Describe it in detail."

"What? I can't." Her face heated at the thought. She had no idea why having his face between her thighs didn't bother her but the thought of describing the sexual activities of the other couple mortified her.

"Do it or I stop." He gave her another lick and she shivered. "You don't want me to stop do you?" He sucked on her clit for one fast moment of pure bliss.

"No." Her knees trembled and her body shook. She'd die if he stopped.

"Tell me what they're doing." He waited, his fingers spreading her wide, his hot breath teasing across her aching pussy, but his mouth and tongue doing nothing.

"The man is…fingering her." Her face had to be beet red.

"Like this." He ran his fingers through her wetness but didn't dip inside.

"No." She rocked against his hand. It felt good but it wasn't enough. "He's inside of her. Touching her from the inside." She wanted Patrick inside of her too.

"Like this." He slipped one and then two and then three fingers into her.

"Oh…yes. He's moving them." She needed Patrick to move his fingers, to touch that spot again.

He smiled against her thigh. "Of course. How remiss of me." He began a soft steady stroke. "What else is he doing?"

"Ah..ah. I don't know." And she didn't care. All she cared about was what Patrick was doing to her.

"Tell me or I stop."

"He's kissing her." He wasn't. He'd stopped. The woman was turning over but she wasn't going to tell Patrick that because she didn't want him to stop.

"Like this." His tongue darted out stroking across her clit.

"Yes. More. Faster."

He did it again and again. Her body began rocking against his face and hand.

"You can't come yet." He stopped flicking her clit and gave her a couple of long, slow licks as he slowed his fingers down too.

"Please, I'm so close." She pushed toward his face. "Make me come. Let me come."

"Watch the show. What's the guy doing now?" His words were rough and rumbled through her cunt.

She couldn't stop the whimper of need as she turned and looked into the other room.

"Ah…" The guy had the woman's ass spread and was guiding his dick into her. She couldn't say that. Patrick didn't want to do that, did he? The couch shifted as Patrick moved.

"Describe what he's doing?" His words were at her ear now, his large, strong body leaning over her, surrounding her.

"You can see." She didn't want to describe it, but she couldn't tear her eyes away. The man's dick was slowly slipping into the woman's asshole. She'd never done that. She wasn't sure she wanted to do it.

"I want you to tell me." He kissed her neck and then bit down as he rubbed his erection against her butt cheeks.

"He's fucking her ass," she whispered. The man was all the way in now and thrusting, his face tight with focus and passion.

"Do you think she likes it?" he whispered, teasing and tempting her with the thought.

Her eyes went to the woman's face and it was bliss. "Yes."

"Would you like to try it?" His hand stroked between her ass cheeks, skimming over her butthole.

"I..I don't know." Her body was aching for release but this was different. It could be painful, but the woman did seem to like it.

"We won't if you don't want to." He kissed her neck as his finger rimmed her asshole.

"Do you want to?"

"Very much." He tipped her face toward him and kissed her. "But you have to want to do it too."

"Will it hurt?" She wanted to please him and she kind of wanted to try it.

"A little, maybe, at first but then no."

"Will I enjoy it?" If it didn't hurt she'd do it for him, even if she didn't enjoy it. However, she'd rather get pleasure too.

"Some women like it a lot. Some like it a little and some don't like it at all." He kissed her again; it was warm and gentle. "But I think you'll enjoy it."

"Do you like it?"

Now he grinned. "I do."

"Do you do it that way a lot?" She couldn't help it she was jealous.

"No. I prefer vaginal sex but this is fun on occasion."

"We could do the other." She wanted him inside her but she'd prefer the conventional way.

"No, we can't." He kissed her again. "I told you, I won't have sex with you."

"But this isn't sex?" She looked back at the couple. The man was thrusting hard and fast now and the woman's mouth was opened, screaming her release. It sure looked like sex to her.

"No, it's not." His finger stroked around her butthole, pressing down a little.

She shivered. It was taboo and dark and she wanted to do it. She wanted to do it for him and for her. "Okay."

He handed her the glass. "Drink. It'll feel better if you're relaxed." He straightened so he knelt behind her and his hand skimmed downward to her pussy. His fingers slid into her and she moaned into the glass. His touch was firm but fast as he trailed his fingers back up to her asshole. "I need to make you wet here." He pressed down on her hole with his thumb. "Finish your drink, Annie."

She gulped it down and put the glass back on the table.

"Relax and watch the show. They're almost done." He continued to stroke between her cheeks and down to her vagina. His rhythm was slow and steady, dipping into her and sometimes twirling around her clit. She began arching her back, trying to follow his touch as she stared through the mirror.

The man was still pumping into the woman. His hands were clenched onto her hips, his fingers digging into the soft flesh, and then he stiffened as he shoved into her one more time before collapsing on her. Patrick continued to play with her pussy and her asshole, letting his thumb press her hole a little more each time. It felt weird, forbidden, but it didn't hurt. Her limbs were languid as the whiskey worked its magic. His fingers found her clit again and the tension that'd built before revved back up. His hand left her ass and the couch shifted. Something cold and wet dropped between her butt cheeks and she jumped.

"More lubricant." He smeared it around her asshole and pressed in with his thumb, this time letting it slide inside of her.

"Oh."

He pushed in farther. "You okay?"

"Yeah." It still didn't hurt. It felt odd, making her feel full back there.

His other hand, moved to her front, teasing her clit. He slipped two fingers into her vagina, stroking against her g-spot. "Relax baby. You feel so good." His voice was thick with desire. "So tight and hot."

His thumb pushed in all the way as he tickled her g-spot and she moaned, rocking against him and feeling him with both her back and forward movement. He was filling her completely. It was glorious.

"You like it don't you?" He bent and kissed her ass, open mouth and wet.

"Yes." She did. She really did.

He pulled his thumb out of her asshole.

"What? Why?" She was so close to coming. He couldn't stop.

"Shhh." His finger replaced his thumb, pressing down and then sliding inside of her. It was longer and felt better.

"Good?" he asked.

"Stroke me, please." She needed him to move his fingers, on both hands.

He chuckled as he withdrew the finger in her ass until only the tip remained inside her and then he shoved it back inside.

"Ohh." God, that felt good.

He did it again but this time when he pushed back inside, he added a second finger.

"Ouch." It was too much, too fast. He was stretching her and it hurt.

"Sorry." He didn't move the fingers in her ass, but he stroked her g-spot and kissed down her back. "Tell me when you're good."

Soon, the pleasure of his stroking overtook the fullness in her ass and she began to move. She wanted him to move. "I'm good. You can…Yes."

He began a gentle thrusting into her ass with both fingers, matching the pace of the ones in her pussy. She felt full and her body tightened. She had nowhere to go to escape the pleasure.

"Oh, God. Patrick." It felt so good. "Faster, please. I'm so close."

"Not yet. Wait." He removed his fingers from both her openings.

"No…please." Her body twitched in protest. She wanted to come. She needed to come.

He kissed her lower back. "One minute baby and then you can come, I swear."

He unzipped his pants, the sound reverberating through the room and even more wetness pooled between her thighs. He was going to penetrate her. She turned to watch him over her shoulder. He filled his hand with lube and then stroked it along his large, hard cock.

"Please hurry." She wanted him inside of her. Now.

His eyes locked with hers for one moment as he spread her ass cheeks and ran his dick across her cunt.

"Yes, there. Please." She wiggled against him. "I need you inside me." She wanted him. She reached behind her and grabbed his cock.

"Fuck, Annie. Don't. I have to go slow and if you…"

She stroked him, leading him back to her pussy.

"Fuck." His hips surged forward as if they had a mind of their own and the tip of him slipped inside of her cunt.

He was hot and hard and so big, filling her. She pushed back, taking more of him into her.

His hands clasped her hips, his fingers digging into her but she welcomed the pain. He was inside of her. She rocked against him, trying to take more of him in but he wasn't cooperating.

His breath was coming in great big pants. "God, I want to. You feel so fucking good."

He shoved into her all the way and she screamed. He was too big. She hadn't had sex in a while and she was tight.

"Fuck, I'm sorry." He pulled out

"No. Please. It's okay. I just need a minute…to adjust. Please…"

But now, his dick was poking at her ass. She stilled as he entered her, a little and then a little more. It'd hurt when he'd entered her pussy, this was going to kill her.

He began to stroke her clit again, rubbing and pressing. "Tell me when to stop. You have to tell me." He pushed in a little more as his fingers slid into her pussy and began to fuck her.

She didn't know where to focus. Her ass hurt as he continued his forward movement, with every breath encroaching into her, but his fingers were sending sparks of pleasure through her and igniting her desires. He began to pull out and push into her, each time going a little deeper. It didn't hurt anymore, not really. She felt full and then he'd press down on her clit a little as he pushed into her and she found herself rocking back against him, matching his rhythm.

"Good? Can I go more? I need more?" His words were gritty and raw. He was close to coming.

"Yes. Faster too."

His hand tightened on her hip as he thrust into her, burying himself deep.

"Oh. Ouch." Pain shot though her backside. That was too much too fast. She was being torn in half.

"Fuck. Sorry." He held still. "Tell me when it's good." His fingers continued to work her labia and clit.

She tried to focus on them, the pleasure but her ass still hurt.

"You okay?"

"No." A tear trickled down her cheek. This hurt.

He backed out a little and rested his head on her shoulder. "How's that?"

The pain was still there, but more like a memory, as the pleasure from his fingers was taking over, pushing it aside. "Better."

He pulled out and pushed back in, slow and steady, but not going as far as before. "Did that hurt?"

She shook her head. "No."

"Thank God." He kissed her shoulder. "Now, I know. This is as deep as I can go. It won't hurt again. I promise." He moved his hand from her hip and stroked her hair. "You ready?" His voice was rough, on edge.

"Yeah." It didn't hurt with him there. "Just no deeper."

"I won't." He started to rock into her, back and forth, in and out, never going any farther than she could stand.

She rested her head on the couch as the sensations washed through her. He was hard and firm in her ass as his other hand stroked her pussy.

"You feel so fucking good. So tight. So sweet." He tangled one hand in her hair as he increased his tempo.

Pleasure filled her from both holes and she began pushing back against him. "Harder, please. Faster." She was going to come.

He tugged her hair, pulling her head back, and kissed her. It was hard and rough, out of control. "Come for me baby. I need you to come. I'm so fucking close."

He dropped her hair and grabbed her hip again. His pace was frantic now but so was hers. The little pain he caused only intensified the pleasure.

"Fuck, I'm coming." He gave her clit a soft pinch as he thrust into her ass.

She screamed as she came, bucking and thrusting against him. Her movements caused him to go deeper and she screamed again as she came a second time. He grabbed her hips with both hands and shoved into her one more time as his body stiffened and he came.

A moment later, he collapsed on top of her. He kissed her neck. "Okay?"

"Yeah." She was still kneeling, her breath coming in gasps. She'd never come twice so close together.

He pulled out of her ass and dropped onto the couch, pulling her into his arms and resting his head on hers. "You really okay?"

She kissed his chest. "Yeah." She looked up at him, his eyes were searching hers. "I came twice. I didn't think I would from anal."

"I'm glad you enjoyed it. Not all women do." He kissed her and shifted until he was on his back and she was half on top of him. His hand wandered up and down her spine as she drifted off to sleep.

CHAPTER 12: PATRICK

Patrick let out a big, weary sigh as his hand wandered down Annie's sleeping frame. "What am I going to do with you, my little voyeur?" He kissed her head. They only had a few days before Ethan came back. He didn't want their time to end and yet he had to stop seeing her, touching her, even sooner. He'd felt her around him. She'd clutched his cock in her hot, wet pussy and it'd been heaven, perfection. There was no way he could stay out of her now. He'd barely kept his dick away from her sweet cunt today. She wouldn't be happy, but this had to be their last day of play.

"I'm going to miss you." His chest tightened. He'd done it again. He'd fallen in love with someone he'd never be able to keep. He kissed her head as his hand trailed between her butt cheeks.

Book 4

Loving The Voyeur

CHAPTER 1: ANNIE

When her shift was over, Annie hurried and changed into her street clothes. She couldn't wait to get Patrick to her house and fool around again. He'd been inside of her, both her back and her front, and she wanted him there again, especially her front. Anal had been better than she'd expected but she wanted conventional sex with him. She slipped into the hallway and there he was, leaning against the wall. Her gaze raked over his frame. She wanted him, right here, right now. Her eyes trailed up his body and she almost gasped from the look of longing on his face. Oh, yeah. They'd do it tonight. She fought a grin as she glanced around. There was no one in sight, so she strolled up to him.

"Annie." There was a warning in his tone but she ignored it.

"Patrick." She ran her hands up his chest and leaned into him as she put her arms around his neck.

"What are you doing?" His hands immediately came to her ass and pulled her closer.

"Kissing you." She raised her mouth to his.

He hesitated for a moment but as soon as her tongue traced his lips he snapped. He lifted her and spun around, pressing her against the wall as he slanted his mouth, devouring her. She wrapped her legs around him and his hand slipped under her shirt, pushing it up as he went. His fingers found her already hard nipple and he tugged on it.

"Do that again." She rocked her hips, rubbing against his erection.

"Fuck, Annie. You drive me crazy." He thrust against her.

"Please, Patrick." She needed him, now. Her hand came between them and she grasped his cock through his pants.

His mouth moved to her breast, sucking it. She moaned as her other hand unbutton his pants, pushing the zipper down and pulling out his cock. He was so hard, so ready for her. She stroked his length and he tugged on her nipple with his teeth, making her squeeze him. He groaned against her breast.

"Shit." He tugged her shirt down.

"No." She wasn't going to let him stop. Not this time, she needed this. She needed him.

"Someone's coming." He unhooked her legs from around his hips and stepped back.

Her knees buckled, and he grabbed her arm as he tucked his cock into his pants, grimacing as he zipped up.

Two women turned the corner. They were maids for the next shift.

"Morning," he said. "Annie, are you ready to go?"

She nodded, her head still fuzzy with passion. He led her to the garage and put her into his car.

"We can't do things like that," he said. "We almost got caught." His jaw was tense.

She wasn't sure if he were angry or if it was only frustrated passion. "Sorry. You're right." He was. She didn't want her co-workers to know about this…arrangement.

He glanced at her nervously and she almost laughed.

"I admit when I'm wrong."

"That's good to know." His lips twitched. "It's not a common trait among women."

"Hey!" She slapped his arm.

"Sorry, but I speak the truth."

"I'm not most women."

"No, you're not." His gaze landed on her for one, hot moment.

She wanted to jump him right there, but doing anything like that when he was driving was dangerous. However, as soon as she got him in her house he was hers.

He pulled into her driveway and moved around the car to open the door for her. She stepped out and stood so close that if either of them took a deep breath they'd be touching. She took his hand.

"I should go home." He shut the car door.

"You can. Later." She'd rather he stayed the night but she'd focus on one battle at a time. She tugged him toward her house but he didn't move.

"Annie, we can't."

She wanted to stamp her foot in annoyance. "We don't have to do anything." She bit her lip and his nostrils flared. "Or we could do other things...you know like we've done before."

"Fuck, Annie. Don't." He stepped away from her as if she were toxic. "We've already done more than we should have and I...I can't not be with you anymore."

She walked up to him. "Then be with me."

"You know I can't."

"Please." She moved closer, letting her fingers skim up and down his chest, going lower with each passing. "I want you and you want me. We're adults. We're not hurting anyone." This time, her fingers caressed his cock, which was once again pressing against his pants.

He grabbed her face between his hands and kissed her, long and deep, making her head spin from the intensity. He pushed her against his car pressing into her and then he lifted her and strode toward her house.

She wrapped her legs around his waist and pressed against him. "God, Patrick, I want you so bad."

"Keys," he said against her lips.

She looked in her purse but couldn't find them. "They have to be here." She shoved items out of her way. If this gave him time to change his mind, she'd kill someone. "Hold this." She pulled out her wallet, handing it to him and then some papers. She almost whooped with joy as her fingers grasped the metal. "Here they are."

He yanked them from her hand and opened the door. He stepped inside, slammed the door behind them as his mouth came down on hers, his tongue claiming her as his. He stumbled to her bedroom and dropped her onto the bed.

She tossed her purse on the floor and he put her wallet and papers on her nightstand.

"I need you inside my mouth, now." She got on her knees and grabbed the waistband of his pants. Her eyes met his but there was no hesitation, nothing but lust, pure raw lust. She clenched her thighs together as she unbuttoned his pants, letting her fingers skim lightly against the tip of his penis. He inhaled sharply. She drew the zipper down slowly. The throbbing between her legs increased at the desire on his face. She shoved his pants and underwear down, allowing his dick to spring free. It bobbed right in front of her face, as if begging her to have a taste. She had no plans on disappointing it. She slipped her hand into her pants and his eyes narrowed with desire. She pulled her hand out and rubbed her wetness along his length.

"Do that again," he said.

She licked him as her other hand dipped beneath her waistband. Her lips parted as she stroked herself.

"Take your pants off. I want to see you."

She let go of his cock and unbuttoned her pants and pushed them and her underwear down around her knees. She rubbed herself and then grabbed his dick, covering him with her juices. She licked her lips. "I don't think you're wet enough."

"Please, Annie." His breath was coming in pants now.

She'd done this to him. She'd brought this great, big, sexy man to the edge of lust and she wasn't even naked yet.

"Annie." It was a word of worship and he grasped her head. He didn't push her onto his cock, but the trembling in his grip told her he wanted to. "Please."

"Please what, Patrick?" She gave him a quick lick and a guttural groan rumbled through his chest. "You have to say it or I'll stop."

"That's not funny."

"I'm not kidding." She wasn't. Kind of. She'd stop but not forever. She wanted to taste him again. Bring him right to the edge with her mouth. She ran her tongue over the head of his dick. "Say it."

"Suck me. Suck my dick, baby."

She licked up and down his length, while her hand stroked him. She lowered her mouth to his cock, taking him in. Now, his hand did push her down as his hips thrust upward. She bobbed her head, finding her rhythm as she sucked and licked, stroking his length and playing with his balls.

His fingers wrapped in her hair and then gave her a gentle tug. "Enough, or I'm going to come."

She stopped, pulling his cock out of her mouth with a pop. He grabbed her face and kissed her, pushing her back on the bed and then his hands were everywhere—on her breasts, her stomach, removing her shirt and bra and then her pants as he suckled her tits. It was too much sensation, too much pleasure. She spread her legs and wriggled against him, trying to get closer. She shoved at his shirt, he'd already removed his pants, but she wanted him naked. He stopped kissing her but only long enough to pull his shirt over his head and then his mouth was on hers. He used his knee to shove her legs farther apart and then he was there—hard and throbbing—right where she wanted him, right where he belonged.

He grabbed his cock and positioned himself at her entrance. "Are you sure?" His words were a whispered groan.

"Yes." She locked her legs around his waist and shifted her hips, causing him to slide inside a fraction.

"Oh, God, you feel so good." He buried his face in her neck and pushed in a little more.

He was going too slow. She needed him inside of her now. "Please, Patrick." She ran her hands down his back and squeezed his ass.

"You feel so good. So, fucking tight." He pushed into her a little more.

He was so big. He was stretching her and filling her. It hurt but in a good way, in the best way. He rocked, pushing in more and more with each thrust—a constant unwavering invasion. Her breath was coming in pants as her fingers scratched at his back.

"You okay, baby?"

"Yeah. Just do it quick." She pushed on his ass with her feet and he slid into her all the way. She groaned. It hurt but she knew in a moment it'd feel better than anything.

"Shhh." He brushed the hair from her face. "Give it a minute. Breathe, baby."

He kissed her, taking her mind off the pressure inside of her, and then he moved, just a little and it felt wonderful.

"Ohh." She moaned.

"You like that." His eyes sparkled as he did it again but this time pulling farther out before pushing back inside of her.

"Yes."

"Good, because I'd die if you made me stop."

"Don't stop. Ever." She kissed his cheek and then lips as he turned his head.

His tongue thrust into her mouth as his dick thrust into her pussy. He moved his lips to her neck as he picked up the pace, moving faster and harder. Her body hummed as she rocked with him, meeting him thrust for thrust, taking him deeper and deeper until she wasn't sure where he ended and she began. Her body spiraled and tightened as their movements became more frantic.

"Oh, God, Annie. You're perfect. You feel so good." He nipped her ear and she burst, clinging to him as she came. He kept pounding into her until he groaned and shuddered his release.

He collapsed on top of her, his face buried in her neck, his breathing ragged. She turned, kissing his cheek, and skimming her legs down his as she untangled her limbs from him.

CHAPTER 2: PATRICK

Patrick stretched, his hand encountering soft curves and his dick hardened. He never wanted to move, except maybe to get closer, to get inside her again. He nuzzled his face into her neck. She smelled good—warm and rich with a hint of flowers. She smelled like Annie. His eyes popped open and memories of the night, well, morning raced through his head like a fantastic porno. He'd been insatiable. Ever since he'd slipped inside her during lunch he'd been unable to think of anything besides getting back in there. The way she'd squeezed him and the hot, wet warmth of her. His dick stiffened even more and his hand moved from her hip to her breast.

She moaned slightly in her sleep. He should leave her alone. She had to be exhausted. He grinned and kissed her softly. After the first time, they'd fucked four more times. He hadn't become aroused that quickly and that easily since he'd been sixteen. His fingers trailed down her belly to her pussy and he began to stroke her. He lifted her leg, placing it over his hip and opening up for him. The head of his cock teased her entrance and she moaned again.

"Let me in, baby," he whispered in her ear. "Open for me."

She wrapped her arm around his neck and shifted her hips closer. He leaned up on his elbow so he could see her face as he buried himself inside her in one long thrust. Her eyes stayed closed but her mouth opened on a gasp. He rocked into her as his hand came down, pressing on her abdomen so he could more easily hit her g-spot.

"Ohh…" She moaned again, as her eyelids fluttered open.

He kissed her neck, sucking on the sensitive spot where it met her shoulder, as he increased his pace, hitting her g-spot over and over. She felt so fucking good as she squeezed him, clasping him inside her as if she never wanted to let him go.

"Fuck, Annie, do that again." He thrust into her hard and she clamped down on his cock. "You feel too fucking good. Come for me, baby. This one's going to be hard and fast."

His finger found her clit and he caressed it, using his nail to rake it gently. She gasped and her body tightened. Her hips bucked and her mouth opened on a silent sigh as her pussy tightened around him, sending him over the edge.

When he could breathe again, he kissed her neck. "I'm going to get some water. You want something?"

A soft snore was his only answer. He kissed her again. She'd just given him one of the best fucks of his life and she was sleeping. Jesus, he couldn't get enough of her. He rolled over and hopped out of bed, accidentally kicking her purse across the floor. He walked over to it and bent, gathering the items that'd fallen out on the trip. He stared at a picture of Vic, Ethan and himself. It was from when they'd first joined the marines. Vic had been so young. They all had.

Guilt slapped him in the gut, twisting his heart. Vic was a mess, lost to the world and it was his fault. He'd been assigned to that mission. It should be him with the memories too terrible to function. He grabbed his clothes and went into the living room. He dropped on the couch, cradling his head in his hands and staring at the picture of his friend. He'd destroyed Vic's life and then he'd fucked his baby sister in every way imaginable.

He couldn't be around her. He stood, pulled on his pants and shoes and headed for the door, stopping with his hand on the knob. He couldn't leave like this. She'd be confused and God, he couldn't hurt her like that. He'd still hurt her but he wouldn't be a coward and sneak away. He put on his shirt and sat down on the couch, waiting for Annie to wake.

CHAPTER 3: ANNIE

When Annie woke she stretched and winced. She was sore in the most wonderful places. Her breasts were tender and her leg muscles throbbed as well as the place between her thighs. She grabbed the pillow that Patrick had used and hugged it. She wished he'd stayed, but last night had been better than excellent. She needed to soak in a hot bath because she had every intention of a repeat performance tonight.

She crawled out of bed and headed for the bathroom. A movement in the living room caught her eye. Patrick was fully dressed, sitting on the couch and staring at something in his hand. She bit her lip. He was still here. He was overdressed but she could work with that. She hurried into the bathroom and brushed her teeth and hair. The bath would wait, or maybe she could convince him to join her. She'd never had sex in a tub—shower yes, but not the tub.

She wrapped a towel around herself and strolled into the living room. "Morning." He looked delicious with his five o'clock shadow. She couldn't wait to feel it on her breasts and between her legs. "I'm going to take a bath. Want to join me?"

As he glanced at her she let the towel drop. He inhaled sharply, his eyes roaming over her body, sending heat shooting through her. She moved toward him.

"Annie. Don't." He stood and stepped behind the couch. "We need to talk."

Her chest constricted as if she were bound in a corset and someone strong was pulling on the laces. Those four words were the worst ones in the English language. "Don't. Don't." She wanted to say, don't do this to me or don't hurt me again, but only that one word would come out.

"I'm sorry."

She shook her head, trying not to cry. "Why?"

He handed her the picture he'd been looking at. It was the one of Vic, Ethan and himself.

"You went through my purse?"

"No. I kicked it when I went to get some water and this fell out."

She stared at her brother, so young and determined, nothing like the broken man who'd come back from the war.

"I...I have to tell you something." He started to move toward her and stopped. "Can you put some clothes on? Please."

She flushed and hurried into her bedroom. She shut the door and let the tears fall. "Damn you, Vic. You're not even here and you're still chasing away my boyfriend. It's not fair." This thing with Patrick was too special to throw away. She was crazy about him. Her heart skipped a beat. No, she was in love with him. He was kind, honorable, and sexy as hell. She wasn't giving up without a fight. She threw the picture on her bed and pulled on a pair of sweatpants, bra and T-shirt. She went into the bathroom and splashed water on her face to hide the fact that she'd been crying. She took a deep breath and walked into the living room, prepared to argue with the most stubborn man in the world.

He was sitting on the couch again, looking like he was ready to bolt. She sat down next to him and he took her hand.

"I didn't mean...We shouldn't have done..."

"Don't you dare apologize for what we did."

"But I shouldn't have touched you." His fingers caressed her knuckles. "Not last time and not the other times either."

"Why? And don't say it's because of Vic because that's bullshit."

"It's not bullshit." He dropped her hand and stood. "You don't understand. I ruined his life and now I've ruined you."

"Ruined me? Are we living in the 1800s? You didn't ruin anything except today, right now."

"You don't get it." His fists clenched at his sides. "It should be me, not him. Me." He hit his chest.

"What should be you?"

"I was supposed to go on that mission, not Vic." His face twisted with anger and regret.

She took a deep breath to steady her nerves. That last mission had destroyed her brother. Vic wouldn't talk about it, but he'd come back broken. "Why didn't you go?" She was glad he hadn't, glad he wasn't ruined like Vic and she felt guilty.

"My father died."

"That's not your fault."

"I should've been back. I could've been back in time. I could've let my brothers and sisters help Mom with the estate but…I stayed and I didn't go on the mission. Vic went instead." He stopped pacing his eyes meeting hers. "He told me to stay home and take care of my family. Family first he said."

He ran his hand over his face, wiping at his eyes. She didn't remember moving but she must've because she was pulling him into her arms. He rested his head on her shoulder, his face buried in her neck.

"He said I'd do the same for him and I didn't." He shoved away from her. "Instead I fucked his sister, his baby sister." He laughed. It was coarse and angry. "In every way imaginable."

"Patrick, I wanted you to—"

"Did you? Did you actually want me to fuck you in the ass?"

"I…I liked it." Her face was red hot now and she hated this. She shouldn't be embarrassed by the pleasure they'd shared.

"Jesus, that's worse. Now, you're a voyeur and you like it in the ass. What's next? Two men? Is that what I should do with you next? Or would you like two women? How about tying you up? I've already spanked you and you liked that too."

It was like he was hitting her again and again. All those wonderful things they'd done together, all those wonderful feelings he stirred inside of her, were dirty to him, vile.

"I..ah, shit, Annie…" He took a step toward her.

"Stay away from me." She stumbled backward.

"Annie…." He reached for her and then dropped his hand. "I should go."

She didn't move as he turned and left. She had no idea how long she stood there feeling used and like a slut. At some point she made it to the couch and collapsed, too hurt, too numb to even cry.

CHAPTER 4: ANNIE

Class was almost over. Annie's stomach twisted. She wanted to see Patrick, but she didn't. She was still mad at him, still hurt by what he'd said. She moved toward the door, Chelsea behind her.

"Don't forgive him too quickly," said Chelsea. "He needs to suffer for being so stupid. Actually, you shouldn't give him another chance. Any guy who'd make you feel bad for having a good time is the kind of guy you should avoid."

She'd filled Chelsea in on everything when her friend had picked her up for school. Chelsea was not happy with Patrick. "He was upset." She walked out the door and froze.

"Who's that?" whispered Chelsea, more than a hint of interest in her voice.

"Remember me? I'm Nick. Patrick sent me to pick you up." Nick stepped forward.

"Is he single?" whispered Chelsea in her ear. "Please, tell me he's single."

Nick grinned. "Actually, I'm not." When Chelsea's eyes dropped to his hand he laughed. "I'm not married but my heart is taken."

"Oh, that is so…" Chelsea almost melted into a puddle on the floor.

"Where's Patrick?" She was amazed her voice was steady. Maybe, he had a family emergency or a work emergency, or something besides just not wanting to see her.

"He couldn't make it." Nick's eyes darted away from her face.

"Today or ever?" Dread settled in her stomach. It wasn't only today. She didn't have to hear the words to know.

"Ah…why don't we talk in my car?"

"You okay?" asked Chelsea.

She nodded and followed Nick out of the building. As soon as they were inside his car, she said, "Patrick's not coming again is he?"

"He thinks it's better if he stays away from you." He pulled out of the parking lot.

She tried really hard not to make a sound, not to breathe funny or sob but she must've done something because Nick said, "It'll be okay. He'll come around. He's just being an idiot."

She wanted to agree but she also wanted to defend him. Patrick was being an idiot but she didn't like anyone but her calling him that. It didn't matter though because she couldn't speak. Her throat was too tight, filled with sorrow. They'd had sex, made love and it'd been great, the best time she'd ever had and now he couldn't stand to be around her. Her brother had been right to protect her from guys like him because she obviously couldn't protect herself.

"I'm really sorry about this. Patrick…is torn about the war and Ethan and your brother…but I know him and he'll do what's right."

Her throat loosened and she laughed, a short burst of absurdity, quickly followed by a sob and then another. Nick drove into the Club garage, got out and opened her door, grabbing her hand and pulling her out of the car and into his arms.

"It's okay. I swear." One of his hands held her head to his shoulder and the other one patted her back. "I'll kick some sense into him."

"He hates me," she mumbled against his chest.

"No, he doesn't." Nick moved away a little and tipped her chin up toward him. "He's crazy about you."

She shook her head, the tears coming faster now. "No. Vic was right. He only wanted sex and now he thinks I'm…I'm…" She couldn't say it. It was too embarrassing.

"I'm going to kill him." Nick pulled her to his chest again.

"Leave him alone. It was my fault. I chased him. He tried to stay away but I…" She didn't want to be here, couldn't be here, not tonight. "I want to go home."

"Of course." He opened the car door for her and she cried harder.

CHAPTER 5: PATRICK

Patrick paced in the Club's garage. He was going to kill Nick. He should've known better than to ask him to take over chauffeuring Annie. She was attractive and vulnerable—perfect prey for a guy like Nick. He'd been watching the cameras, needing to at least see her and she'd fallen right into his ex-friend's arms.

Nick's car pulled into the garage.

As soon as Nick stepped out of his car, Patrick slammed his fist into the other man's face. "You son-of-a-bitch!"

Nick stumbled backward and then ducked, ramming into Patrick's gut. "Me? You're the bastard."

He shoved Nick away, breathing heavy and waiting for an opening. He was a former marine. If he couldn't find one, he'd create one. "Sarah's going to love hearing you lasted an entire what? Two months and then decided she wasn't worth it."

"Don't even say her name you ass-wipe. And I didn't touch your—"

"I saw you on the cameras. You touched her." He jabbed, connecting with Nick's face again before darting away.

"You're a fucking asshole." Nick spit blood onto the concrete. "I comforted her because you made her feel dirty and ashamed."

"What?" Annie wasn't dirty she was beautiful and perfect.

Nick lunged forward, punching Patrick in the mouth.

"What are you talking about?" Patrick blocked the next blow but didn't strike back.

"We done here?" asked Nick, his fists up and ready.

From what he'd seen on the camera Nick had only hugged her and then he'd put her in the car and left. He should've been the one to comfort her but beating the snot out of his friend wasn't going to make him feel better. "Yeah, we're done."

"Good," said Nick. "Let's get a drink and I'll tell you what she said."

As soon as they were in Ethan's office, each with a drink, Nick said, "I knew you were being stupid but I had no idea you were such a jerk."

"I told you, I can't be around her. I can't stop myself from...being with her."

"You shouldn't stop being with her if—"

"You know why I—"

"Stop." Nick held up his hand. "I don't want to hear that bullshit about Vic again."

"It's not bullshit."

"It doesn't matter. This isn't about that. It's about what you said to her. She's convinced you think she's a dirty whore."

"What? No." He dropped onto the sofa his mind playing back what he could remember of their conversation. "I never said anything like that. I wouldn't. She's not..." She was perfect—sexy and sweet and eager to experiment. "She's...I...I have no fucking idea where she got that. I never said that." He tossed back his drink. "I wouldn't. I was the one who showed her...this world."

"And do you think this is dirty?"

"Well...yeah. It is. Some of it anyway."

"Why? It's people getting their kink on. No one is hurting anyone." Nick smirked. "Unless that's what they like, of course."

"You really going to bring Sarah here?"

Nick sipped his drink. "To watch a few shows? Absolutely." He tipped his cup. "Thanks for that by the way. I'd never thought about adding that to our games."

"Will the two of you join in?" he asked. Nick enjoyed ménages and orgies a lot more than he did.

"Fuck no. Sarah's mine."

"Exactly."

"Annie wants to join in?" asked Nick.

"I think so." And that killed him. If he hadn't shown her, helped her enjoy it then she'd have found a nice, normal guy and gotten married. Now, she'd always have this kink.

"Are you sure? She doesn't seem the type." Nick shrugged. "But you never can tell. You did ask her, right?"

"No, because it doesn't matter. There can't be anything between us."

"Right. Nothing besides you fucking her and showing her some scenes."

"Yeah and it wasn't right." The things he'd showed her and done with her when he should've been protecting her from guys like him, tore him up inside.

"Didn't you meet when she was watching another couple?"

"Yeah, but she'd stumbled into that room on accident."

"Really? I told you she'd stumbled into my room when I was with Sarah." Nick took another sip of his drink and grinned. "I think your little Annie had a kink before you met her. You just helped her explore it."

"I guess it's possible." That didn't make him feel any better.

"You being with her is actually a good thing." Nick leaned forward. "You're crazy about the girl and you can help her explore this side of herself."

"I can't." He walked to the bar and filled up his drink.

"Why because of Vic and Ethan or because you're scared?"

"I'm not fucking scared." He was terrified. He was half in love with her and it'd kill him when she realized that he wasn't enough for her. He couldn't share her, he just couldn't.

"Right." Nick finished his drink. "I'm going home to my lonely bed. You think about the real reason why you're staying away from her. You'll have plenty of time because she's not coming back to work until Ethan returns."

"What? She isn't really sick is she?" If she were sick, he could go over and take care of her. He'd be able to keep his hands to himself if she wasn't feeling well.

"Heart sick because you dumped her and made her feel like everything you guys did was sick and dirty." Nick hesitated at the door. "At least man up and tell her the real reason you won't see her."

"I did."

"God, talking to you is like talking to a brick wall. Fine. Keep lying to yourself, but call her and tell her you don't think she's a whore and what you guys did isn't dirty. Don't fuck her up like this. She likes sex and she likes to experiment sexually and from your reaction, I'd say she's quite good at it."

"Shut the fuck up." He was going to punch Nick in the mouth again.

"Don't ruin that. You may be too much of a coward to appreciate it, but some other guy won't be." Nick's eyes lost a bit of focus. "I love that Sarah is so willing to try new things with me. She comes up with some of the hottest fantasies. I'd never want to change that about her."

"Even if she were with someone else?"

Nick's eyes snapped to his. "That is never going to happen." He paused. "But yeah. Even if we break up, a long time in the future, I wouldn't want to destroy that about her."

"Liar."

"I'm not lying. I lo…I care that much about her." Nick strode to the door and hesitated. "I think you feel that for Annie. Grow some balls and do the right thing." He left.

CHAPTER 6: PATRICK

Patrick clutched the phone. "You found him. You found Vic?"

"Yeah. It's him. I made sure before I called you," said Hunter.

"I'll be there in"—he glanced at his watch—"thirty minutes, forty tops." The Club was quiet he could leave for the night. He'd tell one of the bouncers to keep an eye on the place.

"I'll be here."

"Wait," he said before Hunter could hang up. He needed to tell Annie, but he couldn't risk seeing her. He missed her. These last few days, it'd taken every ounce of will power he had not to go to her house and beg her to forgive him. Instead, he'd sat at the Club watching the monitors, hoping she'd come back to work so he could at least watch her. If it wasn't so pathetic he'd laugh. She'd turned him into a voyeur. "Pick up Annie…but don't bring her to the hospital until after I leave."

"I'm not doing that. You need to tell her."

He shook his head, as if Hunter could see him, and then cleared his throat. "I told you to do it. I'm your boss."

"I don't care. I'm not going to tell your ex-girlfriend—"

"She's not my ex-girlfriend."

"Your ex-fuck buddy then—"

"Don't call her that." His fist tightened on the phone. She was so much more than that.

"Stop being a chicken shit. You found her brother. Tell her."

"You found him."

"Under your orders. You need to tell her."

"I can't." He hit his head against the door.

"You can. Vic's in pretty bad shape. She doesn't need to come here with a stranger. You owe her that much." Hunter hung up the phone.

"Mother fucker." He should fire the guy, but he wouldn't. Not only was Hunter excellent at his job, he was a friend. He could wait to tell Annie until Ethan came back to town tomorrow, but that wouldn't be right. He took a deep breath and punched her contact on his phone. She didn't answer, of course, so he left a message. He texted her and Ethan. He called her again, still no answer. He called Nick.

"Hey, I need you to call Annie and tell her we found Vic."

"You found him! That's great." Nick's tone sobered. "How is he?"

"He's in the hospital but he'll live."

"You're going to take Annie, right?" There was a warning in Nick's tone.

"Unless you'll do it." He held his breath, hoping.

"You need to do that. Did you ever apologize to her?"

He counted to ten. "No. I figured it was better if she were mad at me."

"That's bullshit. You need to apolo—"

"Call her and tell her we found Vic and I'll be there to pick her up in about thirty minutes."

"You call her."

"I tried. She's won't answer my calls."

"Don't blame her."

"Me either." He'd hang up on the asshole if he didn't need this favor. "Can you please call her?"

"Yeah and Patrick..."

"Yes." He wasn't in the mood for the lecture that was coming.

"Apologize to her."

He hung up the phone.

CHAPTER 7: ANNIE

Annie peeked out the living room curtains, waiting for Patrick. Her hair was still wet from her shower and she'd barely put on any makeup. She refused to try and look nice for him. He was a jerk and she was done with him.

As his car pulled into the driveway she hurried out of her house. She was at the vehicle as soon as it stopped. She hopped into the car as he was getting out.

He climbed back into the driver's side, frowning at her. "I would've—"

"I don't need you to open the door for me." Her eyes locked with his. "I don't need you for anything." She turned away, blinking to stop the tears. She may not need him but she still wanted him. He looked so good in an old T-shirt and jeans and he smelled delicious. His hair was still damp and his shampoo was dark and spicy. He hadn't shaved and she wanted to run her fingers along his face, feeling the rough stubble.

"Annie…"

"Just drive. I want to see Vic." She clung to the fact that he'd made her feel dirty and perverted. She wouldn't be with anyone who treated her like that.

He stared at her for several moments before starting the car and pulling into the street. She couldn't stop from steeling glances at him. His jaw was tense and his hands gripped the wheel as if he wanted to yank it from the car.

"Nick told me you thought…I never meant—"

"Please, don't. You said enough the other day." She stared out the window. "Thank you for finding Vic, but…" These words were hard. "That's all there is between us now. We should forget everything else."

He stopped at a light.

She glanced at him, forcing a small smile. "Pretend it never happened." If only she could convince her body. She ached for him, remembering the pleasure he'd given her. Her nipples were already hard and all she wanted was to hold on to him and let him tell her everything would be okay, but she couldn't.

He stared at her for a long time. A car honked and he looked out the windshield and started driving again. "I don't know how badly Vic's hurt."

"What happened to him?" She was glad for the change of subject.

"Got rolled."

"Rolled? Like they do to bums?"

"Yeah. According to Hunter, he was living on the street and got jumped and beaten. Ended up in the hospital when someone saw him."

"Why would anyone do that?"

"World's full of shitty people."

That was an understatement. Her brother, the man who'd sacrificed himself for this county, had gotten attacked by a bunch of losers. It wasn't right.

He pulled the car into the hospital parking garage. She jumped out the door and hurried toward the elevators. He trailed after her and when she glanced at him, his eyes were narrowed and his jaw clenched. He hated when she didn't let him hold the door for her. Good, because she...she couldn't hate him so she'd settle on annoying him in any way possible.

He leaned in front of her, aiming for the elevator button and she quickly pressed it. The muscles in his forearm bunched but he straightened without saying a word. The doors opened and she put her arm against the side, motioning him to go first.

"That's not going to happen." He had his arm against the other side. "So, if you want to see your brother, you're going to step into that elevator because I'll stand here all day."

"Stubborn idiot," she mumbled as she walked into the elevator.

"Like you can talk," he said under his breath as he joined her.

She glared up at him but he only raised his eyebrows as he pressed the number four. She wanted to slap the smug look off his handsome face but instead she stared straight ahead. The elevator stopped and the doors opened. He put his arm against the side and waited.

He wouldn't go first and that was fine. He'd won this battle but she'd win the next one. She stepped out of the elevator. "Which room?"

"Follow me." He smirked at her as he headed down the hallway.

There was a tall, lean man standing outside one of the doors. He was an attractive guy with brown hair and brown eyes. He smiled at her. "Annie? I'm Hunter."

"Thank you for finding my brother." She shook his hand.

"It was Patrick's doing."

"I already thanked him." It was ungracious and she felt a twinge of guilt but at Hunter's widening eyes and Patrick's soft chuckle, she realized how that'd sounded. "Not like that."

"Is he awake?" asked Patrick.

"Barely." Hunter stepped aside. "If it's okay with you, I'm going to go."

"Yeah. Thanks," said Patrick.

She pushed past the men and hurried into the room. She stopped several feet from the bed. It didn't even look like her brother. His face was a mass of bruises and cuts and he was so thin, but he was staring at her out of the one eye that wasn't swollen shut and she knew. It was him. It was Vic.

"Annie?" he rasped.

She moved toward him, stopping by the side of the bed. Her hand fluttered above his. She wanted to hug him but he looked so frail, so breakable.

He turned his hand over and her fingers intertwined with his.

"Vic." Tears streamed down her cheeks and she bent and kissed his hand. "Vic." There were no other words. She wanted to yell at him, hug him, hit him and hold him close to keep him safe.

Vic turned his head. "Patrick..."

"Hey." Patrick stood at the foot of the bed, tall and strong like her brother used to be.

"Good to see you," said Vic.

"You too." Patrick's voice cracked.

"You should see the other guy." Vic tried to smile but his face was too swollen.

"I bet." Patrick laughed.

"When can you come home?" she asked.

The question killed the little life that'd been in the room. Vic's eyes dimmed as he looked at her.

"You're not going back to the street." She squeezed his hand. "Look what happened to you. You could've been killed." Her words were flying from her mouth in panic.

"Annie, I can't come home."

"Yes you can." She turned to Patrick. "Tell him. Tell him he has to come home." If there'd ever been anything special between them, he'd support her on this.

"I think Vic's right." Patrick's eyes pleaded with her to understand. "He needs—"

"No." She dropped her brother's hand and stumbled backward. "Don't do this."

"Annie…"

"Why did you bother finding him, if you were only going to let him disappear again?" She fled from the room. Vic was going back to the streets and then he'd die. She'd lose him all over again.

CHAPTER 8: PATRICK

Patrick stared after Annie, his heart being torn in two. He turned on Vic. "You're going into a treatment center and getting help." He strode to the side of the bed. "You are not going to keep doing this to her."

"I know. I already talked to one of the doctors. When I'm released, I'll go right to Mercy Ward for Veterans."

He exhaled in a great whoosh. "Really? And you'll stay?" He wanted to go to Annie, but he needed to get this settled first. "She can't lose you again. She doesn't deserve that."

"No, she doesn't." Vic watched him closely. "She deserves a guy who'll be there for her all the time."

"She deserves that and more." He stared at the door. She deserved everything that was good, everything she wanted.

"She does," said Vic. "Do me a favor and look out for her until I get out."

"What?" His head snapped toward Vic. "Ethan is watching out for her."

"I asked you, not Ethan." This was the old Vic, the one in command.

"I know and I would." His throat tightened. "I owe you."

"You don't owe me anything but I'm asking anyway."

"I would but…she…we don't get along."

"You can barely keep your eyes off her."

He felt the blood rush to his face and he wanted to bury his head somewhere or turn around but that'd be even more obvious. "I wasn't….I mean…I was just worried about her."

"Is there something going on between you two?"

"No." He held up his hand as if pledging a truth. "I swear." There wasn't, not anymore. He'd blown that.

"Are you involved with someone else?"

"No"

"Then you can look out for her until I'm released. I should be able to come home in a few months, six maybe."

"Is that what the doctor said?" he asked. Vic had a tendency to check himself out of places.

"Yeah. That's what the doc said. If I work the program, I should be able to start outpatient services in four to six months."

"That's great." He couldn't help but smile. His friend looked bad but his head seemed to be on a little straighter. "I think they may have knocked some sense into you."

"Yeah, I think they did." Vic's face took on a haunted expression for a moment and then he said, "I'm glad I took your place. You had a chance to be there when your family needed you and"—his hand trembled—"now, I'm asking you to help me, my family."

His life was going to be hell, but he owed Vic and he always repaid his debts. "I'll keep an eye on her but…I'm telling you, she hates me."

"Annie's got a temper but she also has a soft heart. Why would she hate you?"

"It's complicated." There was no way he was explaining that to Vic.

"Then uncomplicate it. Apologize for whatever you did or she thinks you did." Vic's eyes darted to the door. "I let her down. I need someone I can trust to look out for her until I get better."

"Okay." It was going to kill him but he'd take care of her and not touch her. He was a man. He was a marine. He could do this.

"Thanks." Vic tried to smile and then winced. "Go after her and tell her I'm going into treatment."

"I'll bring her back and you can tell her yourself."

"Make it quick. The pain's coming back and I'm going to have to dose myself." Vic tapped a device that'd shoot him full of drugs.

CHAPTER 9: ANNIE

Annie stood in the hospital hallway, her hands trembling at her sides. She was so mad and hurt and sick to her stomach. Vic was going to leave again and there was nothing she could do. Next time she saw him, it'd be in a morgue.

Patrick came out of the room and headed toward her.

"Go away." She couldn't be near him right now.

"Annie…" He stopped next to her.

"You didn't even try to talk to him." She shoved him. "Get away from me. I hate you."

She shoved him again but he caught her hands and pulled her against his chest.

"Let go of me." She squirmed but it was like fighting a boa constrictor. "Let me go." It came out like a whimper.

"Never," he said against the top of her head.

A sob broke from her. He didn't mean it, but her arms wrapped around him and she buried her face in his chest.

"It's okay, baby. Shhh." He stroked her hair.

She wanted one man to stay with her, one man for who she'd be enough. She hadn't been for her father or her brothers and she wasn't for him. He'd made that clear. She forced the tears to stop. "I'm okay now. You can let me go."

He loosened his hold but kept his arms around her. He moved one hand and tipped her chin upward. He looked so concerned, so dear. She bit her lip to keep from crying.

"Are you okay?"

"Yes." She moved back a little and this time he let her go.

"You should talk to Vic. Listen to him."

"No." She stared at Vic's room like there was a tiger in there. "I...I can't. I can't lose him again."

"You won't. I promise." He took her hand.

She wanted to clasp onto him, borrow his strength but relying on someone like him was dangerous. She'd grown up around this kind of guy but she'd only now realized that men like him and her brothers protected the world, not any one woman. "He'll disappear again and—"

"Annie. Trust me."

Her eyes flew to his and by the slight hint of color in his cheeks he also realized what they'd done the last time he'd said those words to her.

"I did that once and it was a mistake."

"Don't say that." His face was a mask of anguish but she hardened her heart.

"Tell Vic that he's welcome to come home anytime." She started to turn but he grabbed her arm.

"Tell him yourself."

"I can't." She fought but tears filled her eyes again. "I can't go through this again."

He jerked her closer. "We lose people all the time. People die. They leave. This is your brother and he needs you."

"We tried that. I tried being there but he won't get help—"

"Talk to him." He dragged her down the hallway.

"Patrick, let me go." She was going to kill him.

He ignored her and pulled her into the room. "Vic, tell your sister what you told me."

"Couldn't wait." Vic's eye was somewhat dazed. "Had to take the meds." He smiled slightly. "Give us a minute alone."

Patrick nodded and left the room.

Vic mumbled something.

"What? I didn't hear you." Now that she was in here, she couldn't walk away from him. She moved over to the bed.

"Be nice to Patrick."

She gritted her teeth. That was the last thing she wanted to do.

"He's a good guy."

Obviously, her brother didn't know him as well as she did. Her face heated with the memories of exactly how well she did know him.

"He's in love with you."

"No, he's not." He thought she was a kinky, perverted slut. He did not love her.

Vic remained silent.

"Goodnight." She kissed his head. "I love you but you're wrong. As usual."

"Not wrong," he mumbled. "Patrick will look out for you."

"I don't need him to look out for me." She was pretty sure she over emphasized the "him" in that sentence.

"I can't come home, baby girl. Not yet." His eye drifted shut.

"You need to get help."

Vic remained silent, lost to sleep.

She kissed the top of his head again. "Whenever you're ready, I'll be home waiting for you. I love you." She turned and fled the room.

CHAPTER 10: PATRICK

Patrick hurried after Annie but she ducked into a bathroom. He leaned against the wall. She wasn't going to get rid of him that easily. He had a mission and he was going to honor it, even if he ended up with a chronic case of blue balls or, with the mood she was in, she might remove them entirely.

After what seemed like an hour, Annie came out of the bathroom. She'd been crying again and he stuffed his hands in his pockets to stop from pulling her into his arms.

"Take me home." She flushed slightly.

He couldn't stop his eyes from raking over her body. He wanted to take her home and take her—in many ways and many positions.

"You know what I meant. Actually? Forget it." She headed down the hallway. "I'll get an Uber."

"I'll take you home." He trailed after her.

"You don't have to."

"I know but I will and I'll bring you back here tomorrow."

"No." She stopped and stared up at him. "I think it's best if we cut ties now."

It was like she'd stabbed him right in the heart. "Can't. I promised your brother I'd look out for you." He took her arm, leading her into the elevator.

"Too bad. I don't need you or anyone to take care of me." She pressed the button for the garage.

He barked a laugh. "Oh, I beg to differ. You need someone to take care of you more than any woman I've ever met." She'd gone too far now. He was an easy going guy but she pushed all his buttons.

"Yeah, and you big, strong guys are the ones to do it." The elevator doors opened and she stormed to his car.

"Yep." It didn't take much effort for him to beat her to the vehicle. He held the door open and raised his brow, waiting for her to argue.

She shook her head and glared at him as she got into the car. He slammed the door and got in the other side. He glanced at her as he started the car, waiting for her to say something. She remained silent, her jaw jutting out stubbornly and her arms crossed over her chest, making her breasts push against her shirt. His mouth watered and his dick hardened. She definitely pushed all his buttons, especially his fuck-button.

He pulled out of the garage. The sooner he dropped her off at her house the better. He needed a breather from her.

She huffed a few times during the trip, obviously fuming but she didn't say a word.

"Vic seems to be doing okay," he said, tired of her silence.

"Yeah, until he disappears again."

"Didn't he tell you?"

"Tell me what?" she was staring at him now, her big, expressive eyes wary.

He didn't want her to look at him like that—like he was going to hurt her or disappoint her. "He's going to get help. Go into treatment. That's why he can't come home."

"What?" Her expression went from surprised to happy to angry.

"I told him to tell you. I thought that's what he wanted to talk to you about when he asked me to leave."

"Are you sure?" She touched his arm and it was like an electric current straight to his dick, making it stand and salute.

"Yeah, I'm sure." His voice had deepened with desire and he glanced at where she touched him.

"Sorry." She dropped her hand as if he'd burned her.

It pissed him off. "Don't. Don't do that."

"What? Touch you? Don't worry. I won't let it happen again."

He pulled into her driveway. "That's not what I meant and you know it." He threw the car into park. She grabbed the door handle. "Don't you dare open that door."

Her eyes locked with his. He opened his door and she opened hers.

"I'm telling you…" He'd turn her over his knee and paddle that sweet ass of hers. His dick pushed against his zipper, trying to escape.

"And I'm not listening." She got out of the car and slammed the door. "You're not my keeper. You're not my father. You're not—"

"I promised your brother I'd look after you." He stormed around to her side of the car.

"You both should've spoken with me because I don't want some sanctimonious prude making me feel bad about myself. Go find a nun or a virgin to watch over." She shoved past him.

His temper dissipated like an ember dropped in the ocean. He hurried to catch up with her. She fumbled with her keys and was slipping inside when he stuck his arm in the door.

"Go away. You're not welcome in my home. Not any more." She shoved his arm. "Get out."

"You're going to listen to me first."

"You can't make me." She turned and walked into her house.

If he went in there, he'd jump her. He wanted her more than he'd ever wanted anyone. He took a deep breath. He'd promised Vic. He took a step and his dick almost leapt with joy. He froze in the doorway. He couldn't risk it. He was only a man, a horny man. "Annie, I never meant to make you feel like that." He peeked inside but he couldn't see her. She was probably in her bedroom. He raised his voice. "The things we did…God…I've never…they were fabulous and I…never thought you were dirty or slu—"

She stormed from her bedroom, still wearing the same clothes. There was a slight twinge of disappointment from his cock who'd envisioned her in lingerie.

"Be quiet. You know Mr. Johnsbrick is nosey and I told him you found Vic. He's going to want an update."

Now he had her. "Then stand right there and listen to me or I'll yell again."

She crossed her arms over her chest and his eyes dropped to her breasts.

"Are you going to say what you have to say or stare at my tits all day?"

The word tit coming from her soft, pink lips made his throat go dry. He wanted to beg her to talk dirty to him but he forced his eyes to her face.

"I never meant to make you think that…that I thought you were a slut."

"You made it perfectly clear how you felt about me…and the things we did." She cleared her throat. "The things I let you do to me."

"Annie." He stepped toward her, unable to stop himself.

"Don't." She took a step back. "I'm not ashamed. I wanted you to do those things and I liked it."

His jaw clenched. "Annie...stop. Okay? I didn't mean—"

"Let me finish."

His hands shook so he grabbed the door frame, keeping himself in place. He could not go to her. He could not fuck her again.

"I enjoyed what we did and I..I like watching the others. I'm not embarrassed." Her chin stuck out with stubborn pride.

"And you shouldn't be."

"That's not what you thought before."

"It is what I thought about you." He inhaled, almost panting with his effort not to touch her and show her how he felt about her. "But not what I thought about me. I'm the one who should be ashamed. I'm the one who touched...more than touched his friend's baby sister."

"Oh, my God! Stop using that as an excuse." She shook her head. "Actually, just leave. You said what you wanted to say, now go." When he didn't move she said, "I forgive you. Please leave."

His heart twisted with indecision. His gut and his cock were telling him to grab her and kiss her. Wipe away any doubt she had about how he felt but his head was blaring a warning. She was into watching. Soon, she'd want a threesome or more. He couldn't do that. Not with her. He lov...cared for her too much to share. He turned and walked across the porch.

He flinched as the door slammed behind him. He started down the stairs and then turned back around. He tapped on the door. "Annie, I'll pick you up at eight tomorrow morning. Okay?" There was no sound. "I'm not leaving until you answer me. I'll yell again." He smiled slightly. "I'll apologize for….things we did in a very loud voice and in very explicit detail."

"Okay. Eight tomorrow."

His knees buckled. She was crying. He turned the handle and the door opened. Obviously, she did need him to look out for her.

She spun around. She'd been heading to her bedroom.

"Annie, don't cry." He closed the door behind him, locking it and then his feet, or maybe his cock, led him toward her.

"Go away." She took a step back.

"I can't." He stalked her until she backed up against the door to her bedroom. "I tried but I can't." He lifted his hand and she turned her head. "Don't be like this, baby. I'm sorry." He leaned down and kissed her cheek.

"Patrick…I can't do this again." Her hands came to his chest and her thumbs caressed him before pushing him away. "Go home and leave me alone."

"I can't do that." He moved closer until barely a breath separated them.

"I'm sure you can't right now, but as soon as you come, you'll find your honor." She almost spat the words. "And then you'll leave me like before. Just like Vic and my dad." She shoved him. "I don't need a man to look after me. I need a man to stand by me, be with me." She shoved him again. "And that's not you."

He caught her hands. "I'm sorry for how I acted. I am. I…I didn't want to be with you."

"Thanks. I feel much better now." Her voice cracked.

He kissed her hands. "But I couldn't stay away. You're like a drug and I needed more and more but I was scared."

"Scared?" Her eyes lifted to his. "Why?"

He took a deep, shaky breath. It was time to come clean. "Because of what you like, sexually."

"No. No. You don't get to do this." She jerked her hands free and tried to move away from him but he blocked her by putting his hands against the wall, boxing her in. She punched him in the gut, catching him off guard and scurried away from him. "Get out. You don't get to make me feel bad about what I like."

He rubbed his stomach. Her little fist had hurt just a tiny bit. "That's not what I'm doing. If you'd let me finish…" He walked toward her but she slipped around him. "I'm not going to chase you all over the house." His arm snaked out grabbing her around the waist and he lifted her, carrying her into her bedroom and tossing her onto the bed.

Before she could roll over he was on top of her, pinning her beneath him. He grabbed her hands, holding them at the sides of her head.

"Let me go." She was panting, causing her breasts to press against his chest.

Her nipples were already hard and that made his cock grow. She was as turned on by this fight as he was. He wanted to shift so he was between her thighs, instead of having one leg tossed over her legs, but as soon as he was in that position all bets were off and he needed to confess before they made love.

"Now, you're going to listen to me."

"I am n…"

He kissed her. It was hard and his mouth was shut but the softness of her lips, made his balls tightened. He moved his face back a fraction of an inch. "Every time you interrupt, I'm going to kiss you. Each time, it's going to be longer and deeper." His hips twitched. The part of his body that most wanted to go deeper, grew longer and harder. "Understand?"

She opened her mouth to speak but then shut it and nodded.

"Good girl."

Her eyes narrowed and he grinned.

"As I was saying, I was frightened because of how I felt about you and what you liked. You like all the kinky stuff"—at her hurt and angry expression he continued—"and I love that. I do, but there are some things that…that I can't do with you."

"Why?" She turned her face away as he lowered his mouth toward hers. "I didn't interrupt. You paused."

He kissed her neck and she shivered. It gave him hope that she didn't truly hate him. "Because I can't share you with another man or another woman. Even if I'm there too. I can't let anyone else have you...touch you. I won't."

"I...I never said I wanted to do that?"

"No, you didn't but do you?" He stared into her eyes. "The truth, Annie."

Her face heated and his heart felt like there'd been an explosion in his chest. He could never satisfy her, not completely. She wanted things he couldn't give her.

"I'd like to watch it but I don't want another man or"–she wrinkled her nose—"another woman." She leaned up and kissed his chin. "Only you."

He fought his desire to kiss her and sink into her. "I'm serious, Annie. If you want that stuff, I need to know now before we...before I fall for you more."

"You've fallen for me?" Her mouth curved into a smile.

He couldn't stop himself. He kissed her, running his tongue against her lips until she opened for him. He thrust into her mouth, tasting her sweetness and his body automatically shifted so he was between her thighs. She wrapped her legs over his calves, opening to him. He pulled back from the kiss. "Hard."

"I noticed." She rocked her hips.

He groaned, burying his face in her neck. "Yeah, obviously that, but I meant I've fallen hard for you."

"Good because I feel the same way."

He leaned up, studying her face. "So you don't, won't want anyone else? A threesome?"

"No. Just you." She tugged on her hand and he let her wrists go. She reached between them and stroked his cock. "This is plenty for me."

"I'm fucking glad to hear that." His lips came down on hers as his hands tore at her clothes. "I need you naked, now."

She shimmied out of her pants and then her hand went to his zipper. He kissed her unable to keep from tasting her as she pulled his cock out from his pants and ran her hand along his shaft.

"You're so fucking wet already." He stroked her pussy. She was hot, wet and ready for him. "I need you, Annie." He should take his time, taste her, suckle her but he couldn't. He hadn't thought he'd ever have her again and his body needed her now.

"Yes." She guided him to her opening.

"Fuck. Thank you, God." He'd make up the foreplay later. Right now, he needed to be in his heaven. He shoved into her, balls deep.

She gasped at his intrusion. He wanted to slam into her, again and again until he came, but she wasn't ready. He stopped, closing his eyes and trying to grasp a thread of control as she held him tight, clenching around him and pushing him toward the edge. He needed to slow down, but she felt so good.

"You okay?" *Please say yes. Please, please.*

"Yeah." She rocked her hips and tightened her inner muscles squeezing him in the best possible way.

"Fuck, baby. Don't do that," he panted. She was playing with fire.

"You don't like it." She did it again the little tease.

"I'm going to come if you keep it up."

"Come then." She tightened around him as he tried to pull out.

He kissed her hard, nipping her lip. "You first." He pulled out of her.

"Patrick," she moaned, reaching for him as he got onto his knees.

He grabbed her and flipped her onto her stomach. He wrapped his arm under her waist and lifted her. He bent her knees and pressed down on her back, pushing the top half of her to the mattress. He knelt between her legs and guided his cock back inside of her. She moaned into her pillow as she pushed her ass toward him. He shifted his hips as he moved in and out of her.

"Oh…oh, my God." She stiffened, clenching down on him.

"Found the sweet spot, did I?" His hand caressed the satiny skin on her back as he thrust into her. "Should I stop?" He hesitated but only for a second. His body wouldn't let him stop the motion. It was too pleasurable and he was too close.

"If…you…stop." She rocked against him. "I'll…never….for…give you."

His balls were tightening. He needed to come but she had to go first. He slapped her ass as he pulled her hips back and shoved into her to the hilt. She screamed, her body thrusting uncontrollably with her release.

"That's it, baby." His fingers dug into her hips, holding her in place as he fucked her. He'd lost all his skill, all his finesse. All that was left was pure lust. His movements were frenzied and hard, she moaned below him and his body tightened. His dick got longer and harder and then he came, groaning.

He rolled to his side, so he wouldn't squish her. He pulled her into his arms, his dick still partially inside her. He didn't want to ever pull out of her. "You good?" he whispered in her ear.

"Perfect." She grabbed one of his hands and pulled it to her breast, keeping her hand on top of his.

"Yes, you are." He kissed her cheek and held her close. "I was thinking."

"Dangerous."

He nipped her neck. "Watch it."

She laughed and wiggled her bottom against his groin.

"I'm not a machine." He kissed her ear. "I need a few minutes to charge back up."

"Good, because I'm tired."

"Then stop rubbing against me, or you're going to be awake all night." He growled. "I think you should come and work for me."

"What?" She stiffened in his arms and tried to pull away.

He almost whimpered as his dick slipped from her pussy. "Don't get mad." He tugged her closer. "Listen to me." He rested his chin on her head. "I could use a chef at my office."

"Really?" She didn't sound like she believed him.

"Yes. Everyone works crazy hours and they're always eating fast food. It's not healthy and in this line of work, they need to be in good shape."

"And you suddenly decided this?" She elbowed him in the gut a little as she turned in his arms.

"Actually, no. I've been thinking about it since you cooked for me."

"That long ago, huh?"

"Yeah."

"And this has nothing to do with you not trusting me or not wanting me to work at the Club?"

"No," he said. She was too perceptive for her own good, or at least for his.

Her brows were raised. He already recognized that as a warning sign.

"Okay. You're right. I don't want you working there. Ethan will be back in a few days and I can't be there with you."

"And you think I'm going to find someone else?" She sat up.

His eyes dropped to her fabulous tits. It wasn't a good sign when she pulled the blanket up, covering herself.

"No. I don't think you'd do that." He didn't, not really, but he'd been cheated on before and it was hard to trust.

"You'd better not." She leaned down and gave him a quick kiss. "I told you, I want you and no one else."

"Good. Then you can work for me." He tugged on the blanket. It wasn't right that she was hiding all that beauty from him.

She let the cloth fall away. "I don't think working for you is a good idea."

"Why not?" He leaned forward and ran his tongue over her nipple. She shivered. "I think it's an excellent idea." His hand crept up her thigh. "We can have private meetings and conferences." He wrapped his arm around her waist and pulled her down, rolling on top of her. "I'll make sure there are locks on every door."

"I can't work for you." She spread her legs, making room for him.

He pressed against her, his cock resting heavy on her thigh. He wanted to be inside of her, but they needed to get this settled because he didn't want her working at the Club. "Why?"

"Mixing business and pleasure doesn't work."

"Ethan would disagree." He kissed her quickly, because he had to taste those lips. "What are you really afraid of?"

She shoved on his chest. He rolled off her and she sat up again. "I don't want to work for you. I won't be your subordinate." She flushed. "Except sometimes in the bedroom."

"Only sometimes?" His gaze roamed over her. He wanted to teach her the true meaning of submission.

"Yes." Her fingers ran down his chest toward his dick. "Sometimes, I want to be in charge."

He gasped as she wrapped her hand around him. "I can live with that."

"Good. It's settled. I'll stay at the Club until I graduate and then I'll find a different job." She ran her hand along his length in long, firm strokes.

"It's not settled." He sat up, breaking her hold. She almost huffed in annoyance. Good, now she knew how he felt.

"I'm not going to work for you." She crossed her arms over her chest, lifting her breasts and his mouth watered.

"Then work for yourself."

"What?"

"Start your own catering or cooking company and I'll be your first customer." The more the words slipped out of his mouth, the more he realized it was a great idea. He took her hands, pulling them away so he could have an uninhibited view of her tits. "You'll be your own boss. You won't work for me. I'll have Terry, he's a lawyer, draw up a contract and we'll start with a year. After the year, if we're both happy we can renegotiate another year contract or a longer one." He'd go longer because he wanted her away from the Club and in his office. They could fuck and then have lunch together every day.

"I don't have the money to—"

"I've got plenty—"

"I am not taking your money." She scooted off the bed, grabbing a sheet and wrapping it around herself. "I won't take Ethan's money and I'm not taking yours." Her eyes were snapping with anger and his dick hardened to a point of pain. "You're just going to have to live with me working at the Club until I finish school."

That wasn't going to happen. "I'll loan you the money." He held up his hand. "Hear me out. Okay?"

Her mouth tightened but she nodded.

"Terry can draw up that contract too. It'll be legal and binding. You'll pay me back the money with interest." He didn't care if she ever did but if it'd convince her to leave the Club, he'd do it.

"Even if we stop seeing each other, I'd pay you back."

The tension was easing from her body. He was winning. "Every penny."

She bit her lip and he wanted to lick it. He patted the bed. She climbed in but didn't move into his arms.

"What if I fail? What if I can't do it?"

He unraveled the sheet from her body and pulled her close. "You won't fail. It'll be a lot of work, but your food is excellent and you're smart and hard working."

"A lot of businesses fail even with smart, determined people running them."

"That's true, but I'll loan you enough so you can hire Nick."

She tipped her head up and looked at him. "Nick?"

"Yeah. He works with small businesses. Helps them establish their brand. He's very good at what he does."

"I like Nick." She smiled slyly at him.

"You'd better not like him too much." He swatted her ass and she squeaked.

"I like him just enough." She pushed on his chest and he flopped down on his back. "But I like you more and in a different way." She kissed his chest and moved lower.

"Yeah?" He leaned up on his elbows, watching her make her way down his body.

"Yeah." Her hair was mussed, her eyes were dark and her lips were lush and red. "You want me to show you how I like you?"

"Definitely." His voice was raspy. He was almost ready to come just in anticipation.

She licked her lips and he groaned. She wrapped her hand around his cock.

"Fuck, Annie."

"I like to taste you." She ran her tongue over the tip of his dick and his arms trembled under him. She licked up and down and all around.

"Jesus, Annie. Please." He needed her mouth on him.

"And I like to suck you." She kissed the tip, licking the precum off the top.

"Yes, suck me." He wanted to flop down and enjoy the feelings but he couldn't take his eyes from hers.

"Mostly, I like to make you beg."

"I'm begging. I'm fucking pleading with you." He should've moved to lean against the headboard. In the position he was in, he couldn't watch and grab her head to push her down on his cock.

"Yes, you are." She opened her mouth, her gaze never leaving his, as she took him between her lips. Her hand stroked him as she sucked.

"Fuck," he groaned. She sure could suck cock.

She increased her pace, and his hips thrust up to meet her. She gagged a little but kept sucking.

"I'm gonna come." He dropped back on the bed and grabbed her shoulder. "Annie. I'm gonna come."

She pulled her mouth off him with a loud pop. "Not yet." She moved up his body. "I need you inside me."

She straddled him, but he was out of patience. He grabbed her and rolled over, positioning himself between her legs. He pushed into her in one long thrust and she whimpered.

"You okay?"

She wrapped her legs around him and grabbed his ass. "Fuck me, Patrick."

He pulled one of her legs up and put it on his shoulder as he rocked into her. She pushed against him, moaning. She was as close to coming as he was.

"This is going to be fast and hard."

"Yes. Please." Her nails dug into his back.

His hips moved on their own. He was lost to the feel of being inside of her. She was so tight and he was so close.

He fucked her harder and faster and she screamed, her body clenching around him and he shuddered as he climaxed.

He dropped her leg and rolled to the side, pulling her close. She snuggled against his chest and he kissed her head, waiting for her to fall asleep.

As soon as her breathing was steady he buried his face in her neck. "I love you, my little voyeur." He was pretty sure she wasn't ready to hear him say that, but that was okay. He could wait. He wasn't going anywhere.

CHAPTER 11: ANNIE

When Annie woke, Patrick's arm was draped over her waist. She wanted to smile, to kiss him, to jump him, but she crawled out of bed and went into the bathroom. Last night had been great, but so had the other times before he'd bailed.

She turned on the shower. As soon as the water was hot, she stepped inside, closing her eyes and letting the heat soak into her sore muscles and boy was she sore. They'd made love three times last night. He'd been insatiable and she'd loved it. They'd tried several positions, causing her to use muscles she hadn't even known she had. She jumped as the shower door opened.

"Good morning." He said as he stepped in behind her.

"Morning," she mumbled, her eyes roaming over him. He was even more handsome than last night. The scruff on his face made him look dangerous and oh so hot.

He grabbed the shampoo and squeezed some into his hands. "Let me help." His strong fingers slid onto her scalp, massaging. She tipped back her head, giving him better access and tried, unsuccessfully, not to moan.

"You like that?" He said against her ear, his stubble scraping along her cheek and sending bolts of desire straight between her legs.

"Uhm…yes." She wanted to feel that stubble against her inner thighs.

He turned her around, using his fingers and the spray from the shower to rinse her hair. He turned her around again and grabbed the conditioner, squirted some in his hands and ran them through her long tresses. She leaned back, wiggling her ass against his erection.

"Tease." He nipped her ear. "Two can play that game." He reached around her, grabbing the soap and squeezing it into his palms before stroking her body—down her arms, her waist, her belly, and up and around her breasts. She wiggled against him more. His hands were strong and slippery, but his touch was too light, too fleeting. She needed more.

"What's the matter?" He kissed her neck.

"Please." She grabbed his hand, dragging it up to her breast.

"Is that what you want?" He caressed her, squeezing and plucking at her nipple, making it harder.

She did but she didn't. It felt great but she was greedy, she wanted more. He pinched her nipple and chuckled as she gasped. His hand drifted between her thighs.

"I bet you need cleaning here." His finger slid along her crease. "Don't you?"

"Yes." She turned her head and captured his mouth.

He tangled his tongue with hers as his finger slid into her, again and again. He added another finger.

"Oh…" Her hips rocked to the rhythm he set with his hand. "Please…" Her legs tensed. She was so close. He curled his fingers, hitting that one spot. "Oh, God." Her body started to tremble.

He pulled his fingers from her and stroked her belly soothingly. "Not yet, baby." He was calming her down, bringing her away from the edge.

"No." She didn't want to wait. "I want to come. Please, Patrick. I need to come."

"You'll come when I tell you." His voice was a rough caress against her ear. "Put your hands on the wall."

She'd do whatever he said, as long as he let her come. He pushed on her back until she was leaning slightly, then he grabbed her thighs and pulled them apart. He bent and kissed her ass, his stubble rubbing roughly against the soft skin.

"You're so beautiful." His finger skimmed along the folds of her pussy. "I'm gonna eat you out." He flicked her clit and she trembled. "Later." He straightened. "Now, I'm gonna fuck you."

The water poured down her back as he moved closer. The tip of his penis rubbed against her ass and then slid between her thighs as he positioned it at her entrance. She spread her legs wider as she shifted backward, wanting, needing him inside her.

He put his hand on the small of her back and slipped inside of her just a little. He stopped. She needed more than that. She needed all of him. She pushed back, taking more of him into her and he slapped her ass.

"Stay still."

"Please...I can't. I need you." She hated this waiting, but she loved it too. It was such sweet torture.

"You can." He grabbed her breast and pinched her nipple. "Don't move or I'll go slower."

"Oh, God, that's not possible. Is it?" She'd die if he went slower. She'd melt into a puddle of desire and need and flow down the drain.

He chuckled, but there was a strain to it. "Disobey and you'll see." He leaned down to whisper in her ear. "If you don't behave, I may have to tie you up."

She shivered. "Yes, please." The idea of being completely at his mercy almost made her come. She pushed backward and he slid inside a little more.

"You...will"—he shoved into her all the way—"be punished for that." He stroked in and out of her, harder and faster.

She moaned, pushing against him, searching for her release. He felt so good, so big and hard, exactly what she'd needed. She trembled around him, clasping onto him with her inner muscles, trying to keep him inside of her.

"Fuck, Annie." He ran his finger between her butt crease. "I'm close…come, Annie, come for me." His body surged into hers as he pushed his finger into her asshole.

She screamed, breaking apart with pleasure as he pumped into her and then wrapped his arms around her holding her tight as he came.

Too soon, he pulled out. He kissed her neck. "You'll pay for that."

She turned in his arms and kissed him. "I can't wait." She stepped out of the shower and squeaked as his hand landed on her ass.

CHAPTER 12: PATRICK

Patrick washed his hair and body and then followed Annie out of the shower. Oh, she was going to pay. He'd wanted to make her pant for him, beg for his cock and she'd pushed him over the edge too fast. He couldn't get enough of her. He ran his hand over his dick and stroked it a couple of times. It was already hardening for her. If they didn't have to go see Vic, he'd make sure she couldn't walk tomorrow.

The thought of telling Vic about them should bother him, but it didn't. He wasn't just fucking her. He was in love with her and he'd be good to her. He'd treat her like a queen.

He went into the bedroom and leaned against the door frame, watching her. She already had her panties on. They were a pretty blue pair and she was applying lotion to her skin, in long strokes. His hands itched to help her. He grabbed his phone from the nightstand and checked the time. The hospital wouldn't open for another few hours. He strolled across the room toward her. Her eyes caught his in the mirror and they darkened with longing. He wanted his fingers inside her so he'd know exactly how closely her desire matched her eyes.

"Again?" Her voice was breathless as her eyes darted to his groin. "We just…"

"Let me help." He put his hands over hers and started to help her apply the lotion. He bent and kissed her shoulder. "Yuck." He wiped his mouth. "That tastes horrible."

"It's lotion. Of course it tastes horrible." She kept applying the vile stuff.

"You need to find some that tastes good."

"You weren't complaining last night." She gave him a cocky grin over her shoulder.

"Last night, you tasted great." His hands rested on her waist.

"And I'm sure I will again, once it soaks into my skin."

"I can't wait." He pulled her back so her ass cradled his erection.

"You'll have to." She turned and ran her hands down his chest. "I have lotion everywhere."

"Challenge accepted." He picked her up.

"What? Put me down." She laughed as her hands went to his shoulders.

"Your wish is my command." He dropped her on the bed and before she could move, he grabbed her ankles and pulled her to the edge. He knelt at the side and tossed her legs over his shoulders. He kissed one side of her pussy. "You didn't lotion here."

She leaned up on her elbows. "Do we have time?"

"Plenty." He ran his tongue along her inner folds. "I was right. You taste delicious without that disgusting lotion."

"Oh..God." She dropped back onto the bed as he buried his face in her cunt.

He lapped and licked and sucked, drinking up her juices. He'd never get tired of this. Her hands grasped at the bed sheets as her hips thrust toward his face. She was so receptive to his touch but this time, he was going to make her beg for it, if he could wait. The whimpers coming from her were causing his dick to jerk in anticipation. He stood. He couldn't take any more. He had to be inside her. He held his cock at her entrance and shoved into her.

"Yes," she screamed as she tried to move her legs, but he held them straight up along his chest.

He pulled almost all the way out and shoved into her again, making her moan long and loud. He rolled his hips as he fucked her. Her hands grasped at the blankets as her hips rocked against him.

"I'm going to make you scream when you come." He increased his pace.

The doorbell rang. Patrick shoved into her again. Whoever it was would go away. It rang again and again. He stopped, his hands clasping her thighs.

"It's six thirty in the morning. Who the fuck comes over here at this hour?"

"No one." She stared up at him, her eyes glassy with passion.

The doorbell rang again.

"Well, it's someone."

"It might be Mr. Johnsbrick. He probably wants to ask about Vic. He'll go away."

He pulled out of her.

"No. Please. Stay." She grabbed his arm.

She was desperate to come. He loved seeing that look on her face. He could fuck her right now, make her scream and she wouldn't give two shits who was outside listening, but he did. He didn't need the nosey neighbor getting an earful. The old guy paid way too much attention to her as it was.

He bent and kissed her thigh, blowing across her pussy. He folded her legs at the knees and put her feet on the bed. He pulled her legs apart a little more and then took her hand. He kissed her fingers, sucking on each of them and she shivered.

The damn doorbell rang again as if someone was holding it down.

"In a minute," he bellowed and the sound stopped. He kissed her fingers again and then put her hand on her pussy. "Don't move your legs, but keep your engine going." He bent and sucked gently on her clit for a second and then headed out of the bedroom.

"Your clothes." She was looking at him, her big eyes pleading.

He'd didn't give a shit if Mr. Johnsbrick got an eyeful, but he'd do anything to make her happy. "Stroke yourself and I'll put something on."

Her fingers began massaging her clit. Her mouth opened in a silent gasp. God, he wanted to be inside of her. His dick got even harder. He'd come outside of her if he didn't do something soon. The doorbell rang again.

"Fuck." He grabbed the towel she'd used after her shower from the back of a chair and wrapped it around his hips as he strode for the door. "Keep playing with yourself." He glanced back at her. "I'll know if you stop."

"How?" She hollered after him.

"You won't be as hot and wet." He yelled back, no longer caring if the old guy got an earful. He opened the door. "What do you…"

Ethan's fist connected with his nose. He staggered backward but his years of training kicked in and he blocked the next punch. Ethan charged, ramming into him like a freight train and sending the two of them barreling across the living room.

"You bastard," yelled Ethan as he threw punch after punch. "You lousy, mother fucking bastard."

Ethan landed a solid blow to Patrick's torso and he grunted, but he wasn't a novice at hand-to-hand combat. He blocked most of the punches and managed to land a few to Ethan's side and face.

"It isn't what you think." He didn't want to fight his friend. He grabbed Ethan in a bear-hug. "Listen to me."

"I heard you." Ethan head-butted him and now his nose was definitely broken. "I heard her!"

Annie rushed out of the bedroom, wearing her sweatpants and T-shirt. "Ethan, stop. Don't hurt him."

Hurt him? He could take care of himself. He started fighting in earnest now. He didn't need her, his woman, thinking he was the kind of guy who got his ass whooped. He spun and kicked. Ethan dodged, causing Patrick's foot to hit the other man's shoulder instead of his face.

Annie launched herself between them. He tried shoving her behind him, giving Ethan another opening which he didn't hesitate to take.

"Annie, get out of here." He shifted to keep her behind him and Ethan's next punch landed on his stomach. He bent over but he charged forward, catching Ethan off guard, and the two of them hit the couch and landed on the floor.

"Stop it! Both of you." Annie jumped on top of his back as Ethan pummeled his abdomen.

"Annie, you're killing me." He tried to buck her off him but she clung to him like a fucking monkey.

He grabbed her hands, leaving himself vulnerable to Ethan's punches as he yanked her from his neck and shoved her away. He turned to focus on his opponent, who was now kicking his ass. They rolled on the floor and then

Ethan was on top. Ethan's fist flew back, getting ready for a powerful blow. Patrick brought his legs up to wrap them around Ethan's neck but Ethan dodged as Annie rushed in again. Ethan's arm caught her on the shoulder and she flew backward.

"You hit her." All he saw was fury. He shoved Ethan aside, his fist flying, hitting the other guy over and over. "You fucking hit her."

"Annie, I'm sorry," yelled Ethan, barely trying to defend himself.

She sat up, groaning. "Patrick, stop." Her tone was soft and pleading.

He hurried over to her. He fumbled with her shirt, trying to see where she'd been hit. "How bad does it hurt, honey?"

"God, Annie, I'm so sorry." Ethan was staring down at her.

"Get her some ice." He pointed to the kitchen.

Ethan hurried out of the room and came back a moment later with a rag filled with ice. Patrick snatched it from him and gently placed it on her shoulder.

"Ouch." She winced and then she touched his face, her fingers gentle. "Oh, Patrick."

"I'm fine." He probably had a broken nose and his eye was going to swell shut, but he'd be fine. He'd had worse injuries.

She glared around him at Ethan. "What in the hell were you doing?"

"I...I came to take you to the hospital."

"At six thirty in the morning."

"I didn't know how long it'd take you to get ready and I brought breakfast." Ethan nodded at the food lying on her front porch. He shrugged. "Plus, I couldn't sleep. I couldn't wait to see Vic."

"What are you doing back already?" He took Annie's hand and helped her up off the floor. He sat on the couch and pulled her down next to him.

"Put some fucking clothes on," growled Ethan. "We're not done discussing this."

"There's nothing to discuss." He didn't move. He'd lost his towel during the fight but he had no reason to cover up. Annie didn't mind.

"Nothing to discuss? What about how I left you to look after her, to take care of her and you ended up fucking her."

"Ethan, stop it." Annie stood and took Ethan's hand. "I'm a big girl. I don't need either of you to take care of me."

"Too bad," they both said and then glared at each other.

"That's enough." She took a deep breath. "Ethan, sit. I'm going into the kitchen and get some towels and ice. You both need them." She stared hard at each of them. "Swear you'll behave." At their nods she clarified, "And by behave I mean stay exactly where you are and do not hit each other."

"Fine." He said, although he'd love to punch Ethan once more for interrupting some of the best sex in his life.

"Until we leave here." Ethan clenched his hands.

She shook her head and went into the kitchen.

Ethan gave him a disgusted look. "I thought we were friends."

"We are." They'd been through too much together not to be.

"Not anymore."

That hurt. "It's not what you think."

"Really? So, that wasn't Annie moaning and screaming when I came to the door? At first, I thought someone was hurting her. I almost broke the fucking door down but then...I realized."

He ran his hand over his face, wincing slightly. "I tried to stay away from her. I did, but I couldn't."

"She's Vic's baby sister."

"I know." He took a deep breath. "I shouldn't have touched her."

CHAPTER 13: ANNIE

Annie's stomach twisted as she stared into the freezer. Patrick was doing it again. He was second guessing what they had. She wasn't sure if she could go through this fight over and over, but worse she wasn't sure she could let him go. They needed to sit down and have a long talk—no sex, just talking—and they'd do that after she killed Ethan. She dumped the ice into a pan and tossed some rags in a bowl of water. She grabbed both containers and headed into the living room.

"I tried to stay away from her. I did." Patrick took a deep breath. "But I can't. I love her."

The two containers slipped from her hands and clattered to the floor. Both guys turned and stared at her.

"You...love me?" Her hands were shaking at her sides.

Patrick's eyes widened in panic and he glanced at the door but then he sighed. "I know it's soon and it's okay if you don't feel that way…yet, but—"

"Do you love me? Really love me?" She still didn't move. She hadn't even considered that he might be in love with her. Even after Vic said it, she'd dismissed it. They'd been so busy fucking and fighting, but her heart melted at the thought because if he did, it explained a lot.

"You don't even know her," snapped Ethan.

"But I do." Patrick's eyes were locked with hers. "I've known her for years. Vic shared every letter she wrote. Some of them, I read over and over. She was funny and sassy and I…I think I've been somewhat in love with her since the letter she wrote about not making the cheerleading team. My heart broke for her. I wanted to hug her and protect her. If I'd been there, I would've done anything to make her happy."

"She was a teenager." Ethan's tone dripped with disgust.

"I know that." Patrick turned and glared at him. "I didn't have sexual feelings for her then, but I cared about her." His gaze went back to her. "And when we met, all these years later, she was the same girl only better." His eyes darkened as they dropped to her chest and back to her face.

"You really do love me. Me." She couldn't believe it. This couldn't be happening but it was.

"Yeah." He swallowed. "I do."

Her feet flew across the floor and then her arms were around him and she was straddling his lap. "I love you too."

"Really?" He searched her face for the truth. "You don't have to say it just because I did."

"I can't think straight when you're near. I think about you all the time. I hate it when you're mad at me and all I want to do is touch you and feel you inside of me."

"I'm out of here." Ethan stood. "I'll see you at the hospital." He stopped at the door. "If you hurt her, I'll beat the shit out of you. Again."

"I can't hurt her. She's my heart." Patrick's hands wandered from her waist to her hips, pulling her closer to his erection.

"Oh my God. You've turned into a damn woman." Ethan slammed the door as he left.

She bit her lip. "I want to kiss you but I'm afraid."

"Of what." He tugged on her sweat pants.

"Of hurting you. You're bruised everywhere."

"Risk it." He brought her mouth down to his as he lifted her, pulling her pants off.

A second later he'd put her back on his lap and she was lifting up on her knees. She grabbed his cock and held him at her entrance. "I love you." She slid downward, filling herself with him. "Oh, you feel so good." She lifted and lowered herself.

His fingers tightened on her waist, helping her set the pace. "You're heaven. My heaven." He thrust upward hard and fast. "And I'm right where I belong."

CHAPTER 14: PATRICK

Patrick and Annie arrived at the hospital an hour later than they'd planned. He held her hand as they walked down the corridor. It'd been an hour well spent, but he already wanted her again. Just being near her drove him crazy with lust. He wasn't sure how Ethan was going to handle him signing her up as a Club member, but his friend would have to deal with it, because she liked to watch and he still had things to show her—a lot of things.

When they walked into Vic's room, Ethan was already there. He'd been bandaged and cleaned up but his shirt was still full of blood. A cute nurse was dabbing some antiseptic on his knuckles. The man could attract a female from a hundred miles away. Patrick pulled Annie closer to him.

"Wow!" said Vic. "Ethan, you didn't lie. You kicked his ass."

"I'll talk to you later." Ethan smiled at the nurse who smiled back before turning and leaving the room. He turned toward Vic. "I told you. You owe—"

"He didn't kick my ass." But they were right. He'd taken a lot more punches than he'd given.

Vic looked better today. He was still too thin and his face was swollen and turning color from the beating, but he was sitting up and alert.

"Have you looked in a mirror?" Vic laughed. "Really guys? Just because I don't look so pretty any more is no reason for you to do this. You're taking this solidarity thing a little far."

"He would've won if I hadn't helped," said Annie.

Vic's dark eyes landed on their hands. "What's going on?"

"I...I..." Patrick moved closer to the bed, dragging Annie with him. "I'm in love with your sister and if you want to beat the crap out of me for that, you can. As soon as you get better."

"Don't worry, I will."

Part of Patrick's heart died. Annie had told him that Vic suspected he had feelings for her. He'd hoped to get his friend's blessing. He'd thought Ethan and Vic knew him better than anyone but Nick was the only one who'd realized how terrified he'd been about falling in love again.

"If you ever hurt her." Vic smiled. "Otherwise, it's about time."

"What?" said all three of them.

"I knew you were in love with her when I saw you together last night. Why do you think I asked you to look out for her?" Vic gave them an incredulous look. "I'm not an idiot. Asking you to look after Annie is like asking the fox to look after the hens. She's exactly your type." He paused. "No. She's better than your type. She's loyal and faithful."

Annie glanced at him, her dark eyes curious. Great, now he'd have questions about his past relationships to answer.

"Back me up here, Ethan. Only an idiot would ask Patrick, who didn't know Annie and didn't think of her like a sister, to look out for her. I mean, we both know the ladies love Patrick."

His eyes darted to Annie. The curiosity in her eyes had been replaced by irritation. He was going to clamp his hand over Vic's mouth if his friend didn't shut up.

Vic continued, "And Annie's cute as a button. Throwing those two together is sex waiting to happen. Right?"

"Well…" said Ethan. "I don't think I'd say only an idiot."

Annie walked over to Ethan and grabbed his shirt, pulling his head down. She gave him a quick kiss on the cheek. "Thank you, idiot."

Thanks for reading The Voyeur Series and I hope you enjoyed Annie and Patrick's story. If you did, please take a moment to leave a review.

If you liked your glimpse into La Petite Mort Club, I have many more stories to tell about that place and its sexy men.

Find out how Nick and Sarah met by reading the beginning of Interviewing For Her Lover – Book One in the Six Nights of Sin Series (below) or get the ebook version FREE.

Amazon = http://myBook.to/SixNSin_Book1

Other Retailers = https://www.books2read.com/u/mlKVj9

If you're not already a member, join my Readers' Group.

Here's What You Get When You
Join My Readers' Group

Win Before You Can Buy
Exclusive Giveaways
Free Books
Sneak Peeks

Go Here to Join my Readers' Group

https://dl.bookfunnel.com/wci5hhjt8p

Go to my website or email me for details:

http://www.EllisODay.com

authorellisoday@gmail.com

Now for the sneak peek at Sarah and

Nick's story.

Sneak Peek:

CHAPTER 1: SARAH

"Do I have to take off my clothes?" Sarah tugged on the hem of her black dress. It was shorter and lower cut in the front than she normally wore, but the Viewing was about finding a man for sex and according to Ethan men liked to look.

"No." Ethan turned her away from the door and forced her to look at him. "You don't have to do anything you don't want to do."

She stared into his blue eyes. Why couldn't he be interested in her? She'd only met with him five or six times, but she trusted him. He ran his business, La Petite Mort Club, very professionally and he was gorgeous with his sandy brown hair, strong cheekbones and vibrant blue eyes. Sex between them would be good. Easy. He was attractive and…not for her. She didn't want decent sex or good sex, she wanted mind blowing, screaming orgasms and that wouldn't happen between him and her because there was no chemistry, no attraction.

"Listen to me." He moved his hands to her shoulders and gave her a gentle shake. "You aren't selling yourself to the highest bidder. You're looking for a partner. One who'll"—he grinned—"turn you on in ways you can't even imagine."

She glanced at the door where the men waited. Waited for her. Waited to decide if they wanted to fuck her. "I'm a bit nervous."

317

"About what?"

This was embarrassing but she'd been honest with him up to this point. She'd had to be. He was helping her...had helped her to choose the five men in the other room. "What if none of them..."

"They will want you." He touched her chin, turning her face toward him. "A few of them may back out after this but not because they don't want you."

"Yeah, right."

"I'm only going to say this once. You're beautiful and different, unique."

"That's not necessarily a good thing." She had long legs and a nice body—trim and firm—but with her auburn hair and green eyes she was cute at best, not gorgeous. The men she'd chosen were all rich, good looking and powerful. They could have anyone they wanted.

"It's exactly what they want, or most of them anyway." He took her hand and led her closer to the door.

She leaned on his arm, hating these shoes. She should've stuck with her flats but Ethan had given her a list of what she should wear and high heels were on the top. She'd found the smallest heels in the store and by Ethan's look when he'd first seen her she might've been better off going barefoot. He'd met her at the private entrance and his gaze had been appreciating as it'd skimmed over her dress, until he got to her feet. Then he'd frowned and shook his head.

"Finding the right men for you wasn't easy." He stopped at the door.

"Thanks a lot." She shifted away from him, his words hurting a little. She hadn't been sure of her appeal to the opposite sex in a long time, not since the early years with Adam.

"It's not because you aren't beautiful but because you want to be dominated and you want to dominate—"

"I do not want to dominate." All she could picture was a woman in black leather with a whip and that wasn't her, not at all.

"If you say so." He smiled a little. "But, you do want to lead the scene. Right? Because that's what—"

"Yes." Her face was red. She could feel it. She didn't want to talk about her fantasies again. It'd been embarrassing enough the first time, but he'd had to know what she wanted to compile a list of candidates.

"Most at the club are either doms or subs. Very few are switches." His eyes raked over her. "That's what's so special about you. You want it all and…that's what made choosing these men difficult."

He'd given her a selection of twenty-two men who might be interested in what she wanted. She'd narrowed it down to seven. Two had been uninterested when he'd approached. That'd left her with the five who'd see her in person for the first time tonight, but she wouldn't see them. That'd come after the Viewing when she interviewed any who were still interested.

"Remember what you want. This is your deal. You call the shots. At least a little." He kissed her forehead. "But don't refuse to give them anything. You don't want a submissive."

"No." That didn't turn her on at all and she only had eight weeks. One night each week for two months before she'd go back to her lonely life, her lonely bed, dreaming of Adam.

"You can do this." He pulled a flask from his jacket and unscrewed the lid. "For courage."

"Thanks." She took a large swallow, the brandy too thick and sweet for her taste but it was better than nothing.

"Now, go find your lover."

She laughed a little but sadness swept through her. There'd be no love between this man and herself. This would be sex, fucking. That's all. The only man she'd ever love, her only lover, was dead. This was purely physical. "Thank you again." She stood on tip-toe and kissed his cheek. He may be gorgeous and run a sex club but he was a good man, a good friend.

She turned and opened the door and walked into the room, trying to stay balanced on these stupid heels. Men wouldn't find them so attractive if they had to wear them. The room was dark except for one light highlighting a small platform. That was for her. She stepped up onto the small stage. The room was silent but they were there, above her, hidden behind the one-way mirrors, watching and deciding if they wanted to take the next step—to eventually take her.

She stared into the blackness of the room. It wasn't huge but its emptiness made it seem vast. She glanced upward, the light making her squint and she quickly stared back into the darkness. This was arranged for them to see her. That was it. She'd get no glimpse of them yet. She'd seen their pictures, chosen them but meeting them in person would be different. A picture couldn't tell her their smell or the sound of their voices.

She tugged at her dress where it hugged her hips,

wishing the questions would start, but there was only silence. She shifted, the heels already killing her feet. Ethan hadn't liked them and if they weren't going to impress, she might as well take them off. She moved to the back of the stage, leaned against the wall and removed her shoes. As she returned to the center of the stage a man spoke, his voice loud and commanding almost echoing throughout the room.

"Don't stop there. Take off your dress."

She bent, placing her shoes on the floor. That wasn't part of the deal. She wasn't going to undress in front of five men, only one. Only the one she chose. She straightened. "No."

"What?" He was surprised and not happy.

"I said no. That's not part of the Viewing."

"I want to see what I'm getting."

She stared up toward the windows, squinting a little. She couldn't tell from where the voice had come. The speaker system made it sound as if it were coming from God himself. "And you will if I pick you."

Another man laughed.

"It's not funny. She's disobedient," said the man with the loud voice.

"Not always. I can be obedient." These men liked to be in control but sometimes, so did she.

"Will you raise your dress? Just a little," asked another voice.

"Didn't you see enough in the photos?" She'd applied a few months ago for this one-time contract. She'd been excited and nervous when she'd received the acceptance email with an appointment for a photography session. She'd never had her picture professionally taken, since she didn't count school portraits or the ones her parents had had done at JCPenny's. She'd been anxious and a little turned on imaging wearing her new lingerie in front of a strange man, so she'd been disappointed to find the photographer was an elderly woman, but the lady had put her at ease and the photos had turned out better than she'd expected. She glanced up at the mirrors, hoping she wasn't disappointing all the men. That'd be too embarrassing.

"Those were...nice, but I'd like to see the real thing before deciding if you're worth my time."

She raised a brow. "You can always leave." She shouldn't antagonize him. She was sure the bossy man had already decided against committing to this agreement. Disobedience didn't appeal to him. That left four. If she didn't pick any of them, she could go through the process again, but she didn't think she would.

The man chuckled slightly. "I know that, but I haven't decided I don't want to fuck you. Not yet, anyway."

The word, so harsh and vulgar excited her. It was the truth. That was what she, what they were all deciding. Who'd get to fuck her. It was what she wanted, what she'd agreed to do, and as much as she dreaded it, she wanted it. She was tired of being alone. She missed having a man inside her—his tongue and fingers and cock.

"Do any of you have any questions?" She clasped her dress at her waist and slowly gathered it upward, displaying more and more of her long legs. She ran. They were in shape. The men would like them.

"Lower your top," said the same man who'd told her to take off her dress.

She didn't like him. If he didn't back out, she'd have Ethan remove him from her list. He was too commanding. He'd never allow her to be in control.

"I don't know if he's done looking at my legs yet." She continued raising the dress until her black and green lace panties were almost exposed.

"Very nice and thank you," said the polite man.

"You're welcome." This man might work. She shifted the dress up another inch before dropping it, giving them a glance at her panties.

"Now, your top," said the bossy guy.

She lowered her spaghetti string off one shoulder, letting the dress dip, but not enough to show anything besides the side of her bra.

"More," he said.

"No." She raised the strap, covering herself. She didn't like this man and wished he'd leave. She'd kick him out but that wasn't part of the process and they were very firm about their rules at this club.

"He got to see your pussy. Why don't I get to see your tits?"

"You got to see as much as he did." She was ready to move on. She bent and picked up her shoes. "If there's nothing else, gentleman, we can set up times for the interview process."

"Turn around," said another man.

It was a command, but she didn't mind. There was a politeness to his order and something about the texture of his voice caused an ache between her thighs. There was a caress in his tone but with an edge and a promise of a good hard fuck.

"Are you going to obey?" His words were whisper soft and smooth.

"Yes." That was going to be part of this too. Her commanding and him commanding. She dropped her shoes and turned.

"Raise you dress again."

She looked over her shoulder at where she imagined he sat watching her.

"Please." There was humor in his tone.

She smiled and slowly gathered the dress upward. She stopped right below the curve of her bottom.

"More. Please." There was a little less humor in his voice.

She wanted to show him her ass. She wanted to show that voice everything but not with the others around. This would be just her and one man, one stranger. That was one of her rules. "No. Only if you're picked do you get to see any more of me than you have." She dropped her dress, grabbed her shoes and walked off the stage and out the door.

She was going to have sex with a stranger. She was going to live out her fantasies for eight nights with a man she didn't know and would never really know, but she wasn't going to lose who she was. She'd keep her honor and her dignity which meant she had to pick a man who'd agree with her rules.

Continue Reading for FREE
Amazon = http://myBook.to/SixNSin_Book1

The Voyeur Series Books 1-4

Other Retailers = https://www.books2read.com/u/mlKVj9

Coming soon:

ETHAN'S STORY
TERRY'S STORY

Email me with questions, concerns or to let me know what you thought of the book. I love hearing from readers.
authorellisoday@gmail.com

Follow me on Facebook, Twitter, and Pinterest.

Facebook
https://www.facebook.com/EllisODayRomanceAuthor/

Twitter
https://twitter.com/ellis_o_day

Pinterest
http://www.pinterest.com/AuthorEllisODay

ABOUT THE AUTHOR

Ellis O. Day loves reading and writing about love and sex. She believes that although the two don't have to go together, it's best when they do (both in life and in fantasy).

www.ingramcontent.com/pod-product-compliance
Lightning Source LLC
Chambersburg PA
CBHW070832280626
47161CB00015B/478